See Me

CONSUMED SERIES
BOOK 1

Tris Wynters

Tris Wynters Publishing

Contents

This series is for those BookTok ladies who dream of multiple men consuming your mind, body, and soul. Who enjoy seeing good men raze the world to protect their woman. And for those who love to see a woman come into her own power, and take control of her own demons.

Enjoy,
XOXO Tris

See Me

Playlist

(Playlist available on YouTube Music)

1. **Climax-** Usher
2. **Love The Way You Lie (feat. Rihanna)-** Eminem
3. **Sunflower-** Post Malone & Swae Lee
4. **Lose Control (feat. Ciara & Fatman Scoop)-** Missy Elliot
5. **Pour Some Sugar On Me-** Def Leppard
6. **Rack City-** Tyga
7. **Pony-** Ginuwine
8. **Down On Me (feat. 50 Cent)-** Jeremih
9. **When We- (Remix) (feat. Ty Dolla $ign & Trey Songz)-** Tank
10. **Touch Me-** Ann Marie
11. **Earned It-** The Weekend
12. **Middle Fingers-** ASTON
13. **Mad Hatter-** Melanie Martinez
14. **Been to Hell-** Hollywood Undead
15. **Popular Monster-** Falling in Reverse
16. **Voices in my Head-** Falling in Reverse
17. **Victoria's Secret [The Metal Version] (feat. Harper)-** Jax
18. **The Beautiful People (Burlesque Original Motion Picture Soundtrack)-** Christina Aguilera
19. **Joke's On You-** Charlotte Lawrence

Warning

The Consumed Series is a dark, contemporary romance with adult themes. The female main character has multiple love interests and will not have to choose between them. The present love interests are not the dark and broody types but, her past and future have plenty of darkness that will force our female to shine.

While I would love for you to enjoy this book, please keep your own mental health a priority. By the end of this series, all five main characters will have revealed dark traumas, gained new scars, slayed their demons, and have blood on their hands. This book is a slow burn while our characters build their relationship. The next two books will have heavier trigger warnings, and our MCs will do a lot of damage in the name of love. This book will end with a cliffhanger but there will be an HEA; eventually.

Please be aware of your own triggers and limitations.
A more defined list of content/trigger warnings can be found on the next page.

If you are someone you know is struggling with thoughts of suicide, please reach out to 988.
You are worth it.

Content/Trigger Warnings

Violence
Adult Language
Stalking/Harassment
Graphic Sexual Scenes
Homophobic Slurs
MM
FM
Physical, Mental, and Emotional Abuse of Person
Physical Abuse of Animal
Rape
Forced drug use
Sexual Assault
Pregnancy from SA
Anxiety and Panic Attacks
Kidnapping
RH
Gang Violence

If you have any questions about content or trigger warnings, please reach out to triswyntersbooklover23@gmail.com.

1

Annie- 10 Years Ago

Staring out at the dancefloor, my mouth drops open. Lukas is grinding on a beautiful girl with mocha skin. I am frozen where I stand as I watch his hand slide to the front of her pants and he moves her jet black hair away from her neck.

Just as he sucks on her neck and dips his fingers into her pants, my body jolts to action. Steering through the sweaty, alcohol-infused bodies, the bass thumping is drowned out by the ringing in my ears. I vaguely hear the lyrics to Usher's Climax. *Figures and oddly appropriate.*

I make my way through the bodies grinding on the dance floor and step up behind him. There was no way I was going to interrupt his very public display. Not bothering to stop and think, I found my hand slipping in his back pocket, freeing him of his wallet. As soon as it's in my hand, I turn and high-tail it off the dancefloor. His cousin, Joey, sits on a barstool at our table, wide-eyed and mouth dropped. I find my ID, since Lukas always insisted on carrying everything I had, and toss the wallet to him. "Congrats, you are officially his ride home. Have a good night."

Not pausing to say my usual goodbyes to our group, I head straight for the door. My ears are ringing, my head is spinning from the mix of Tequila Sunrises and the overwhelming sense of shame and embarrassment coursing through me.

You idiot.

You know better.

He is just like the others.

I pass through a cloud of smoke and hear my heels clack on the rusty wooden floor near the door. As I reach my hand out to push the door open, a firm, yet sweaty, hand grabs my bicep and turns me so fast I land on my ass. I sit for a moment trying to wrap my head around what happened. Before my mind can catch up, Lukas is bending down and tugging me to his body. "Baby. Are you ok? I didn't mean to make you fall. I told you not to wear those heels."

Numbly, I raise my head and take in the man-child in front of me. Lukas looks down on me like he is truly worried. His piercing ice-blue eyes are wide, his brows furrowed in worry, and his dirty-blonde hair, shaved on the sides and longer on top, is stuck to his head with beads of sweat dripping down. "Annie. Are you ok?" For some reason, hearing my name snaps me out of my stupor. I flinch my arms out of his hold and push his solid frame back an inch.

With heels on, Lukas is only a couple of inches taller than me. A fact I originally loved since I rarely wore heels and enjoyed the way his lean, muscular arms would wrap around me. Now, I feel small, insignificant, and just plain stupid.

Mustering up every ounce of courage I raise my chin, roll back my shoulders, and look him square in his eyes. "I'm fine. I am leaving now. Enjoy your night." Before I take my next breath I am turning back around and shoving the bar door open. The night air is humid but the light breeze cools my skin after being inside drinking and dancing for the last 4 hours.

Stepping off of the wooden porch, my heels begin crunching across the gravel parking lot. Crossing the clearing to the first row of cars, I hear Lukas screaming for me and begin to walk faster. I refuse to do this with an audience. Knowing most of our friends had front-row seats to what he was doing was enough to make me push this place from my mind forever.

"Annie! Talk to me! What the hell?" Lukas stops me by tugging my hand and whirling me back to him.

My brows furrow and my head tilts as I take him in. He looks genuinely confused. Panting heavily, slumped shoulders, and cheeks tinged with pink splotches. The man I always thought was too hot to be in this town is looking at me like I told him aliens were real.

"Lukas, I don't want to do this with you. We all saw what you were doing with that girl. It is what it is." His look of befuddlement apparently sent my brain into word-vomit land. "I had a feeling you had been seeing other girls when you were out of town for work but seeing how easily you were able to forget about me, after you brought *my* drink back to *our* table, that confirms it. It's fine. You haven't been happy with me in a long time so I'm going home and you can go live your life."

I'm not sure what I expected once it all came out. His breathing stills and his fists clench then unclench. "What are you talking about? I love you, Annie. I don't understand what's going on!" His voice raises with every word. I could feel my shoulders turning in and my head dipping down praying for the ground to swallow me whole.

"Lukas," I almost whisper, officially unsure if I have lost my mind or if he has. "You went to buy me water when I went to the bathroom. When I came back, my water was there but you weren't. Joey, Kenny, Eric, and Tina didn't see where you had wandered off to so I headed to the other end of the floor to see if you went to play pool. Instead, I saw you, with that girl. You were not even 10 feet from me so I saw everything." The longer I talk, the more my shock wears off and I begin vibrating from the sheer amount of anxiety, embarrassment, and heartbreak coursing through my system.

Lukas brings his hands up in a placating gesture as if approaching a wounded animal. "Baby, I would never hurt you. You are my girl. I fought hard for you and we are meant to be. I drank too much. I really thought she was you!"

That. Right. There.

"What?" My voice rings out through the dark as my system overloads. "Are you insane? She is half my size and black! I look like Casper compared to her. I may not be smart, as you have told me so many times, but I am not blind."

I chuck off my heels and sprint through the parking lot towards the 6th row where my car is. I am so done. I am done with being the sad girl; the fat girl; the lonely girl; the stupid girl. I can't do this anymore.

As I hit the key fob and open the cranky door to my little, black hatchback, I realize another door opens. Feeling exhausted already, I sigh, "Lukas. It's done. It's fine. Just go."

Lukas throws himself in the passenger seat, buckles his belt, and turns those stupidly mesmerizing eyes on me. "Please baby. Please just take me home and I will explain. We can talk this out. I am drunk and I am so sorry. Please, just take me home."

I take a deep breath, feeling the tears beginning to form as the last five minutes come barreling forward. Too overwhelmed to argue, I slide into my seat. As I start the car, "Love the way you lie" by Eminem and Rhianna seeps into the car. Great. My favorite artist has now been tainted. *Could anything else go wrong?* Before the chorus even ends, Lukas slaps the radio off, plummeting us into silence.

Ten minutes into our twenty minute drive, our silence reaches a breaking point. Silent tears have been streaming down my face making the night drive down country backroads more difficult. "Annie, baby, I love you. I really didn't know. Maybe I should have stopped drinking when you did. I don't cheat. I'm not a cheater. Ask Rory. Rory would never be my friend if I cheated. I need him like I need you, Annie. I wouldn't do anything to hurt you. I'm so sorry." He went from calm and collected to spewing and hysterical. *What does his best friend have to do with this? Did I miss part of a conversation?*

I keep my thoughts to myself, not wanting to rock the boat. We are half-way to his house and I still have a thirty minute drive in the opposite direction. *Why am I taking him home? Oh, because you can't say no and are a people-pleaser. Idiot.*

My thoughts are interrupted when I hear sniffling and realize he is crying. Like, honest to God, tears down his face, snotty nose, crying. *Maybe he really did just get too drunk. We've all done that. Maybe I overreacted.*

I'm lost in my thoughts and more confused than when we first left the bar. Maybe my two drinks were stronger than I thought? Maybe I didn't work them off as fast as usual. But, that *was* a girl. I saw her, and so did everyone else. Why is *he* acting so hurt? Does he really love me so much the idea of me being done genuinely hurt?

Just as I begin to spiral, I pull onto the long dirt driveway leading to his parents' property. We have been building a house out here and he currently lives in a small trailer near the driveway.

I loop around the grass area we all use to turn around and pull up outside of his trailer. Suddenly, my mind turns completely off. It's like someone flips a switch and numbs my thoughts, body, and heart. I don't even know how long I sit there, completely shut down.

Movement to my right pulls my focus and I see Lukas unclipping his seatbelt and lean over the seat. My eyes process that he is moving towards me but it's like my body isn't my own. I just stare at him, allowing myself to be swept away in his ice-blue eyes; again. He reaches over and cups my face with his hand and slides his thumb across my chubby cheek. Leaning his forehead on mine, his stupid-perfect eyelashes flutter closed as he inhales deeply. "Please, kitten." He rasps out the pet name that I've always hated; his voice hoarse from crying. "Please come in and we can talk. I know you need to get home tonight but please, just come talk with me for a little bit."

His eyes flutter open and he leans in, placing a gentle kiss on my nose. For a moment we just stare at each other and I lose myself in his soothing heat, his eyes that make me weak in the knees, and the flutter of my heart that has been present ever since this incredible man set his sights on me.

I close my eyes, steal a deep breath, and utter the words that will become my greatest mistake. Bringing my hand to lie on top of his, I open my eyes, put on a slight smile and give him my acceptance. "Ok, Lukas. Let's talk."

* * *

I grit my teeth as my bare feet contact the dirt-laden floor. The grisly, fine pieces of rubble indent my heels and toes as I make my way over to the small corner that contains a few of my things. Lukas and I have been together for almost 2 years but we hadn't taken the step to officially move-in together. We started making plans for building a house on his parent's property since 5 acres is plenty of room for all of us. Lukas travels frequently for different contracting gigs. This latest job has him and his cousin maintaining, fixing, and installing atm machines in various states.

I still have 6 months on my apartment lease and there was no way I could fit his stuff, and our 2 dogs in the small space I have. I do, however, keep a small bag of essentials here for when I stay over just like he has a few things at my place.

As part of our "future" plans, he built a huge outdoor kennel with a covered area for our dogs to be able to play and stretch their legs daily. Letting Mable live here instead of with me was a terrifying decision but she seems to love the open space. I visit her often and know that Lukas' mom is always looking out for both dogs.

The small trailer he stays in when he is home was originally built as a guest room. The door that leads in is the only entrance or exit. When walking in, you can easily see that three areas are sectioned off by mini-walls about 4 feet deep.

The area on the left is the "bedroom", which also showcases the only window. The thrum of the AC can be heard throughout the small space. The room originally didn't have it but Texas summers proved to be too much for anyone to be in here comfortably without one.

Near the window unit is his Queen mattress, a small dresser, and a fan. The middle area, between the two mini-walls is the "bathroom". Just a toilet, a toilet paper holder and stand, and some hand sanitizer. It is set-up similar to a porta potty and is easily accessible on the outside for regular cleanings.

The right side of the space acts as a changing area/closet. The entire trailer is 12 feet wide and 20 feet long. It works for him since he works a lot and can get anything else at his parents' house which is just a two minute walk down the drive.

I move on auto-pilot, grabbing my clothes and the small bag of essentials I keep here and begin rolling them up to make it easier to hold. The silence is oppressive and makes my skin tingle. I stand, clutching my belongings to my chest. Sucking in a deep breath, I turn towards Lukas and plaster a gentle smile to try and show I'm fine. However, that's not the look I am receiving in return.

I feel myself flinch as I come face-to face with Lukas. His eyes are red-rimmed, brows furrowed into a scowl, cheeks are flushed, and his normally perfect hair is sticking up in every direction. Sweat is dripping from his goatee as he pants heavily. "You stupid bitch."

"Huh?" I flit through my mind to try and remember if something happened since we returned. *Did I disassociate while grabbing my clothes?* Usually that only happens when he is raging or during our so-called sexual encounters.

"You are such a hypocritical whore. I know you've been sleeping with Kenny. Who cares if I have a little fun knowing you are fucking Mr. Muscled Best Friend all the time." His voice becomes louder as he spits each word. I feel my face contort trying to figure out what on Earth he is talking about.

"Don't play dumb with me you fat slut." He takes a step closer to me as I shuffle back. His voice becomes a menacing growl. "How dare you embarrass me in front of my friends." Step. "How dare you run away from me." Step. "How dare you think you can do better than me." Step.

Now, I'm backed against the far right wall. I take in his eyes and our erratic heartbeats seem to be in sync. I am not sure what to say or what he's talking about. I never cheated. Where is he getting this?

"Lukas, I don't know what you're talking about but I have never cheated on you. That's not who I am. When we started this, I told you I would rather you leave me out of the blue than ever cheat. I don't respect cheaters. Kenny and I have been friends as long as we have known each other but we never hang out alone. Either you are there or his girlfriend, Tina, is. Whatever it is you think I have done, you're wrong."

Lukas shoulders begin to relax as he takes a couple of stuttering breaths. "You're right. I'm sorry. Let's just go to bed."

Wait. What?

"No, Lukas. I'm done. I told you I would bring you home but that's it. I'm taking my dog and going home. You cheated. I am done and I am leaving." Squaring my shoulders I lift my chin and look straight into his eyes. The dim light near the bed has turned them from an ice-blue to an ocean blue. His eyes are wide and bloodshot.

In the moment it takes me to catch my breath, he closes his eyes and starts crying. He pulls me into him, hugging me so fiercely I have no idea how to move. I stand there frozen as sobs rock his chest. "I love you, kitten. Please. I am so sorry. I need Rory and I need you. Please, kitten. It's ok. I love you." His words begin to jumble as he sobs into my neck. Feeling tears streaming down I do the only thing I can think of; I hug him back.

After a few moments, his sobs turn into hiccups and he begins walking backward to his bed, bringing me along with him. My body moves without my permission. Too confused to comprehend what is happening. I feel like I am missing something. Like I'm only hearing parts of a bigger conversation.

One that I'm not even part of.

When we reach the bed, he pulls me down with him and curls around me so tightly I can barely breathe. "Lukas" I gasp. "Stop. If you're worried about Rory finding out, I won't say anything. Ok? But this is done."

"No kitten, I love you!" His cries have turned into strangled rage. "We belong together. It's me and you. No one else will ever give you what I can. You know you can't be without me. You know that before me no one even looked at you. You were one of the guys. Period. I saw past that. *I* did!" With each passing word, his rage grows and I feel my mind retreating.

Not again.

"You would be *nothing* without me. I helped push you to finish your degree. *Me.* I gave your stupid dog a place to stay. I opened your eyes to how good sex can be. Do you think anyone else would have done that? Do you really think anyone else could see past your rolls on your belly or the moles on your face? No! They wouldn't. They never did and never will. We've talked about this before. No one will ever see you as more than one of the guys or like a little sister. It's me and you baby." His voice begins to shift into a quiet whimper. "Me and you."

"It was," I began. "But, not anymore. You haven't been happy with me in a long time. It's time for me to let you go."

Just as I begin inhaling a ragged breath, I'm tossed off the bed and onto the wooden floor. My elbow cracks and pain radiates through my arm. Lukas pounces off the bed in a move I swear he was too drunk to pull off. He pulls me up, yanking me by my arm and I fall into his chest. "You stupid bitch." *Whap!*

It takes a moment for my body to register the pain across my cheek from his backhand. But he's already started screaming again. "I do everything for you! You are nothing without me." Moving like a whip, the hand that hit me comes out and holds my left arm in a punishing grip. Shock forces me to move with him as he rams me into the opposite wall.

Woah. How did we get across the room so fast?

As the thought surfaces, my head bounces off the wall. I quickly realize he has his left forearm stretched across my neck, pinning me to the wall. My whole body begins trembling but my brain seems to have lost all ability to react normally. Shocked, I stare into Lukas' eyes. I swear my heart stops when I see endless pools of blackness where the blue used to reside. The fear entangles itself through me and I release a whimper.

Leaning in, Lukas sneers and growls, "You are nothing without me". His low voice takes on a menacing quality I have never heard before. It's like a demon has possessed him. Each word he enunciates with a press into my throat, a subtle shift closer, or a squeeze of my arm. "No one else. Will. Ever. Love you."

Gasping around his arm slowly cutting off my breathing, I let my thoughts tumble right out of my mouth. "You are crazy. You're completely insane."

The cackle he releases sounds more like a villain's laugh than the light laughter I've come to love. A shudder racks my body but my brain still forgets that in fight or flight, I'm more of a freeze kind of girl. *Why did it choose now to change that?*

"You will never get away with this. Let me go. Let me get Mable and leave and you will never have to put up with us again."

"Ha!" He barks. "Rappers get away with beating their wives all the time and I will too. I own you, Annie. You *are* nothing and *have* nothing without me. Even your own mother loves me and she would hate you if you left."

"Of course my mother loves you" I spit. "She's a minister, she's supposed to love everyone."

Shut up, mouth!

The sneer on his face becomes deeper and the shadows take over his face as he steps impossibly closer. His angry words come out just higher than a whisper, "If you step so much as one foot out that door, I will shoot you before you reach your car."

What the hell?

"What? Why? Just let me go! This isn't like you. Just stop!" Panic rises in me and I begin to claw at the arm still pinned to my throat. He switches his left arm for his right hand and squeezes. Just as I reach my knee up, hoping to catch him in the balls, I hear a familiar *click*.

My whole world slows to a stop as I widen my eyes and stare into the dark abyss of his eyes. My peripheral shows me the familiar glint of his gun, pressing on my temple. My brain finally loses all fight and I tremble uncontrollably. Tears are streaming down my face as images of my best friend, my mom, grandparents, and brothers flash through my mind.

What story will they get? Will they be disappointed in my decisions?

I haven't talked much to any of them in so long. Lukas said they made him uncomfortable and he preferred his friends and family. I wanted him to be happy. It wasn't until this moment that I realize I no longer have anyone but him. Not really. My friends, now, are his friends. I have seen my family on holidays but that's it. *Would they even miss me?*

Shame and resignation hit me square in the heart. I was never good enough for any of them. It's better this way. Lukas was the only one who looked at me and saw the real me. And he liked me. The areas I needed to work on, he helped me fix or change. He accepted all my messed up pieces, enjoyed when I cooked and cleaned up for him and when I took care of his dog.

I mean, sure he'd get mad if I didn't make his meals perfect and he'd make me do it again. And there are a few holes in the walls but that's because I made him mad. Once I cleaned up the mess, he forgave me. Like it never happened. He even worked around my physical flaws by keeping the lights off and a shirt on when we were intimate. That way neither of us was uncomfortable.

Hell, thanks to him my mind learned its very own superpower. When he wanted to do something that hurt or I hated, I floated. Floated off into a field where Mable and I ran. Or floated through memories of camping and beach days with my best friend.

He's never hurt me on purpose. In fact, it's my fault sex usually hurts anyway. My body doesn't respond like it's supposed to. I'm broken so it's damn near impossible to get wet. Even the times I had to go to the hospital for stitches were my fault. One time was because I disassociated too early and let my ass drop before he had pushed in. And the few times because of me falling or objects hitting me, I wasn't paying attention. He wasn't trying to hurt me. It *was* fine. He loved me. But now, now is definitely different.

Now I have really messed it up. I should have left it alone. I know better than to talk back to him. I know better to embarrass him but I never learn. I've never made him this mad. I ran off and made a scene. I threatened his friendship with Rory knowing cheating is a big no-no for him. *He was right every single time he told me what a fuck up I am. I guess I couldn't change.*

Lowering my head, I take a shuddering breath and relax into his hand. My tears have long since dried up, my body no longer trembles, and my mind has already become clear. "I'm sorry" I whisper and close my eyes as I prepare for the end.

What seems like minutes pass, although it was maybe only one. I jump out of my skin when I hear metal clamber across the floor and hit the wall by the toilet. My eyes spring open to meet Lukas'. Tears are streaming down his face. Before I can question what's happening, he grips both of my forearms, twirls me around, wraps me in his arms, and walks me over to the bed. Lying down he embraces me and begins stroking my hair like he is petting a dog. "It's ok baby. You are forgiven. It's ok. I love you."

My mind is slow to come back online. This man's emotional pendulum has always been volatile but never to this extreme. I blink my eyes open as his voice rings out again, anger radiating through the room as tension coils his body. "I love you! Don't you love me?"

The emotional whiplash has me struggling to respond. He grabs my arm and jerks me from him so he can look into my eyes. A gasp leaves my throat as I see his blue eyes darken, again. "Answer me!" He roars.

"Yes. Yes, I love you." I stammer quickly.

He tsks like I am a disappointing child. "You're only saying that because you're scared." *Well duh.*

"No. I do love you. I'm just tired. It's been a long night. Maybe we both need some sleep." I say it as gently as possible. Usually that helps him calm but tonight has been so intense that I am not sure it will help.

The whole night comes barreling back into my head like a video. *What am I doing? He put a gun to my head! I won't be that girl. If he can just go to sleep, I can sneak out and leave. Once I do, I am never coming back.*

My mind goes into overdrive coming up with an escape plan. I begin to formulate ideas as we sit in silence. Lukas takes a deep breath and snuggles into my neck. He pets my hair and shushes me like *I'm* the one crying. I've never been so terrified or confused in my entire life. My heart beats erratically as I continue working on an exit strategy. My face hurts, my throat burns and I just want to curl up in my bed and sleep for days. But I can't do that. Not yet. I have to get out of here.

Blinking back to myself, I carefully reach for my phone, still in my back pocket, and notice an hour has passed. Lukas' breathing has evened out and his body has relaxed into the bed. He is passed smooth out. *Damn, I definitely disassociated that time.*

Coming back into myself, my limbs feel heavy, my cheek throbs, and my eyes are swollen from crying. He's been mad before. He's said awful things but never, never this. I can't stay here. I won't.

Gently, I steady my breathing and begin to untangle myself from Lukas' arms. He's still lying on his side facing me so I wrap them around the pillow I was using and slowly slip the rest of the way out of bed. With my phone in my hand, I quickly toe across the room and gather my belongings, checking that my keys are still in my pocket, and slip out the door. I shut the door agonizingly slow and wait for the gentle click before running barefoot through the yard and over to the dog cages.

Mable hears me coming and begins barking, wagging her tail excitedly. I try to shush her but she wakes Lukas' dog and they both go nuts. I quickly throw open the lock to the dogs' cage area and begin to fling the door open.

I'm abruptly shoved to the side and plummet to the ground with a grunt. Blood begins to seep from my hand, dripping to the ground. I hop back up, scooping up my phone and belongings as I go. When I turn, I see Lukas has closed himself in the cage with our dogs.

"What are you doing, Lukas? Just give me Mable and I can leave. You don't want me anymore. Just let us go!" I am frantically searching the area to see if anyone has come out of his parents' house. I don't see his cousin's truck here so he must not be home yet. The lights in his Mom's house are all still out. I'm not even sure they would come out to help me.

Lukas' growls low and deep. I whip my head around expecting it to be one of the dogs but see the eerie darkness in his eyes once again. A shudder makes its way down my spine as I feel his anger surge higher. "You want to leave me cunt, you can. Go on. But Mable is mine now."

"No! She's mine! Give her to me, Lukas. You don't even like her!"

I've had Mable for almost 2 years now. When she was just a few months old, she was dropped off at a vet clinic my friend worked at. She had been burned and held tightly with a collar or rope, leaving behind spots on her body and around her tail that hair could never grow. She was there for me when no one else was and I refuse to leave her, now.

Thankfully, I remember I still have my phone in my hand, hidden under my things. I quickly find the buttons for the recorder I use for class just as he starts yelling, again. "I don't like her? What are you talking about?" he sneers, eyes wild with rage.

"Lukas, you hate her. You're always yelling at her and popping her in the face or butt for little things that dogs do. She's a dog, not an adult, and you treat her like shit. Just, let me get her out of your hair. I can take her to my family and you won't have to deal with her anymore."

Time seems to slow. Lukas' chest is puffed out and panting with adrenaline and pure rage. He looks completely unhinged. "I don't like her? Huh? Is that what you think?" He slowly steps backward towards his own dog and away from Mable.

As soon as I think he's going to let me open the gate and get her, he scoops up his dog and begins hitting her in the head and bottom. The dog yelps loudly and I start screaming for help. "I. Treat. Them. The. Same." Each word is carried through with another swat. *Jesus, he's lost his mind.*

At this point, it's so loud that I know our voices have carried to his parents' house. Of course, no one shows. Heaven forbid anyone in his family say or do anything negative to him. The squeals from the dog cage reminds me to focus and try to come up with a plan to save not only Mable, but his dog as well.

"Lukas. Just listen." I try to speak gently, calmly, hoping he will relax. "I am not trying to take your dog. I would never do that. But please, please give me Mable. I need her." A whimper leaves me at the possibility that I will never see her again. Lukas snarls and tosses his dog behind him. She lands on her side with a yelp and my heart shatters. Mable is cowering in the front corner of the cage and pawing at the gate to be released.

"Lukas. Please. I won't say anything about what you did. Just, please, let us go. I will take Mable right now and I swear no one will know anything. I won't go to the bar anymore. I won't come around your friends. We'll just disappear. Me and her. *Please*."

I am pretty sure I have never begged this much in my life but I am also too scared to try and run for the car. My nerves are shot, my head is pounding and my stomach feels like concrete has been poured into it. *How did we get here?*

My wide eyes implore him to do this one thing; to let go. His eyes swirling with malice and pure hatred. After what feels like an eternity, frozen in fear, he lifts his arm and points toward my car. "Go. Now." He grits through his teeth. His command cracks across the night and echoes around us.

"Not without Mable." I sniffle and force myself to stand a little taller, even though my lips and hands are trembling, and slowly make my way to the cage to unlock the door.

"Don't fucking try it you disgusting whore. You leave representing what you are. Nothing." He growls. Actually growls. Like a bear right before it rips your face off. "Drop your shit. I've put up with enough from you. Useless cunt. They always said fat girls are the best lovers because they'll do anything to please. And I have to say, they were right. But I'm over it. You may suck a cock like a porn star and cook like a 50s housewife but that's where the good things end. Drop your shit and get off my property before I call the cops for trespassing."

WHAT?! He can't be serious? Did I die earlier? Am I in hell? None of this makes sense.

"Now slut!" His voice makes me jump straight out of my stupor. This has to be a dream. This is nuts.

It's at that moment all rationale takes a flying leap right out of my head. My eyes flit to the gate door and I jump towards it, unhooking the latch as I do. The metal on metal creaks as I swing the gate open and Mable comes bounding out.

Lukas seems to be momentarily frozen by my audacity as he just stares at me. The moment Mable barks and takes off, Lukas snaps out of his stupor with a roar. I take the pile of belongings in my other arm and whip them towards his face. I immediately jump back, sling the door closed and flip the hatch down.

Twisting around I run like I have never run before. Lukas' roar of anger vibrates through the property but I don't dare look back. I can hear the clanking of the gate as he tries to get the lock free from the inside. Adrenaline races through my body and my feet don't even process the pain of running across rock, gravel, and patches of stickers. All I know is my car is just, this, close.

About ten feet before I get to the car, I hear the cage door crash loudly behind me and Lukas screams across the property "Fucking bitch!"

The moment the words leave his mouth, a loud bang whips through the air and I hear a ping like something hitting metal. My brain doesn't process it as I reach into my pocket and begin fumbling for my keys. Clicking the key fob multiple times to unlock the door I see Mable reach the car just as another bang/ping combo strikes out. And then my brain catches up. *Holy shit. He's shooting at me! The crazy bastard is actually trying to kill me.*

Sliding towards the car I reach the handle and open the door just enough for Mable and I to leap in. I don't even bother with securing her or myself. A ping hits the side of the car just as I flip the ignition and punch it into drive. Gravel and dirt whips into the air as I make the fast turn to head out of the rocky driveway. I push my car as fast as I can without hitting trees or the perimeter fence.

As we hit the paved road another ping and a spark flies from the light pole to my left. "Shit." I shove Mable down into the passenger floorboard and press the gas harder as I approach the curve of the road that will officially put us out of sight. Right as we begin the turn, my rear window shatters, causing me to scream out. My car swerves a little and I work to correct it. As soon as the curve turns into a straight, I blast off into the night and dial my best friend.

Christina and I haven't spoken much since I got together with Lukas but I am hoping that she forgives me. At least for one night. There is no way I can go back to my house. Not tonight. Maybe not ever. I'm not sure what to do from here but I do know, I can't do it on my own.

2

Annie- Present Day

The wildly oppressive heat from the Texas summer sun beats down on my shoulders. The kids just started school again a couple of weeks ago but we're still dragging out their giant inflatable water slide every weekend. It keeps them moving, out of the house, and gives me some time to listen to music or read.

I lie back in my lounge chair with my trusty bearded dragon catching rays on my tankini-covered stomach. We adopted Reginald last year when the guy at the pet store said he was going to be euthanized. His tail had been broken when he hit something so people weren't interested in buying him. Apparently, he had out-stayed his welcome.

I couldn't handle that so I became the woman who stopped by the pet store for dog food and ended up with an addition to the family.

The sounds of my kids splashing around their inflatable water course fill the air and mix with the booming bass of the outdoor speaker. Sunflower by Post Malone rings out while contentedness washes over me.

My phone chirps, alerting me of a message. I'm perfectly happy ignoring it for a few more minutes but my kids decide to choose that moment to complain of hunger.

Scooping up my phone then placing Reginald on my shoulder, I walk into the house to grab the watermelon I had cut up earlier. After getting the bowl out, I decide to go ahead and heat the oven for lunch. *Might as well since this watermelon will be demolished in 10 minutes.* By the time I had the oven preheating and the watermelon in hand, the kids are drying off on the towels they laid out for their daily lunch picnic.

"Yes! Watermelon. My favorite." My youngest, Josh, exclaims. I chuckle as I place the bowl between the three of them, shaking my head as they all stick their hands in and excitedly talk about their favorite fruits.

Sometimes I wish I was a kid again. To be so carefree, no worries other than whether or not it will rain, and to see the world through their eyes. Joy, amusement, and happiness can be found around any corner. Something I frequently struggle to remember. Thankfully, my kids do a pretty good job of reminding me. Just watching them interact and listening to their antics can bring a smile to this worn-out mama's face.

"Mom, can Reginald eat with us?" One of my twins, Cheyenne, asks. "Sure, why not? Let me go grab his salad and creepy crawly bugs. Do you guys want that for lunch, too?" A chorus of "ew" and "no" rings out and I laugh at the look of sheer horror on their faces.

"Oh, alright. No bugs for you, then. Reginald can have them all to himself." I boop my little dragon on the nose for good measure as the kids giggle.

"Thank goodness for that" Samantha states between giggles.

Back in the house, I watch my littles through the kitchen window as they eat their snack and chat happily about whatever game they're talking about. The nice thing about having 8-year-old twins and a 6-year-old is they're all pretty interested in similar things. It makes it just a tiny bit easier to keep up with the ramblings.

The oven beeps telling me that it has been preheated so I slide out a bag of chicken nuggets onto a pan and pop it in. Then I get started on mixing the greens, basil, and watermelon with a small helping of dubias in a plastic bowl for Reginald to enjoy. I grab his clear carrier and stroll out so I can set him up with his own lunch next to the kids. They all begin laughing and talking about how fast he's eating and even clap when he runs around the small space chasing a dubia.

Remembering I need to set my timer for the oven, I go to open my phone and see the message notification at the top. Assuming it's from my mother, I open the messaging app and raise my brow at the words I find.

Unknown- Must be nice walking around your little house with your little kids. It would sure be a shame if anything happened to them.

Panic claws up my throat. *What the hell? Is this a joke?* I feel the familiar heating of my cheeks and chest as the beginning of an anxiety attack comes on. Closing my eyes, I take a deep breath and refocus my mind.

5 things I can see: Sam's drenched brunette hair, falling from her braids; Josh's mouth covered in red from the watermelon juice dripping everywhere; Reginald's baby blue carrier; Cheyenne's bright red ladybug swimsuit; The black phone case that protects my phone.

But why do I feel like I am going to need more than a case for protection?

"Thank you, Officer Daniels. I really appreciate your time." My cheeks flood from embarrassment for even bothering to bring them in. I mean, an unknown number is possibly threatening me. What do I expect them to do?

I for sure didn't anticipate the man standing before me. Officer Daniels looks like he stepped straight out of my favorite smutty books. Standing at least 6 feet tall, he towers over my 5'4". His build looks like he trains in one of those CrossFit gyms on a daily basis. His arms bulge under his blue uniform. Corded veins pulse through his forearms that had to be hand-sculpted by God himself. His shoulders span so wide that I wasn't sure he would fit through my front door without turning.

When he knocked on the door, I peered through the hole and cursed that the porch light was out. I waited until after the kids went to bed to call the police. I didn't want to freak them out and I figure there's not much to go on, anyways. I hesitantly called out asking him to identify himself. I even went as far as asking for his badge number and typing it into my phone. Just in case.

As soon as he gave me something that sounded plausible, I slowly opened the door to get a better look. The relief that flooded me when I saw his name tag and uniform was enough to make me light-headed. When I swung the door open, I realized why his name tag was the first thing I saw. This man is HUGE.

I trailed my eyes up from his chest to his neck. His tan skin is swirled in blank ink spreading from one side, assumingly across the back, and ending perfectly center on the other side. His caramel-brown beard is shaved close and neat. Enough to run your fingers through but not so much that it covers any part of his big, bulging neck.

"Ms. Carol?" I snap my eyes to his as the heat rushes through my cheeks and straight to my ears. Before I can even chastise myself, I am thrown into pools of brown with golden flakes. His eyes make me think of fall days and warm bonfires. *Where the hell did that come from?*

"Hi, yes, sorry. That's me. Just didn't realize the porch light was out. Would you like to come in, Officer Daniels? No use standing out here in the dark."

"Yes, ma'am. Thank you."

As I close the door, I blurt out, "Oh gracious, please don't call me ma'am. I don't think I'm that old, yet." I giggle out then slap a hand over my mouth when I realize how thick my southern drawl came out. I turn away quickly and veer left into my kitchen. I make my way across the small kitchen and turn back when I reach the cabinets on the opposite wall.

Officer Daniels chuckles and removes his peaked cap and crosses it over his body to stick under his arm. His hair is the same caramel color as his beard but with streaks of chocolate. Also like his beard, he keeps his hair trimmed short and neat; slightly longer on top. The length would be the perfect to run my hands through, delighting in the sensation under my fingers without getting caught up in knots.

"Maybe not," he drawls, "but my mama raised me with manners. It doesn't matter if you're 18 or 88, I would still call you ma'am. Heaven forbid my mama hear I wasn't using my manners." His husky voice and southern twang travel down my spine and sends tingles straight to my core. *Girl, get a grip.*

Shaking off his response, or rather my reaction to his response,

I lean against the counter and slump a little while crossing my arms across my body. I try desperately to cover the pudge of my belly that is surely noticeable with how my tee fits. I stare down at my feet for a moment before clearing my throat. "So, do you need a picture of my phone message or just my word? It's been a long time since I had to file a police report so I am not sure of the protocol." Embarrassment floods me, once again. *Am I overreacting? Will he judge me? Pity me? Believe me?*

Officer Daniels clears his throat and I flinch, my eyes jumping to his. He holds his hands up in a placating gesture, his brows furrowed and his forehead wrinkles as he tips his head to the side. His eyes search mine like he's analyzing me or trying to find the secrets in my soul. "I'm sorry Ms. Carol. I didn't mean to startle you. You just looked a little nervous. Please don't be. That's what I'm here for. I want to help. We can start with a verbal statement, then I will get a written one and if you have any physical evidence, I will collect it. Let's just start from the beginning, yeah?" His smirk pops out a dimple that is absolutely drool-worthy. His eyes light up with a sincerity that takes my breath away.

"Yeah, ok. Let's do it. I mean this. Let's, I'll, yeah. I can talk." The more I ramble, the brighter my face gets. I can feel it burning through my face.

I chance a peek at Officer Daniels to figure out how badly I should be embarrassed. His relaxed position, the glimmer of amusement in his eyes, and the light twitch of his lips assure me he isn't judging me. He does appear to be amused but, if I don't get it together, he will surely end up laughing at me at some point. The thought strangely settles me as I take in a deep breath, then lead him to the kitchen table to get started.

3

~

Annie

The rest of the week passed by without incident. Officer Daniels had assured me they would look into the threat but with so little information, we may not get much. Honestly, I knew that. But I learned the hard way a long time ago that evidence and a paper trail can be the difference in life or death.

It's Friday afternoon and I'm running around with the littles trying to pack the last of their bags. My mom wants them for the weekend so I can finally get some time to breathe, catch up on cleaning, and maybe dive a little deeper into the reading list that has grown massively.

As I'm shooing the kids and their bags into the car, I hear my phone ping with a message. Assuming it's my mother being impatient, I get everyone settled in, choose a song for the ride, and begin our journey across town.

When we come to our first red light, I grab my phone to let my mom know we're on our way. Instead of her usual antics at me not getting them to her fast enough, I see **Unknown** in the notification bar. The sharp inhale is my only tell that something is wrong. Opening the message, I prepare for whatever cryptic message awaits me.

Unknown- Don't forget to lock the house princess. Wouldn't want anything going wrong while you drop off the kiddies with Mama.

Oh hell no. This bastard has another thing coming if he thinks he's scaring me. Just as the light turns green, I have my phone open and dialing my last saved number. The music cuts off, much to my littles' dismay, and the Suburban fills with ringing through the speakers. Before the second ring finishes, I'm met with a deep, soothing voice that feels all too good. Like a balm to my tattered soul. "Officer Daniels here."

"Um, hi, uh, Officer Daniels, sir?" *Jesus, Annie, what is wrong with you?* "I, um, sorry. I am in the car with my kids and needed to let you know that I got another message."

His silence stretches for a moment but I pick up the distinct sound of clacking keys on a computer. The seconds tick by before he responds. "Sorry about that, I was just getting back from lunch and needed to log back in. I'm sorry. What did you say your name was?"

Oh, good gravy. Of course, he doesn't remember me. It's been almost a week and I am sure he's dealt with hundreds of people since.

"Annie. Annie Carol. Like I said, my kids are in the car but you told me to contact you immediately if I received another message so, yeah."

"Ah, yes! Annie. It's good to hear from you. I mean, not that it's good you got a message but, you know. Um..." Officer Daniels stumbles for a moment. He is probably just juggling all of his *real* cases and is trying to sort out where he put my measly little file.

"So, the message. I know you're in the car but when you're safe, and not driving, can you screenshot the message and send it to me, please?"

"Yes, sure. Absolutely. I just wanted you to know. I'm dropping off my kids at their grandmother's for the weekend so it may be another 20 minutes."

"That's fine. And, I'm sure they are all excited for a weekend with Grandma. I'll get started on updating your file as soon as I receive the message."

"Thank you, Officer Daniels. I know it's not much but it does make me feel better." Relaxing my hold on the steering wheel that I'm apparently strangling, I take in the tingles that work their way through my fingers. I allow the sensation to ground me, I take a deep breath.

"No thanks yet, Annie. You can do that after we figure this out. And, please, call me Vince." I swear I hear him grinning through the phone.

"Ok. Vince. Thank you. I will message you soon." My brain supplies me with the fact that sounds way too personal so I stammer my way through a more appropriate response. Or so I thought. "I mean, message about that case. Not about anything else. You know what I mean, Officer Daniels. I mean, Vince. Ok, I need to focus on driving my littles. Don't need to be a distracted driver." The more I ramble the brighter my face and chest feel.

It takes me a couple of beats to realize my last statement may have sounded flirty instead of joking like I hoped. "Not that you're a distraction, sir, I just mean, I want to be safe. Kids and all. So, yeah. I will message you the information later."

Seconds tick by with absolutely no response. If I wasn't driving, I would bang my head on the steering wheel. Instead, I am caught off guard by the deep, rumbling chuckle that comes through the line. His next words blanket me like a spell that simultaneously has me relaxing, and clenching my thighs. "No worries, Annie. Take care of those babies. I'll be waiting right here until you get there safely...But only because you called me sir."

The call ends with a click and music fills the vehicle. It takes me a solid minute to figure out if I imagined the words. And the way his voice dropped, good gracious. My panties are now ruined. There is definitely something wrong with me.

Get a grip. I bet that man has women lining the streets to see him. He wouldn't want some frumpy woman with three kids. You have officially read one too many smutty books. Focus. Your life is your kids. Not in the clouds.

The rest of the drive is filled with singing and laughter as we make our way through the city. My mind firmly back where it needs to be and my heart beating just for them.

4

~

Vince

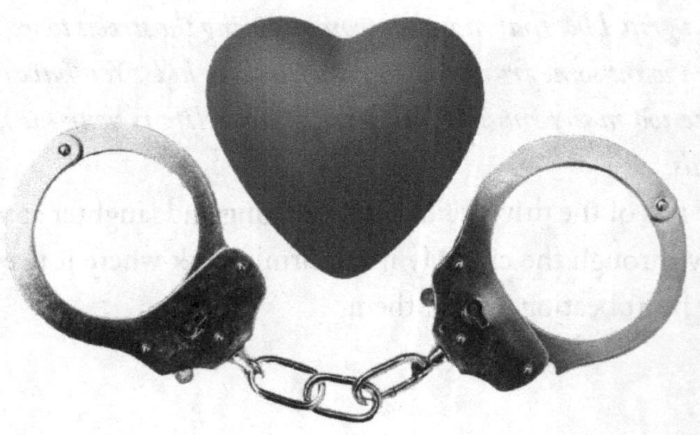

My mind is running a million miles a minute. Between the local gang that thought they could come into town and all the crap I have been dealing with with my dad, I need a break. *Fuck that. I need a vacation.*

I amble over to the coffee machine in the corner of the breakroom and top off my now cold coffee. I check my watch and realize I have been digging into the Black Thorns gang for 3 hours without a break.

But, what a break it was.

Hearing Annie's sweet voice over the line took me by complete surprise. It's like my brain short-circuited and forgot how to function. I knew who she was the moment I answered but didn't want to seem overzealous so, like everything else I do, I screwed it up. Asking who it was probably made her feel crappy. I mean, I spent a solid hour in her little kitchen soaking up every detail about the woman with the sparkling blue eyes. Eyes that hid pain, sorrow, ghosts behind a mask of strength and love for her kids. What I wouldn't give to dive into those depths. Swim through her soul and take away all the negativity.

Her messy-mom bun, as my brother would teasingly classify it, sat just at the top of her head, towards the back. Her darker roots were prominent before they gave way to shades of platinum and rustic blonde. Her heart-shaped face, rounded on the sides and pointed more around her chin, showed lines that told of a life filled with smiles and laughter but also worry.

Annie's nose was the perfect rounded shape with a small jewel glittering on the left side. Because her hair was up, I caught her multiple piercings. Both ears had double piercings in the lobes, which held small, simple studs. A cartilage piercing on her left ear dangled what appeared to be a star from a pink planet. Finally, her right ear had an industrial bar, titanium I assume, stretching from the top to just above halfway down the side.

Seeing those jewels glisten in their simplicity made me wonder what other little pleasures she took part in. I got my answer when we moved from the doorway into the small kitchen. As she giggled about something she said, her hand clapped over her mouth. Her arms were curvy at the top and lean leading towards her wrist. I noticed a tattoo design on her left forearm. I didn't want to stare but I looked forward to knowing more about it. Her right arm held a geometric shape with flowers in the middle. The entire design sat perfectly on top of her arm and drew me in. The line work was amazing. I briefly considered asking who the artist was but shook that from my head. Professionalism was key.

Before we walked to the kitchen table, I got to really see her under the bright lights from the ceiling. She was shorter, maybe 5'4", 5'5', and curves for days. Her tits formed under the black, reptile tee she was wearing. Judging by the way the tee clung to each slope, they would be perfect handfuls. Her stomach was not thin or sculpted but rather soft and inviting.

When she turned to make her way from the counter to the table, I almost combusted like a teenager. The black, ripped jeans she has on showed every curve down to her tiny ankles. Her thighs looked like squishy ear muffs that I want to both bite, and sooth. And her ass. Dear Lord, her ass. It was not your typical bubble butt. It did poke out a bit but instead of rounding out backward, it rounded towards the sides; connecting to her hips with dips and curves I wanted to trace with my tongue. Each cheek was easily wide enough to show off my full hand-print. No wrapping around to the side. A perfect canvas to turn her creamy skin pink.

After an hour with her, it was apparent that her real smiles were few and far between. The plastered-on fake smiles she gives cover everything from shame and embarrassment to fear and acceptance. Acceptance of what? I didn't know. Not yet, anyway. But I know I want to find out. More importantly, I want to find out how to get more real smiles. The ones that took over her whole face and transformed her from beautiful to stunning. Her smile was contagious, making her chin more pronounced and lifting her entire face. The sparkles in her eyes reminded me of precious stones, glittering in the sunshine.

Seeing her porch light out almost made me want to change it for her but I knocked myself down a peg. No need to go all he-man on a woman I literally just met. But, when she opened the door with those big doe-eyes, wide with trepidation and caution, it took all I could not to thump my chest like King Kong and drag her away from anything that could scare her.

Her strength and determination impressed me as we discussed the incident. I have a sneaking suspicion, this isn't new for her. She said as much but it didn't fully register until I was back in my squad car, headed for the station.

One thing I know for sure, this woman is the epitome of strength. She has absolutely been beaten down and dragged through hell yet she frequently reminds herself to be strong for her kids. Her guarded stance when we first entered her kitchen told me all I needed to know. The subtle shift of her hunched shoulders to try and appear small, the way she wrapped her arms around her midsection as if shielding herself from prying eyes and judgment.

Yeah, some jackass, or multiple jackasses, did a real number on her. But the moment she talked about the potential threat to her kids, her entire demeanor changed. She sat up straighter, painted a look of determination on her face and tilted her chin up like she was preparing for battle.

Her phone call today pissed me off. Not because she called, but because I was sincerely hoping that all of this was just a misunderstanding or a prank. Something, anything that wouldn't bring harm to this woman. That fact that some dickwad is scaring her makes me want to hit something. I feel myself begin to vibrate in anger.

What am I doing? I don't get worked up about women. No relationships. Not now. Not after what happened last time.

Trudging back to my desk, I open up the Black Thorns file and begin looking for connections, again. This is the perfect distraction from the blue-eyed angel I can't take my mind off of. *This* is what I'm here for. *This* is what keeps me going. The Black Thorns are going down and it's going to be me that hammers the nails in their coffins.

5

Annie

After dropping off my littles with my mom, and sending Officer Daniels the information, I dial one of my closest friends. Her smoky voice lifts through the speakers and instantly makes me smile.

"Hey, lady. Where have you been? I've missed you!"

Lana and I met a couple of years ago after we moved into the little neighborhood. Her body is the perfect image of a curvy woman. Thick hips and thighs, and boobs that men drool over, even if she's wearing a button-up work shirt. Her brunette hair is always in a high ponytail. Unless we're at her house, then she lets it fall where it wants to. She isn't the dress-up and makeup type; except for rare, special occasions. She loves to live life, drink, hang in her garage, and talk shit.

I've always envied her ability to just accept herself and give others the option to do the same. "If they like me, cool, if not, fuck 'em" she once told me. She is my exact opposite. No worries about pleasing others, no bull-shit covers, she speaks her mind and lets the chips fall. I'm lucky to have someone like her. Unfortunately for her, that also means she has stuck up for me on more than one occasion. She doesn't like drama but refuses to let someone disrespect her friends.

Now that I think about it, I think I felt drawn to her because she is so much like my best friend, Christina. She moved states a few years ago and is living her best damn Hallmark family life. I couldn't be happier for her, but I still miss her like crazy. We may talk as frequently as two working moms can but, it still sucks. I'm just glad I accepted Lana's invitation to hang out. I would be far lonelier without her. I would laugh a whole lot less, too.

"Hey, Lana! God, it's good to hear your voice. Been busy with kids and work but I finally got a rare weekend to myself. Do you want to catch up sometime?" The more I speak, the more relaxed I feel. I know I need to catch up on some chores and chapters but I need people, too. Lana is always my first call on the rare instance I'm "free". "Actually, I have plans tonight."

"Yeah, sure. I mean, maybe even brunch on Sunday before I get the kids? Whenever. Just wanted to put feelers out." I try to sound nonchalant but the truth was, I didn't have many others I rely on.

After Christina moved a couple of years ago I closed myself off, again. My other friendships had been faulty at best. Built on my typical foundation of me playing chameleon and trying to be the person they wanted me to be. But, naturally, they floated away, too. Lana is the one person I know who doesn't expect anything from me and truly accepts me. Broken, damaged, used, and useless. But, for some reason, she likes me anyway.

Her chuckle brings me back to the call, "Girl, if you had waited for me to finish, I would have told you I have plans but you should absolutely join. It's time you got out and had fun."

My brain back-fired. "Out as in, not hanging in the garage? Where are you going?" I am pretty sure my panic didn't come through; or at least, I think it didn't. I don't do well around large crowds. Being open to all the judgment makes me break out in hives. Literal hives.

I can feel my chest and face heating, but am pulled from the swirling doubt when Lana states, "Annie! It's fine. You know I would never put you in harm's way. We always hang out in my garage or yours. Just come out with me. One night. If it gets to be too much, let me know and we will bring the group back to my place. Ok? But you've got to get back out there. You work two remote jobs, take care of your babies, and never leave the house. Getting out will be good for you. You'll see."

She paused her rant long enough for me to gather my thoughts. I mean, how bad could it really be? People went out all the time. Heck, I used to. And, instead of ruining her night, I could always just go back home. However, the moment that thought entered my mind, I recoiled, bringing back my attention to the ominous messages I was receiving. I really didn't want to stay home alone tonight. Yeah, going out tonight was definitely the lesser of the two evils.

"Alright, I'm in. But no trying to hook me up." I added, knowing she's been trying for the last eight months.

Her laughter rang out and I eased back into my seat. "Fine, fine. But come to my house to get ready. Oh, and when was the last time you got tested for STDs?" *Wait, what?*

"Why?" My voice came out as a squeak. I mean, it's not like anything has happened since my husband died but I did ask for one at my girly appointment last month.

"Was it in the last 3 months?" Completely ignore my question. "Well, yeah, last month actually."

"Sa-weet! OK, bring the results, and your ID. We are going to live it up tonight. And Annie?" She pauses long enough to pull me from my fear. "Yeah?"

"Breathe. I promise I would never knowingly put you in danger. Now, get your ass over here and we can get ready together."

The music blaring through the speakers tells me she hung up; most likely not allowing me time to object. As I comb through my thoughts, trying to figure out if I could really do this when my poly-jamorous playlist begins playing Lose Control by Missy Elliot. At that moment, the words spill from my lips and I quickly become overly animated. Before the hook drops my entire body is in it.

Damn, I love music. Feeling the familiar smile that only comes from a good song, in the right moment, solidifies my decision. I want to dance, to move, to feel alive. Tonight may be a huge mistake, but that's Tomorrow Annie's problem. Tonight, I'm going to go with the flow and enjoy the company of my closest friend. What's the point of life without living a little?

Let's do this.

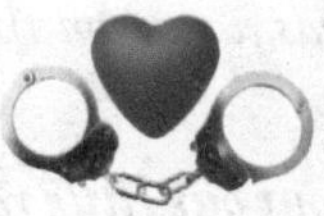

I am neck-deep in Black Thorn's paperwork when my cell buzzes on my desk. Seeing Jenson's name flash across the screen tells me that he sent a message. I pinch the bridge of my nose, feeling my headache tighten around my temples, before responding.

Jense- Making sure you're alive out there. Don't forget we're going to Sky's the Limit tonight. You need it. We need it. Don't even think about pussying out.

My eyes are throbbing and my back is aching from sitting in this damn chair all day, chasing leads that lead to ghosts.

Me- It wouldn't be pussying out because I didn't agree to go in the first place.

Jense- Well who pissed in your cornflakes, Everest?

I know what he's doing. He only uses the nickname to get under my skin. He easily has 4 inches on me but I'm a lot broader than he is. Nick called me Everest when we were leaving the movie theater and complained he couldn't squeeze out the door with me next to him. *Dick.*

Me- You know I don't eat that sawdust, Jen-Jen." I chuckle knowing he hates us calling him that. His hair is forever longer than anyone else in our little group. He either leaves it down in waves or puts it up in the perfect, GQ-worthy man-bun.

Jenson and I have known each other since high school. Tale as old as time and all that shit. He was a star on the swim team while I relieved my anger on the football field.

Nick and Cory rounded out our little rag-tag team of misfits. While Jenson and I had the school cheering when we played, the other two goofballs stayed behind the scenes. Cory had been proactive in planning, organizing, and fundraising every major school function. From Freshman orientation to school dances, there was nothing that didn't pass through Cory, first. He may run around like a stressed out chicken but his final products were always better than anyone imagined. Each event was different, all 4 years. No two themes had been the same but he was a master at reusing decorations and materials.

Nick, on the other hand, was a computer whiz. He was the quiet kid. You know the one. Black hair, black nails, baggie black shirt featuring

Korn's new album image. People didn't understand him so they typically gave him a wide berth. Had they taken the time to look closer, they would have seen a kid wanting to disappear from attention because the only type he ever got at home was negative. He firmly believed that if his family was cruel and abusive to someone they were supposed to care for, everyone outside of that would be the same.

Naturally, Jenson and I first met at an athletics fundraiser Freshman year. The departments split us up into groups to tackle the car wash, advertising, and entertainment. Jenson and I worked on making big, obnoxious signs to catch everyone's attention that came within half a mile of the parking lot we were in.

When we finished making signs, we started talking and quickly realized we had a lot in common. One of the strangest connections was the fact neither of us liked that attention from the sports. We enjoyed the sport itself, how it cleared our minds and pushed our bodies. Anything outside of that was frivolous nonsense.

Towards the end of Sophomore year, the athletes were asked to work together to prepare for our massive end-of-year celebration. Enter Cory. The guy was so high-strung, he had lists for his lists. All the other guys seemed to razz him about it but, just like every other event, Jenson and I just did what we needed to finish the project. In the grand scheme of our lives, it didn't matter.

As the event drew closer, the other groups appeared to take on the "typical jock" stance and pushed Cory over everything, purposefully leaving out small things or adding them just to watch Cory squirm. Jenson and I could tell Cory was about to break and not in a tear-filled manner. Cory's eyes looked murderous as one group "accidentally" filled the balloons with confetti penises instead of the graduation confetti. His shoulders drew up, his fists were clenched and he was noticeably vibrating with barely contained rage.

Seeing a potential for trouble, Jenson and I left our station and asked Cory how he wanted the streamers to hang from the ceilings. It took a moment but he pushed out a deep breath and stalked over towards our table. Once we meticulously drug out each and every confirmation about placement, Cory's shoulders relaxed. Jenson decided validation was the way to go and commended Cory for everything he had done. The more we talked, the more he relaxed. Jenson and I decided he needed to loosen up a little and maybe we could help with that.

After the celebration the following week, we found Cory loading up the last of the storage boxes in the rec room and decided to ask him to come grab a burger with us. He looked like we had asked if he was an alien and searched our eyes trying, and failing, to find any malice. Once he realized we were serious about hanging out, he ecstatically agreed.

He locked up the rec room and said he had to stop in the AV room to make sure all the equipment that was used was stored properly. There, we found Nick backing up files, I guessed, and shutting down equipment. After his initial shock at someone in his space, I took a cue from Jenson's repertoire and complimented him on the sick light show and music production. Jenson and Cory joined in on the praise and we watched as he uncurled from himself.

By the time everything was shut down and stored properly, the four of us had started joking about the drama between some teachers. The banter felt comfortable, right, somehow. We grabbed dinner at a local diner and the rest is history.

My phone buzzes again, bringing me out of memory lane.

Jense- Don't hate because your hair isn't as soft and lustrous as mine. But, seriously, you're coming out with us. It's been months and this case has been draining you. Come on! You haven't been home in days. Please.

The big-teary-eyed emoji pinged in directly after.
Taking a deep breath and exhaling raggedly, I scrub a hand down

my face and run my fingers over my beard. It *has* been a long time since we all had a night out. And I was definitely spinning my wheels in circles with this case. I guess a change of scene couldn't hurt.

Me- Fine. Fine. Stop pestering me. I'm closing down here. Will be home in an hour.

Fireworks and smiley faces light up my screen and I chuckle as I drop my phone in my pocket. Pushing away from my desk, I quickly organize the area for maximum efficiency so I can dive right back in when the next shift starts. I take a moment to clean out my coffee mug and set it on the drying rack before locking my desk and strolling to the elevator.

As I descend to the parking garage, my mind slowly wanders back to the woman with the big blue eyes and the most tempting dips and curves. When the elevator pings, I shake myself to clear my head. Maybe I do need to find someone to play with tonight. It's been long enough. I bet a real release will pull me out of my head. Come tomorrow, I'll be relaxed, clear, and ready to get back to digging up dirt.

6

Annie

After a thirty-minute drive, I slip out of Lana's Chevy and glance around. The lot we parked in is a typical parking lot in an L-shaped strip center. All the doors and windows are covered in black with something that makes them shimmer under the glow of the street lights. The smaller section on my left looks like it had once been 3 separate offices or businesses. There was an additional door right in the corner before the building continues out across the lot in front of me. 6 separate doors are located between sections of large windows; all covered in the same black material.

Lana steps up to my sides and hooks her arm into mine. "Ready bitch? I'm so excited! I've wanted to bring you here forever! I can't believe it's finally happening." She ends with a squeal that sets my nerves alight. *What the hell have I gotten myself into?*

I check my phone for messages but know after the call at 8 that my littles are in bed already. Mom was way too excited I was going "out-out" and told me to live a little. She reminded me that life is short, the kids were covered, and I was allowed to have some fun once in a while.

Nodding to Lana, we stride towards the corner door of the club and I plaster an excited smile that I wasn't sure I felt yet. My nerves are firing and my anxiety is swirling. I used to go out all the time but, I don't know. I grew up, I guess. Life happened. I don't need bars and clubs to have fun. And I will never be in a relationship again. I focus every ounce of my energy on being a good mom to my kids and making sure they know nothing but love, acceptance, and self-confidence.

Lana yanks the door wide and we step into a small, narrow foyer to our left. A huge, burly man is standing with a tablet in his hand and a serious expression on his face. There is nothing in this area that gives me any idea of what is here. The hall was just that. Red crimson paint filled the walls with intricate, black molding giving it a gothic yet sexy vibe. The area is lit with a singular, black chandelier that drips danger and decadence. Other than that, it's just us, and, um, Charles; according to his name tag.

Lana pushes her chest out and smirks wide. "Hey, Charlie. Manning the door tonight?" Charlie snaps his attention to Lana and something swirls in his eyes. Lust, *nothing new there*, and, was that...admiration? He looks like his soul has just been snatched straight from his body and he can't help but stare. Taking a peak at Lana, I'm shocked to see the same, exact thing. *Filing that away for later.*

Lana's grin grows into a real-life genuine smile, her face heating the longer he stares. As if zapped by lightning, Charlie flinches, clears his throat, and then looks back at his tablet.

"Yeah. I'm covering for a bit since Joseph took his kids to the rink for their birthday. He'll be back in a couple of hours." He started with a voice that sounded gruff and detached but ended with it deep and rich.

A spark lights in Lana's eyes before introducing us. "Well come find me if you decide to hang out when he gets back. Until then, Charlie this is Annie. Annie, Charlie." We shake hands with plastered-on smiles and awkward "nice to meet yous."

Charlie asks for my ID and paperwork from the doctor. He briefly explains that exclusivity and privacy are very important. Then, he leads us further down the hall and into a tiny office that consists of a small square table and chairs.

Handing Lana a key I didn't even realize he used, he asks if I want him to go over the NDAs and information or if I would be more comfortable with Lana doing it. Not knowing what the flying fuck he's talking about, I slap on a false bravado and tell him not to worry because Lana and I can handle it. With a smile, and a nod of his head, he glances at Lana one more time before smirking and closing the door.

The moment the door clicks, I whirl on Lana. "Ok. I try to be very understanding and accommodating but maybe that's my fault. Why are we in this room? Why did they need a clean medical record, and why, the fuck, do I have to sign an NDA?"

Lana had taken a seat on one of the benches in the small room. She stays silent as I rant and pace the floor. Once I stand still and face her, her smile lights up and her eyes sparkle with mischief.

"Annie" she states calmly, "You are one of my absolute, bestest friends. I would never do you wrong. But you, my friend, need to live. We have had enough late-night conversations, both with and without alcohol, that I *know* you, and I know how much you try to close off to others. I know you have a wall around your heart, body, and life as high as the Great Wall of China. I know you've been hurt. But I also know that you deserve the world and more. You deserve to live and feel and explore."

"But I do. And I don't want another relationship. Like ever. I don't need all that," she cuts me off with a raise of her hand, effectively silencing me.

"I'm not saying we are looking for forever. I *am* saying I know you and I are a lot more alike than even you may know. And a big part of that is because the moment you tell, even me, something you think you may be judged for, you cut yourself off and change topics. However, we have talked so much that you have slowly given me a lot of different pieces to the puzzle that is you and your curiosities. And, I think this place can help you see where those pieces fit into your life. I know this place helped me feel seen, and safe, and sexy, and powerful and confident. I'm saying, please trust me." The sincerity and hope in her eyes knocks me off balance.

We've always been talkative, jumping from one subject to another. And I know I have sometimes clammed up when a topic becomes too much or I get shy or nervous or embarrassed, but I had no idea she saw, and knew, so much. Add to that how much she genuinely sounds like she cares, I couldn't back out now even if I wanted to. Rolling my shoulders back and steeling my spine I breathe out and say the only words I can think of. "Let's do this."

* * *

When Lana sat me down and explained what this place was, I truly felt like I stepped into the twilight zone. I swore sex clubs weren't real. They were just fantasy destinations in books and stuff. Her chuckle at my naivety made me give her the stink eye before she assured me, once again, we would have fun.

The more she explained, the more I understood why we did our makeup and hair but brought the clothes to change into. Anonymity was a huge selling point for this place. No phones or recording devices are allowed and there was a very wordy NDA. Medical clearance was required every 3 months and you didn't get on the list unless you were a member, or a guest of a member and they are chaperoning you. However, they still ran a background check.

By the time I finished with the paperwork, I asked if they needed a urine sample as well, earning me a swat on my jeans-covered ass. I figured I needed some humor after reading it all. The club policies and procedures are insane. But, I guess they have to be.

First order of business, if you are new, you have to come in at least an hour before opening so they can get everything processed and cleared; which explains why we left the house so early. Additionally, the list for entrance has a limit and is different for each evening. The club is open for this purpose on Thursdays, Fridays, and Saturdays beginning at 10:00 pm. If you want in, you have to call to be on the list before 7 pm that evening or any day before. They do not allow walk-ins.

Before walking out to finish getting ready, we are given masks that must be secured before entering the parking lot and stay in place until after we leave the parking lot. If anyone shows up without the one that is issued, with the exception of theme nights, they can not enter.

From 10-Midnight, the larger area on the right opens as a regular dance club. Drinks flow and people begin to loosen up.

After midnight is a whole different ball game. That's when the more *interesting* things become available. From 12:00-6:00 am, the middle and left sides of the building open up. The middle is supposedly a dance/voyeur-type area. They still have a bar but clothes and inhibitions are apparently optional. The left side of the building holds rooms that are apparently decked out with anything and everything someone, or multiple someones, may need to have a little fun.

That is where Lana first lost me. There's no way I'm going to show anyone my body and I'm definitely not screwing someone I don't know. It took her a couple of minutes but she finally reminded me this place is 100% about consent. I don't have to do, drink, see, or say anything, and, at the first sign of pushiness, people are out on their asses. But, according to Lana, that rarely happens due to the extensive paperwork and legalities involved.

Once she had me calm, again, she explained that each time you check in, you choose your color for the night. Red, Yellow, Green, Black. If at any time you want to change it out, you can. The colors are worn as bracelets on your wrist to show others your availability. Red- Just watching, Yellow- May be interested in playing, Green- Here to play, and Black- Owned. I cringed when she said it out loud but she quickly explained that the club caters to the BDSM community. So, if a woman, or man, is owned, it is a consensual agreement between the parties involved, and that label is highly respected throughout the community.

Taking in all the information was a lot but the key point I focused on was the fact that *I* choose my involvement in all aspects of the evening. If someone breaks the rules and becomes pushy, security gets involved. They are highly protective over their customers and consent was repeated about a thousand times in the paperwork.

An hour later, we're walking back through the door, masks in place, and checking in. Lana requests a yellow bracelet since she doesn't want to make me feel abandoned, and I choose red. Charlie draws open the curtain behind him and my mouth drops. This place screams decadence and danger. Sophistication and depravity. Red paint covers the walls with similar trimming that is in the hallway. The bar is to our left; every bottle you could dream of is sitting on tiered shelves connected to a long-mirrored wall. The front wall, where the outside windows are, is lined with huge black, shimmering curtains.

The wall on the far side in front of us, the right wall, and the front wall are lined with big black sectionals. Each sectional has a small round table in its center with battery-operated tea lights to give a semblance of privacy.

The area in the middle is large enough to fit at least 200 hundred people. Thankfully, the club just opened so it's not packed yet. We make our way to the bar, grab a beer from a man named Jerry, and slide into the buttery couch as we wait for the rest of the group to arrive.

Typical club music is blaring through the speakers, a myriad of lights flash in every direction, enticing customers to let loose. DJ Got Us Fallin' in Love by Usher and Pitbull thumps through the space and I find myself slightly moving to the beat.

About ten minutes later, Lana and I are giggling like school girls, gossiping about neighborhood drama. She glances at the front door and jumps up, making her way through the small crowd on the dance floor. I look up and notice three figures who I assume are Jose, Connor, and James, but I can't quite tell given their distance and the amount of people between us.

As Lana finishes hugging them each, another woman jumps out from behind Connor, I think, sending her and Lana into a squealing fit that carries across the dancefloor. After a moment, she steps back, talks animatedly about something, while the others nod and grin. Then turns back this way, leading the group back to our area.

Once the guys reach us, I jump up and trade hugs with each relishing in their presence and overjoyed that I got to see them all tonight. When I step back, Lana introduces me to her friend Kyra.

Apparently, she just moved back and had turned to Connor for help in a surprise reunion.

In no time we are all laughing, sharing stories, and bantering back and forth. Lana is the easiest girl to hang out with and Kyra seems to be cut from the same cloth. The guys have been at Lana's every time I have gone over there. At one point I asked if they were just going to move in and help with rent. They're all good guys. Loyal, hilarious, and can take as good as they give when we start bickering. It's my own little family; even if I don't get to enjoy their time frequently.

This is going to be a great night. I can feel it.

7

∾

Jenson

Sky's the Limit is packed tonight. Not necessarily unusual for a Friday night but the air seems to be more charged with... something, I don't know. We've all been so busy with work and our personal projects that the guys and I haven't had time to just relax and unwind. We haven't been here in at least three months and haven't played with someone else in longer.

That bitch Amber did a real number on Nick and Cory. Vince and I liked her but I don't think we ever let it unfurl to the depths they had. Since her, Nick closed himself off more than he had been in years and Cory has buried himself in work. He's got to take a break. We all do. Hopefully, tonight will be just what he needs.

Jerry, the bartender, slides over the tray of beers and shots with a

54

nod and I swivel my head behind me to make sure I don't bump any-one. The black leather sectionals that line the walls around the massive space allows every patron a perfect view of the bar, and the entertain-ment floor. I scan the floor and spot the guys in the far corner. A small battery-operated tea light sits in the middle, illuminating their faces, each hidden behind a black mask. They are just far enough away from the main floor that the lights barely reach them and they look like a bunch of creepy motherfuckers.

Chuckling to myself, I walk over and pass out the drinks to start the night. Lifting up our shot glasses, Cory recites our toast, "To the men we are, the boys we were, and the legends we will become. Cheers!" We all clink our glasses and throw back the shot. The fiery tequila burns as it makes its way down and ignites my soul. I slide on the end of the sectional and lean against my knees as I survey the crowd.

"Tommy must be thrilled to see the club fill up like this," Nick remarks as he picks the wrapper of the beer.

"Hell yeah. I bet he and his group will be celebrating tonight in a big way. Jerry told me the list was completely maxed out for the night before 8." Cory grunts his approval and Vince looks a million miles away.

Tapping him on the knee to get his attention, he fumbles his beer before mumbling something and putting it on the table. "What's up, man? You ok?"

He exhales in a rush and scrubs a hand over the top of his hair. I can see the lie on the tip of the tongue. With one glance at me, he knows I'm not playing. "No. Just this gang is kicking my ass and there's other assholes out there. It's just. I don't know, man. I'm supposed to find and catch the bad guys. But once we lock one up, it seems ten more pop right out of thin air." He blows out another breath and takes a gulp of his beer.

"I get that. That's why you needed a break. You are only one person. You can't take everyone down. And humans are just that;

humans. Some are bad, some are good. Some are good but make bad decisions. You can only do the best you can given the resources and abilities you have. You're not trying to save the world. You're trying to make the world better for one person at a time. And hope that causes a ripple."

"Well shit, Jense, if I didn't know what you did for a living, I would think you were some kind of motivational speaker, conning people out of their money," Nick says with a sarcastic grin.

"Fuck you, man," I joke, tossing the wet napkin I pulled from my beer at home. "I'm going to go grab another round of shots. Any requests?"

I rise to my feet and turn back to look at my 3 best friends. My 3 lifelines. Cory's eyes light up with interest. "Ooo, you know what we haven't done in forever? A kamikaze!"

"That's because that's a pussy drink," Nick grunts as he dodges Cory's slap to the chest. I look at Vince to get his input and he's chuckling at the other two clowns, finally looking relaxed. When he faces back to me, he juts out his chin in agreement.

I make my way back to the bar and lean against the end. Knowing it will take some time before Jerry gets a minute, I pull up my work email to make sure nothing strange has happened in the last hour. *Yeah right. This company is a well-oiled machine. I'm just obsessive.*

I tuck my phone back in my pocket as Jerry slides over to me. Leaning over so he can hear me, I order 4 kamikazes and 4 tequila gold shots. As Jerry walks off, I hear the slightest little giggle coming from behind me, and my heart stutters. I turn around, lean back on the counter, and take the most adorably sexy woman I have ever laid eyes on. Yes, those two descriptors don't go together but, by God, she is.

Behind her black mask are the most strikingly ocean-blue eyes. The strobes from the lights dance around her face, making her eyes appear to be glittering. Her platinum blonde hair is pinned back on each side with soft curls falling past her shoulders. Her cheeks are the perfect amount of round to match the curve of a hand but appear to be splattered with pink. Not like makeup, pink. Blushing maybe? Which leads me to believe she's not wearing much makeup since most cake on enough crap that it turns them into someone totally different.

I take in her shoulders and see the lace of her bra strap covering a black tattoo just beside her left collarbone. Her other shoulder is covered by one of those one-sided shoulder shirts. The material looks soft but not shiny. It falls off her shoulders just enough to make you want to explore more. The shirt itself is understated, all black, maybe a size too big, gently clinging to the swell of her breasts before rumpling around her waist. The short-as-sin black shorts come just an inch or two below the apex of her thighs and what a glorious sight those are.

Her creamy skin looks like the sun doesn't regularly destroy it. Her thighs are tantalizingly perfect. *I bet I could see a full handprint just on the top.* The lighting is just bright enough that I see the little handles on the inside. You know the ones. The hot pockets of the thighs that girls hate. Right on the inside. *Mmmm delicious.* They are the perfect size to grab onto when riding around in the car. Close enough to her core to matter but not so close that she gets anything; until I say so.

Oh, Dear Lord. Crap. Now I have a boner.

Shaking myself out of my terribly obvious staring, I force myself to look back at her face. However, any excitement I had vanished in an instant. Her shoulders are pulled back and chin tipped upwards but her breathing seems to be stuttering. Like, she's preparing herself for battle.

As that thought enters my mind, I snap my gaze to her eyes and watch as she pulls back the lighter, carefree look she had just worn; shuttering it behind a wall of disinterest; or maybe that's forced confidence. Either way, I don't like it.

Clearing my throat, I tip my lips into a wide smile and hope she can see the mischief in my eyes. "Were you laughing at me, Sweetness?"

She holds her stance for a beat before her brows furrow in confusion. "Wh-what?" *Oh sweet Jesus. Her voice matches her face. I want, no, I need to hear more of it.*

Chuckling I step forward, just into her space but not so much that we touch, "I heard you giggle. No one is around you, so it wasn't a joke someone told. Were you laughing at me?"

The wheels in her eyes start churning. I can see every single thought play out. She's worried and maybe a little scared. Does she think I'll be mad? Or yell at her? Before I can throw out a joke to calm the thoughts that are clearly wreaking havoc in her mind, she dumps on me, then retreats.

I steal a glance at the floor before meeting his eyes again. "I wasn't laughing at you. I was amused that someone ordered a drink that I hadn't even thought about in over a decade. I just kind of figured that wasn't a thing anymore." I shrug as I finish my rant. My voice came out just loud enough for him to hear me over the music but not by much. I tried to sound confident and bold, maybe flirty, but not snarky.

Fuck, why couldn't I keep that giggle in? I can literally feel my cheeks and ears burning. I can't talk to guys. Let alone guys like him. Shit.

Mr. ManBun seems stunned for a moment while his green eyes sparkle in the light. Those have to be contacts. I have never seen eyes look like actual emeralds. Their depths and the way the lights of the club bounce off them is absolutely mesmerizing.

"Are you calling me old or new? I can't tell which." His lips tilted in a casual smirk and his eyes sparkle with mischief. *I hope. I think that's what that is. Oh God, is he making fun of me? I gotta get out of here.*

I can feel the embarrassment bleeding down my neck and into my chest. Searching for a way out, I quickly apologize, blurt out something about it being funnier in my head, and dash back to the couch that Lana sits at with our friends. Sliding into the sectional, I do everything I can to make sure my back is firmly facing the bar.

Jesus, Annie. One night. You can't keep yourself from saying something stupid for one night?

A snap near my face cuts me off from my own verbal lashing. "Annie, you ok? Did you get your drink?" Connor asks with his brows pinched in concern. Hearing Connor's question, Lana turns away from her conversation with Jose and looks at me.

"Good Lord, girl, what happened? Your whole upper body looks like a tomato."

Thank you Cherokee genes from somewhere in my lineage. I can't make a fool out of myself without plastering it all over my body.

"Nothing," I answer quickly. "Just, um, couldn't decide what I wanted so I came back." I officially have our little group's attention. And from the looks of it, I really am a shitty liar. Jose leans over the table and narrows his eyes, scanning everything from my waist up. "Ooo girl, who is he?"

"What?" The chorus around me says the same thing. Jose looks so smug and I want to punch him in his perfect face. I narrow my eyes at him and purse my lips before taking the high road...sticking my tongue out at him.

The laughter around me lifts my spirits and I remember why I love this little group. They are all nosey, a little pushy, but so damn loyal to the people they care for. It is intense and overwhelming but, also, nice.

The longer I go without talking, the harder Jose stares at me. "Annie, babe, you always drink the same 3 things. Either a beer fully

dressed, a tequila shot, or a tequila sunrise. Don't play with me, girl."
Dammit.

After about a minute, I blow out a breath and start to think about how to explain it. I mean, sure, Mr. ManBun is sinfully sexy. All that thick brown hair made me want to run my fingers through it. And good gracious, his eyes were effing emeralds. Of course, I got lost in them! Not to mention his body. He towered over me even though Lana convinced me to wear a pair of wedge heels. Lower than hers, but high enough I'm certain I'm going to break something.

His beard was shaved close but still long enough to run your fingertips through. In the brief glimpses I got with the dance lights, I noticed small plugs in each ear. His white shirt was tucked into his fitted black jeans and the top 3 buttons had been left undone, revealing a myriad of tattoos peeking out from his collar. His entire frame appeared to be lean muscle. Not bulky with lifting weights but more of a swimmer or a rock climber. The sleeves on his shirt were rolled up to reveal lean, veiny forearms that were wrapped in tattoos. His entire presence screamed money and sex but the glint in his eye screamed of a whole other kind of danger.

Shaking my head from the rabbit hole I fell down, I shrug off the others and go with a simple, "Just some guy who was too hot for his own good and clearly saw me lacking."

I tried to change subjects but Lana went full-blown attack dog. "Who the fuck disrespected you? Where?" Jose and Connor are both trying to get her to sit back down as my eyes widen with shock. I knew she was protective but we never really went out anywhere for me to see how much.

"Lana," I said gently, "Lana, it's fine. He didn't say anything. It was just how he looked to me, I guess." And then, the word vomit. "And he asked me a question and I froze. I mean he was like, sinfully hot, and I couldn't tell if he was joking with me or upset or maybe he was just playing around, you know. Like, 'Let's flirt with the fat girl.

Ha. Ha.' I don't know so my brain just glitched, and I came back here. He did nothing wrong. I don't think he did. I'm not sure. Anyway, I'm here and we're going to have fun. Wanna dance?"

By the time I shut my mouth, get control of my flailing hands, and take a deep breath, I realize my entire little group is staring at me, slack-jawed with a mix of confusion and...pity, maybe? "What?" I mumble. My face and chest ignited all over again.

Connor rests his hand on my knee and I jump at the contact. He pulls it back quickly and holds it up until my mind catches on to who it is. I release a thankful smile towards him before he responds. "Listen, A, you are ok. You are safe. And you are going to have a great time. So what, you got into your head a little? It happens. You haven't been out in how long? It's normal. Stop overthinking everything and let go. Just breathe and know we've got you. Ok? Now, I'll go grab you a drink, and you and Lana can hit the dance floor." He taps his finger on my knee, this time not making me flinch since I saw it coming, and walks away with a wink.

Lana jumps up, shimmies past Jose, and takes me by the hand. "Let's go, bitch. We didn't come here to over think, we came to stop thinking. Woo-hoo!" Chuckling at her antics, I let her drag me to the floor and hope my brain would magically forget the whole ordeal.

8

Annie

The vibrations from the bass and lyrics from the song the DJ plays wind through my soul like tendrils of serenity. It is a high no drug could ever mimic. Pour Some Sugar on Me by Def Leppard is the perfect song to warm up my old, tired mom-bod. Lana clasps her hand in mine and leads me through the bodies swarming the floor. Once we reach a spot we can move around in, she throws my hand over her shoulder and backs up against me as we start swaying our bodies to the music.

The beer I had when we first arrived, along with our mandatory tequila shot when the group arrived, loosened me up enough to close my eyes and get lost in the song. My body moves around with Lana, in time with the music. Within moments, I let the rhythm of the song consume me.

I'm a big woman. The hips, thighs, and hanging belly from 2 C-sections and jacked-up hormones mean squeezing into anything less than a size 18 is problematic. My calves, ankles, forearms, and wrists are unusually smaller than the rest of me so they are the only parts I usually show.

Apparently, not tonight. Tonight, Lana had me squeeze into the shortest black shorts I had ever seen. They legit stop three inches below my ass. I can feel the jiggle in my thighs with every step I take and it makes me cringe. She "graciously" let me keep my one shoulder hanging-tee that shows off my collar bone and one of my favorite tattoos.

Lana also helped me with my makeup; light foundation with something called a setting powder, minimal blush since my face has enough red in it naturally, especially when I actually blush, an under-stated smokey eye, mascara that makes my lashes look full, and my favorite matte ink that enhances the soft-pink rose color of my lips, while also withstanding anything I come in contact with.

She finished my all-black ensemble with a pair of black wedge heels that gave me a slight lift, making my calves pop. A far cry from my norm, that's for sure. Converse and Hey Dudes are my go-to when out and about. And when home, my trusty slippers or double-buckle sandals accompany me. I had to hand it to her, I definitely felt better than my usually frumpy-mom vibe. *If only these shorts could just unroll a little.*

We had my main problem areas covered well enough but having this much of my thighs showing was becoming more and more of a problem. By the end of the song, I was pretty sure I had subtly tried to tug them down at least six times. The moment I gave myself over to the music, I would feel something that would make me cringe and

I'd be back to trying to pull them down, again. I know damn well it won't happen. This is how short they are, but it doesn't stop my brain from trying.

The DJ changes up the tempo and switches over to Rack City by Tyga. The change fills me with giddiness and sends me back to a time where I was free, happy, and found my solace on the dance floor.

Lana easily switches over dancing styles with me as the music envelopes us. I may be big but when I want to move, I do. It might not be sexy, or even something people want to see but in these moments, when I'm lost in the music, I could care fucking less.

-*Nick*-

Jenson has spent the last ten minutes scanning the dancefloor like it has the answers to the world's hardest questions. Ever since Jenson came back with the drinks, he's been unusually quiet. Like, he's lost in his head or something. "He Jen-Jen, what's got you so blue?" Throwing out the nickname was a surefire way to snap him out of his head.

Shrugging, he picks up his beer and swallows back a gulp before setting it back down; never taking his eyes off the floor. I share a look with Cory, then Vince to gauge their input but apparently they are just as clueless as I am. *Ok, different tactic.*

"Hey, Jense, you think the Cowboys will make it to the Super Bowl this year, right?" The three of us snicker knowing that talking in any positive way about the Cowboys will surely send him off on a rant.

We wait for a solid minute before Vince nudges his shoulder.

Jenson jumps out of his skin like he forgot we were here. Taking a breath and glancing between each of us, he shakes his head like he's clearing it. He clears his throat before saying, "Sorry. Just got lost in my head there. What's up?"

"Dude. You have been zoned out for at least ten minutes. That's not like you. Everything ok? Did something happen?"

"Uh...well...no?" His brows furrow like he's not sure if he's asking a question or answering one. "Okay," I hedge slowly. "Why don't you let us in? What's wrong?"

Jense takes a deep breath in before blowing it out, then reaches for his beer and takes a long pull. Whatever happened, he is definitely in his head.

"Jesus," he mutters to himself. "Ok, ok. So, I don't know why I'm letting it get to me but there was this girl. No, woman. She was, is, a woman."

All three of us perk up with equal amounts of confusion and intrigue. For Jenson to be this flustered, she must have floored him.

When he doesn't continue, Vince is the one to push, "And..."

After shaking himself from his thoughts, he tells us about the encounter he had at the bar. According to him, she is perfect and sexy but had absolutely no idea. Her voice got to him and the more she talked, the more he was drawn in. He had noticed her red bracelet and assumed this was probably her first visit.

Judging by the way he rambles on about every detail he noticed, the girl really called to him.

"So what?" Cory begins. "Go find her. Dance with her. Let her see that you were joking and not trying to hurt her feelings. You said it yourself. It seemed like she was wavering between confidence and uncertainty. If this is her first time, she may just have a hard time wrapping her head around it all and, maybe you just caught her off guard." He shrugs like it is as simple as that and takes another gulp from his beer.

For a good long moment, Jenson just stares at Cory, hopefully soaking in his words, then looks over at me. I raise my eyebrows at him in question before he clears his throat, then says he needs to use the bathroom. *Idiot.*

"Alright," I started as I stood up from the ridiculously comfortable couch, "I'm going to get us another round. Any requests?" The other two look at each other before turning back to me and shaking their heads.

Alrighty. Guess we're all going to be moody assholes tonight. Why did we come out, again?

Our couch is a straight shot to the bar. It's relatively easy to skirt around the main dance floor and sidle up to the counter. Jerry nods over to me and I hold up 4 fingers. He gives me a thumbs-up and dashes away.

I idly scan the floor packed with bodies working out the stress from their lives. Just when I'm about to turn and face the bar again, I see her. Now *that* woman is perfection. The crowd splits just enough that I can see her and another woman moving to the music. The woman in front of her is grinding into her front while I have the perfect view of her delicious ass.

Lord give me strength.

Her platinum hair, falling in waves past her shoulders, dips even lower as she throws her head back and absolutely gives herself over to the music. The sway of her hips is like a siren's song. Calling me; pulling me towards her.

My knuckles turn white as I grip the counter to my left and the barstool in front of me. My little siren continues swaying around to the rhythm and moves, just so, granting me my own little slice of heaven. My eyes hone in on her deliciously thick thighs; her little hot pockets, getting warmed up for their next meal.

Jerry slides the beers over towards me and I barely register that I should thank him or something. I nod in his general direction but keep my eyes fixated on the woman before me. The song comes to its end and I exhale the breath I didn't know I had been holding. Turning, I grab the beers and head back to the table.

When I make it back, I'm instantly disappointed that we took the furthest damn table in the room. I set the drinks in front of each of the guys and leave Jenson's in front of his spot. I plop down on the edge of the couch just as the next song begins playing. I obsessively scan the floor trying to find her; irritation creeping in as a mass of bodies moves to the floor.

Finally, there's a subtle break in the crowd and I find her again. Bodies are gyrating all over the dance floor because Ginuwine's Pony just brought us all back to our youth. But I sense something is wrong. My siren looks like someone has just jumped out of a dark room. Even from here, I see the panic on her face.

What is that about sweetness? Did someone hurt her? I'm gunna...

Before I can finish my thought, her friend pulls her hand back and clasps her face in her hands. She is telling her something and it looks kind of like she is reassuring her. Maybe calming her. *Oh shit, are they together?*

All thoughts in my brain cease to exist the moment my siren smiles wide. I kid you not I can see it from here! Her smile brightens up the entire room and her shoulders relax. Whatever her friend says, she chuckles and nods before grabbing her hand, turning around, and moving further into the dance floor; closer to me.

I don't know what's happening. My body feels like it's been activated by a live wire. My siren and her friend stop on this side of the dancefloor with only a few feet of people between us. Suddenly, a hand slapping on my thigh has me jumping out of my skin. The guys start roaring hysterically. "Ha. Ha. So funny. What was that for?"

Apparently none of these ass-clowns can answer me at the moment. I give them all looks letting them know they are less than amusing. "Cory...asked you...if you saw any prospects" Jenson wheezes through his laughter. "Then, then, Vince asked... if you... needed a bib." *These guys are all assholes. I swear.*

Jenson continues his laughter-induced wheezing "You still didn't respond...so, so... I hit your leg and you jumped so, fucking high!" That sent them all over the edge again. The longer I look at the lot of them, the harder is it to contain my own laughter. *Man, we must have really needed a night out if scaring me has them going this hard.*

Rolling my eyes I chuckle at their ridiculousness and take a swig of my beer. "Sorry jackasses. Guess I got a little lost in my head tonight, too." I smile and shrug it off before thumping Jenson on the thigh.

Returning my eyes to the dancefloor, I immediately catch sight of my siren. I have a perfect view of her profile. She and her friend have switched positions with my siren grinding back into her friend's front. The provocative lyrics in the song spur them on. It's like a God-damn porno, but with clothes, and I am here for it. Her hips are rolling, knees bent just so and, is that a tattoo on her forearm? *Fuck me.*

My heart is racing and I feel myself leaning towards them. Being drawn in, summoned, called. Bracing my arms on my knees I take in every inch of her with my greedy eyes. All that creamy, delicious skin, her ass, breasts, and thighs that are perfect for a large hand; or eight.

The longer I watch, the more I want her. And just when I can't take any more, she dips down low, pops her ass into her friend's crotch, and rolls herself back up; sliding her hands up her body, chest, and through her hair.

And *that* is when I learned I could cum without physical stimulation.

9

Annie

The song ends and my limbs vibrate from lack of use. I haven't had this much fun in ages. But, I'm old, and in desperate need of water. "I'm going to grab a water; need anything?" Lana leans in to listen before shaking her head. "All good. I'll meet you back at the table."

Glancing around, I look for the path of least resistance. People are everywhere. I didn't even realize how packed it had gotten while we were dancing until the group of girls bumped into me. The visceral shock to my system almost did me in but, in true Lana fashion, she was able to bring me back down. *Stupid nerves.*

I find my way through the crowd surging with energy as the

chorus to Jeremih's Down On Me begins. I've noticed that the closer we approach midnight, the filthier and sexier the songs get. At first, they switched through genres every few songs but It seems like the DJ is sticking with the songs you can get *very* close with.

Guiding my way through a gap in people, I hear the deep, rumbling laughter of a group of men. The sound sends goosebumps skittering over my arms and up my neck. Whatever is happening over in the furthest corner must be hilarious as the sounds of thumps, either on knees or the couch, produce a visual that someone, or a couple of them, are slapping their hands down. A small smile curves my lips at the thought of others enjoying themselves. Laughter is good for the soul, so, good for them for allowing themselves to let it out.

Turning my thoughts away from the corner, I step out wide and head towards the bar to ask for a bottle of water. I am definitely not in my 20s anymore and if I don't hydrate, I will be useless for at least two days. And, I have a house to clean.

A few girls step up behind me, giggling to each other. "Holy shit Beth, did you see that guy with the blue hair? He looks like a rock God. I wonder if he plays."

"Girl you can have him because Big Daddy in the back is all mine. Could you imagine all the ways he could flip you around like a ragdoll? Yes, please!" The duo dissolves into a fit of giggles before discussing what drinks they are going to order.

When the person in front of me moves away, I step up and wait for the bartender to finish with the next customer. The seductive tempo has me closing my eyes and swaying my hips. Subtle, of course, because I *am* standing in line and not on the floor. Just enough that music extends throughout my body and everything else begins to fade.

"What can I getcha?" I flinch, momentarily having forgotten where I was. The bartender has a wide smile and nice eyes which instantly has me release the breath I had gulped in. "Two bottles of water, please."

"No way. A pretty girl like you can't be in this room and walk away without a shot, at least." The smooth, smoky voice to my left slides over me like warm maple syrup. *Damn, what I wouldn't give to hear him speak to me. Maybe the duo behind me caught someone's attention. Good for them.*

Waiting for my drinks, I reach across the counter in an attempt to snag a few napkins. Of course, I'm short and there's no way I could possibly muster up the courage to yell over this music just to ask someone. I shrug it off and lean back to my original position. At the same moment, the bartender slides over 2 bottles of water to me with a wink. He then nods at the person just over my left shoulder so I smile and turn to maneuver out of the way.

"Hey, Jer. Need the keys to the office. We have a wardrobe emergency." The man chuckles.

When I turn to make my way from the bar, I am met with a chest. A hard chest. A hard chest with a sprinkling of blonde hair that's noticeable only because the top few buttons on his cyan-colored shirt are undone.

I snap my head down, muttering an apology, and try to sidestep him so I can get out of his way. As I start to move to his side, I stumble on my heels. His hands reach out and land on my shoulders like he's trying to steady me.

Before I can override my brain, I flinch, momentarily drawing my shoulders up. His hands fly back up and in front of him. "I'm so sorry. I couldn't back up and I actually thought you tripped over my big feet. I didn't mean to startle you." *Oh. He's the one with the yummy voice.*

"No worries. It's fine. I was just trying to get out of your way. Heh." I rattle off my response and barely glance toward his face because I know that damn voice is coming from a man *way* out of my league.

He chuckles deep in his chest and leans forward, just a little, to talk over the music. "You could never be in my way darlin'. I was already trying to get your attention."

"Huh?" I snap my head up to meet his eyes. "Yeah, you ordered only water. Surely you could use a shot or a beer, or something fru-fru?" His lop-sided grin seemed so genuine and the earth tones in his hazel eyes drew me in. He reminded me of summertime, camping by the lake.

"Wait, fru-fru? Like what?" *That's what you picked up on, Annie? Insert mental forehead slap here.*

"Hmmmm." He taps his chin and walks around me like a predator sizing up his prey. His eyes sparkle with playfulness behind his black mask and his dimples become more pronounced as his smirk grows into a knowing grin. As he comes to a stand in front of me, I notice his sharp nose, angled jawline, and puff of sandy brown hair. The sides are shaved close but the top is much longer but combed back and off to the side. The five o'clock shadow he's sporting makes his look go from businessman to playboy.

He stops in front of me, snaps his fingers, and smiles wide like he just made a brilliant observation. "I've got it. You're definitely a liquor girl but try to stay level-headed for some reason or another. The club scene isn't really your thing but you are more than happy to go out with friends when you can. You don't get a lot of time to yourself so, when you do, you milk it for all it's worth. You definitely seem like you have a few tricks up your sleeve but keep them hidden behind your alarmingly beautiful smile." He pauses for what I am sure is dramatic effect. "I'm going to go with tequila sunrise."

My face falls from my expanded smile in an instant. The past slaps me so hard it's almost hard to breathe. I feel my anxiety rising as memories threaten to take over. *Stop. Annie. You're fine.*

Shaking my head, I plaster on the brightest smile I can muster, chuckle, and roll my eyes. "Ooo that's a good guess. Maybe you should be the bartender instead."

His head tilts as if assessing me. It seems as if we are suspended in time. Forcing myself to continue grinning, I clear my throat before excusing myself.

"Well, as insightful as this has been, I really need to get back to my friends. Enjoy your night. And, good luck with the wardrobe malfunction." I say the last piece with my eyebrow raised and quickly scan him from head to toe. Right before I turn around, I make eye contact and throw him a wink with all the false bravado I can muster. His mouth drops open in shock and his eyes show his widen in surprise. Turning away, I make my way back to my group, just as the DJ announces that when the next song ends, the other sections will officially open.

Great! Maybe all the Adonis-types who keep flustering me will make their way to the back and I can just get lost in myself out here.

10

~

Cory

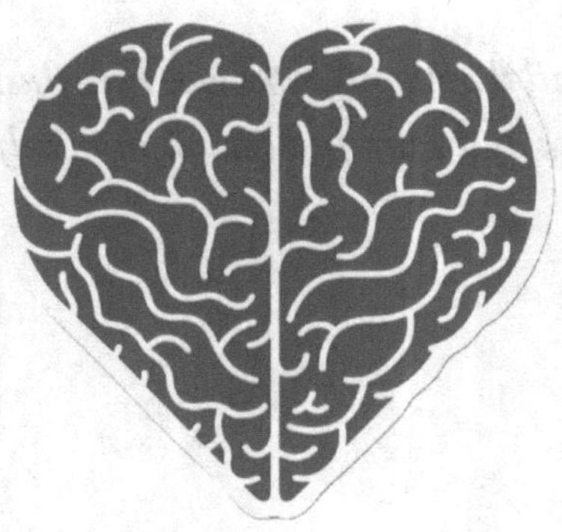

If I was a bettin' man, I'd bet I just met the woman that has Jenson all tied up. *Now I see why.*

After Vince pointed out that Nick had shown signs of his O face, we all dissolved into laughter. It definitely took us longer than it should have to help the poor bastard. Not sure what set him off, *pun intended*, but I know none of us have done that party trick since we were teens.

At some point, Nick stalked off to the back rooms yelling that we were all assholes. Once we sobered up a little, I told the other two I would come over and grab the key to the office we have set up. We always have a change of clothes stored here, just in case. Although, it's usually because Vince tears up the clothes or Jenson spills something. Never for anything this entertaining. I chuckled to myself the entire walk to the bar.

I slid up to the bar on the far left side so I could steal Jerry's attention quickly but I had mine stolen instead. I lingered just behind her and slightly next to a couple of girls clearly talking about Nick and Vince. When the girl with the fire-engine red hair referred to Vince as 'Big Daddy', I almost lost my composure but held in my need to bark out a laugh. Hearing 'Daddy' while any of us was in the room would be a guaranteed stop. None of us had Daddy kinks. In fact, we all cringed at anything remotely symbolizing a father figure. *Ew. Gross.*

Ignoring their conversation, I focused on the woman in front of me. Her fair-skinned, creamy calves were perfectly pronounced and would look so good drenched in oil; or wax. Her thick thighs were absolutely made to take a hand, or a paddle, and that fair skin would pinken up so beautifully. I had to shove my hands in my pockets and squeeze my hardening dick to try and calm it down.

Then she leaned forward across the bar to order some water. It was the perfect opening. I love to mix others' drinks and come up with perfect concoctions based on their personality. I tried, and failed, to make a joke about ordering just water but it didn't land. She either didn't hear me or completely ignored me, so I decided to wait until she was turned around to make my move.

I returned to my, probably creepy, perusal of her body. Her black shorts were snug against her ass and my cock throbbed painfully thinking about Nick having her trussed up with it in the air. Like a beacon to all our dirtiest fantasies. Her shirt sat right on top, rumpled around her waist. It did an annoyingly good job of covering her outer hips but my mind could fill in the blanks.

Just when I began to watch her platinum hair, twinkling in the light, she lifted up on her tip-toes, and bent over the bar, reaching as far over to the right as she could get. I couldn't tell what she was reaching for but, from my angle, I knew I was screwed. The muscles in her calves and thighs were pulled tight and her shirt lifted just enough that I could see where her hips dipped. *Fuck me running.*

She quickly plopped back down into a standing position when Jer showed up with her water. When noticed me, I let him know I needed the key. Then I subtly shifted, just a little, to block her path, leaving her unable to get around me.

I notice she ducks her head down before realizing I am in her way. She comes right up to my chest and I can see the different shades of blonde streaked through her hair.

After a short back and forth with her, I can see how Jenson felt. She is an angel, but she has definitely been broken. She waffles between bravery and being timid. I wanted her to be comfortable so I showed her my drink-matching trick. *Which failed miserably, as well.*

One minute she had this gorgeous smile that brought her light pink lips to life; her glittering ocean-blue eyes wide and filled with intrigue and amusement. The next, she shut down and transported somewhere entirely different. It was like seeing someone physically pull down barriers around their heart and mind. I was either way off or I was dead right and something bad happened to ruin that drink for her.

I hadn't realized I was trying to search for answers in her eyes until the sassy, confident woman showed back up. Her carefully constructed bravado dripped with confidence, sass, and a little bit of brat. She made a few teasing remarks and sashayed away before I could even pick my jaw up off the floor.

Yeah, that girl is a mystery wrapped in a body made for sin. Now I'm left with two questions: how can we convince this little spitfire to come out and play and, can the guys move past the hurt with Amber to even try?

When Jer returns with the office key, a plan is already forming in my mind. Now, to set the plan in motion.

11

Annie

I make my way back to my friends, downing half a bottle of water before plopping down next to James. "Hey! Look who found her inner dancing queen" he exclaims as the group claps and cheers wildly. I roll my eyes at their antics and try to hide my smirk behind another gulp of water.

Lana reaches over James and grabs my hand, "Girl, that was way too much fun! Now I'm going to force you out more often." I chuckle and shake my head at her enthusiasm for dancing with me. "Fine, fine. It's been too long and it felt so good. Even though I'm sure my knees and thighs are going to be pissed tomorrow."

I can't contain the smile that is glued to my face as I take a gulp of my water. When I look back at them, I see their faces changing, just a little, and they all begin to shift in their sits. Like, someone is about to deliver bad news.

"What's wrong? Did something happen?" Their looks of sympathy and curiosity are burning a trail of anxiety through my system.

Lana clears her throat and swats at James to switch places. She grabs my hand again and plasters on a gentle smile. The kind usually reserved for when she is talking me down from an attack. "Ok, so, the other side is opening soon. I don't want to necessarily leave you alone but Connor, Kyra, and James are going to go to the back rooms and Jose will be scoping out someone to play with. I know it's a lot to process but, do you want to come check it out?"

Before I can even finish my inhale, she rushes through her next statement. "I won't leave you. It's all about consent. No names. Just first letters or aliases. You have the red bracelet on so people may talk but no one should push. If they do, we give the signal."

I sit there contemplating for just a few moments. I mean, no one will approach me anyway. I don't look like half the women in here, I never have. And I am obviously a newb so there should be no reason for anyone to expect anything anyways. My internet search would confirm Lana's assumption about me being intrigued by these *activities. For once in your life, Annie, do something just for you.*

I roll my shoulders back, lift my chin, and flash my best conspiratorial grin. "I'm in. Besides, a girl could never have enough visuals in her rub club."

At first, they appear stunned into silence. Just when I think my joke didn't translate well, they all burst out laughing.

Kyra high-fives me and Lana jumps with a "whoop". Jose pulls Lana down next to him and waves his hand to the table that is apparently filled with shots. "Alright. Ladies' choice first. We have tequila anejo, sex on the beach, and pearl necklace." Lana reaches for the anejo and we all join in.

"Raise your glass to our friends, raise a glass to our fun; regrets in the morning? Nah, there'll be none. Cheers!" We all clink our shots together and toss them back. The intense flavor explodes on my tongue and trickles down my throat, burning in the best way.

Kyra chose the sex on the beach for us to shoot next, leaving the pearl necklace last. The sweet liqueur is a balm for my tastebuds. The creamy nature of the two ingredients blended together leaving a pleasant after-taste.

After all three shots are finished, we grab our water and head to the curtain on the other side of the bar. The curtain slides back to reveal a single door. *I guess privacy really is a big deal.*

Once inside, the space opens up to a huge room, about the size of the club, that is decorated with the same color palette and fixtures. The bar is designed the same as the one in the club and sits to our right. But that's where the similarities end.

Directly to our left is a long hallway. Lana says that is where private rooms are. Some have windows to see in, some have windows that let one room watch the other, and some are completely private. Rooms can be reserved but are generally first-come, first-serve.

The rest of the space holds a giant dance floor in the middle with cages placed near the perimeter. They are placed every 20 feet or so and are far enough from the walls that allow larger crowds to get a full view of whatever entertainment is on display. The 6 cages placed around the perimeter are reserved in advance.

The lights in here are dimmer. Even more than the club area. Instead of giant sectionals, rounded booths, benches, and tables are spaced out through the area. The music isn't as loud but is still enough to keep everyone moving their bodies but in a more subtle, sensual way.

People all around the room are in various stages of undress. One couple is in the closest cage; the woman blowing the man with vigor. His face is pinched with lust as he tweaks her nipples, causing her to flinch but never slowing her speed.

A small crowd has already formed and a man is between two women, watching the couple's show. The woman behind him is wearing a barely-there lingerie bodysuit that leaves absolutely nothing to the imagination. One of her hands is pumping his cock through his briefs as the woman in front, only wearing a tight black thong and nipple clamps, whips his shirt off.

Everywhere I look, people are lost in their own pleasure. Pushing, reaching for the high of feeling alive. It is fantastically erotic. I'm biting on my lip, face flushing, and thighs clenching. *Holy shit! I'm actually wet. And not just a little.* That in itself is a miracle.

I steal glances at my friends as we move away from the door and scope out a place to park. James, Kyra, and Connor apparently aren't interested in moving along. Connor has his hand shoved in the back of Kyra's pants, squeezing her ass, and James is kissing Connor with such ferocity it must feel like he's trying to swallow him whole.

It's not the first time I have seen Connor and James kissing heatedly but the sensual rhythm of the music and the way Kyra's eyes are hooded, watching intently, is a whole different level of hot. Tank's remix of 'When We' plays through the speakers. The lyrics seep through the room, cloaking it in sexual tension.

Lana smirks at them and pulls me towards the far end of the bar, hopping up onto the furthest bar stool and patting the one next to her. From this point of view, we can see the entire floor and all the ways people are enjoying their evening. Lana also knows me well enough to remember that I prefer to not have my back facing doors, or crowds, as much as possible. So, spinning bar stools are perfect.

Just to our right, almost hidden in the shadows is a huge security guard. His eyes constantly scan the area but he appears to be completely unaffected by the acts being performed in front of him. I guess he would have to be in order to do his job effectively.

One of the three bartenders working in this area places some napkins on the counter in front of us and takes our drink order. She is adorably petite but carries the confidence I imagine femme fatales possess. Her breasts are adorned with shiny nipple clamps that are connected by a long, silver chain. The chain dips down to her waist and wraps around her. Just below it sits red cheeky panties and absolutely nothing else. *Oh to have that confidence.*

Barely a minute later she slides over my Pink Russian and Lana's Vodka Tonic. We are so absolutely different. Her a vodka girl; me a tequila gal. She's confident, extroverted, and unapologetically her whereas I am unsure, introverted, and a people-pleaser to a fault. But I wouldn't want her any other way.

As we both take a sip of our drink, keeping our backs slightly turned on the crowd, she releases a squeal. Whipping around, I see Charlie squeezing her from behind, nestling into her neck. My brows hit my hairline and I grin at seeing her so carefree with a man. He whispers something to her before she lets out a gasp and pushes him to her right as she swivels in her stool and throws herself at the man standing there. The hug goes on so long, I glance away, feeling as if I'm intruding on something intimate.

Lana steps back, turns to me, and re-introduces me to Charlie. Apparently, he doesn't have a secret name since he helps with all the paperwork and stuff when coming in. The other guy, going by the name David, steps towards me, holds his hand out for me to shake, and gives me a megawatt smile. He kind of reminds me of Ryan Reynolds. Come to think of it, he could pass as his body double. The only glaringly obvious difference is the long blonde hair he has pulled up in a man-bun.

Charlie steps up behind Lana, sets his hands on her hips, and nuzzles into her neck. The smile that takes over her face as she winds her arm up behind her, dragging her fingers through his hair is absolutely stunning. I have never seen that glimmer in her eyes or the look of utter contentment and joy. I mean, we hang out quite a bit in groups and just the two of us, but I have never seen her like that.

"Maybe you should take Elle," her alias in the club, "for a twirl around the dancefloor." I toss out the suggestion with a smirk towards 'David' and glance back at Charlie. "Better hurry up before someone else steps up." My smirk grows as I try so hard to convey my amusement and sincerity with my eyes.

The masks take some getting used to as they cover from the middle of my eyebrows to the edge of my nose. But, it's at least not itching and irritating me so much anymore. Almost like putting on a hat and then forgetting it's there by the end of the day.

Lana steps away and dips her head towards me. "No way. I'm not leaving you alone. It's just good to see these fuckers."

"Watch it, princess," Charlie growls low under his breath. That definitely sounded like a naughty warning and not a scary one. *Damn. Go Lana.*

I reach out towards her, pull her into a hug, and pull back with my most dazzling smile. Speaking in a low tone, I say, "Girl, get your ass on that dance floor with at least one of those two fine specimens who are clearly excited to see you; in more than one way." I lift my brow to convey my meaning and gently push her towards them. She snatches up her drink, downs it in three gulps, and turns to face both men appearing very eager to hear her response. Subtly pushing her way between them, she sashays towards the dancefloor. After six or seven steps, she turns around, raises a brow, and brings up her hand, giving them a come here motion with her finger. One of the guys groans and the other growls but they both step towards her.

Deciding I didn't need to watch any more of *that*, I turn back around, grab my drink, and take a big sip of the creamy, fruity concoction. The thrum of the music mixes with the alcohol flowing through my veins and I allow myself to relax. I take a deep breath and allow myself enjoy a break. A break from my jobs, from being a mom, from trying to be fun and funny, from faking confidence; just, a break.

12

Annie

Touch Me by Ann Marie vibrates through the speakers. After fifteen minutes on the dance floor, Lana and her men had each shed some of their clothing. They are currently making use of one of the round booths on the opposite side of the club.

I feel strangely comfortable here. I'm not necessarily *enjoying* any particular group's activities but I am oddly content. For the first time in a long time, I feel no anxiety about being the weirdo by myself, no pressure to be or talk or act a certain way, no, nothing. Just content.

I'm sure part of this peace has to do with the third Pink Russian since making our way over here. They are just so damn tasty. My body is warm, a serene smile permanently gracing my face, and I sway to the rhythm as I glance out across the floor. Once Lana and her guys moved to the booth, I scooted over to her stool so others could have easy access without leaning over into my space.

Closing my eyes, I sipped the drink Jesse had waiting for me before I even had to ask. The cute little bartender is all smiles, bright and bubbly. She checks in every few minutes but the last time I told her I was good and to just keep the drinks coming. I already know we are going to Uber back home so I'm letting myself indulge tonight.

"Damn. Looks like my assessment wasn't far off the mark. I knew you were a tequila girl." A familiar male voice interrupts my reverie, but the alcohol has calmed my system enough that I don't jump. *Go me.*

I open my eyes to find the sculpted Adonis with hazel eyes smiling down at me. The mask covering the top part of his face brings out the colors swirling in his eyes; like a small town's landscape in the middle of Autumn. He's wearing a lop-sided grin and standing just far enough in front of me that I could stand up and move away if I wanted. But, right now, I don't want to. Something about his presence really does draw me in. What it is, I don't have a clue. But at this moment, I kind of want to figure it out.

My lips tilt into a grin of my own as I find my sassy side. The one I use to banter with the guy friends I'm comfortable with. "Ok, Mr. Mixologist. I'll give you half a point. But don't go thinking you have me figured out just yet." I bite my lip coyly because, holy shit, I was actually flirting!

Adonis chuckles and it sends goosebumps up my arms. He raises his hand to his mouth and rubs his thumb across his bottom lip. It's then I notice his eyes have dropped to my mouth, now sucking on my straw.

"Well, maybe we should change that" he drawls. I snap my eyes back to his, glinting with mischief. Furrowing my brows, I try to remember the last 20 seconds of our conversation. *Stupid Adonis messing with my brain. Or, maybe it's the drinks?* I glare down at my drink like it's done me dirty and immediately giggle at myself, shaking my head.

"What's so funny, Pretty Girl?" Oops, I must have giggled out loud.

Holding in another one, I smile at him and shake my head "Nothing. Just something in my head." He smiles down at me for a beat before looking around. "Where'd your friends go?"

"Ahh, my people. They went off on their own adventures." I smiled fondly as I think about how they're all blissfully enjoying their night. "They left you all alone? Psshh, that's just wrong." He says it in a way I can at least tell he's joking so I grin and shake my head.

"All good. I'm a big girl. I can handle myself. Besides, I am happy they're happy. I have all I need right here. Good music, good drinks, and time to myself."

He tilts his head, assessing me again. I'm not sure what he's looking for but I raise my brow in challenge. "Do you want to join my friends and I? We're in that booth right over there." He points toward the back wall. From that booth I could still keep Lana in my sights. I may be comfortable, but I'm not dumb.

Jesse chooses that moment to check in, "Hey girl, how's the drink treating you?"

I turn towards her with the biggest smile I can manage before responding, "Still amazing, just like the rest." She smiles and nods before looking at Mr. Mixologist. "Do you want me to send over another round to the table, boss?" *Wait, boss?*

I whip my head back to the man standing in front of me, eyes wide and brows lifted in shock. "She's messing with you. I'm not the boss. Tommy is. We're just really close with him and here a lot." He gives Jesse a playful glare.

I get the feeling that wasn't the whole truth but decide not to press it. "And yes, please send us another round to the table. Add an extra for Pretty Girl here, too. She's going to come hang out with us for a bit."

Shock punches in my chest as I register his words. "Oh, no thank you. I don't need another drink. Just a water." I didn't want to owe anyone anything and I could already tell I was probably reaching my limit. "And a water, too Jess." He says with a wink before presenting his arm for me to hook mine through.

I hesitate, for just a moment, before glancing at the security guards dotting the area. Then again, if Jesse jokes about them being bosses, they would probably be the most respectful in the whole place.

Swallowing past the lump in my throat, I drain the last of my drink, set the glass back on the bar, and loop my arm in his. "Ok, Mr. Mixologist. Lead the Way".

* * *

By the time we stop in front of the round booth, my palms have started sweating and I'm scanning every possible exit. *Why did he invite me? It doesn't make sense.* Maybe it's because I am one of the few with a red bracelet on and he's just making sure I enjoy myself. Hoping for that membership fee. Now that makes more sense.

Two men are sitting in the booth. Even sitting down I can tell the one on the left is huge. Big broad shoulders and well-defined pecs are noticeable as his shirt pulls tight across the expanse of his chest. I can barely make out some kind of tattoo near his neck but it's really dark over here. I do see the full sleeves of ink running down both arms and stopping just above the wrist. So many designs together I can't make any of them out. His mask accentuates his brown eyes. The lights bouncing around the room make them look like they're glittering. I suck in a sharp breath as he stares into my own eyes. I've never felt so seen; *or safe*. It's unnerving and kind of makes me want to run away.

I pull my eyes from him to the guy on the right. The shadows from the room make his jaw look like it's been cut from stone. He's about the same height, judging from their seated positions as the other guy but much leaner. He is rocking some bright, blue hair. Close fade running up both sides and significantly longer on the top. Styled perfectly to appear messy but is carefully crafted to stick up, and bend back away. His nose is perfectly angled and above the most beautifully full lips I have ever seen. The lights in the room bounce off something and I realize that it's a silver loop hanging from the left side of his bottom lip. His mask reveals deep, dark eyes. Eyes that see everything no matter how much you try to bury it. Eyes that suck you into their vortex and disseminate your very being. Eyes that have seen more darkness than most, but definitely speaks to mine.

"Pretty girl. Did you hear me?" I jump out of my shameless gawking and look up at him. "Sorry, what?" I squeak out. His smile is so wide, it takes over the entire bottom half of his face. "I said, this is John" pointing at the giant, "And this is Matthew" pointing to the guy with the blue hair.

Moving my eyes to his, again, I realize he looks shocked or surprised about something. His lips are parted and, even with the mask on, I can tell his eyes are wide. I quickly glance behind me but don't necessarily see anything shocking. *At least, not for a place like this.*

I shrug it off and remember my manners. "It's nice to meet you all. Sorry, um, did you tell me your name? I typically remember things better but I'm a little over-stimulated here."

He snorts in amusement before turning that sexy-as-sin grin my way, "Mark".

"Ooo," I start in my most overly impressed voice, "Now all you need is Luke, and could call yourself the Gospel Boys." At first, all I could hear was the music from the club and my heartbeat echoing in my ears. *Damn, I know better than to make jokes. It was pretty bad. Maybe I offended them. Oh, shit. I hope that doesn't get Lana kicked out.*

Deep, rich laughter suddenly shakes me from my mini-meltdown.

I look up, not realizing I was looking at the ground, to see all three of them cracking up. Big bright smiles, rosy cheeks, and chests vibrating with laughter. The collective sounds send electric shocks straight to my core. I was *not* prepared for the way my body was reacting but tried my damnedest to hide my dilemma behind a wide smile.

"Actually," 'Mark' begins, "The fourth member of our merry band of misfits does go by Luke when we're here. He's taking care of some things for the owner, Tommy, but he'll be back in a bit." The amusement sparkles in his eyes and I notice his eyes briefly dip down to my lips before bouncing back again.

"Well, now that you formally know three of the Gospel Boys" he jokes with a grin, "How 'bout we get you on the dance floor and show you that we are definitely *not* good boys?"

"With all of you? At the same time?" I checked since apparently my raging hormones are making me a bigger idiot than normal.

"Sure, why not?" John drawled. "An angel needs her Gospel Boys. No one else would be worthy." The look he gives me is downright sinful; challenging even.

Jess drops the tray of drinks in front of us and disappears faster than I could process. Mark hands each of us a shot, then we raise our glasses. "To new friends, close family, and fun times. Cheers!" We all clink our glasses, throw back the burning shot that comes from a high-end gold tequila, and slam them back on the tray.

"Well Angel, shall we?" John stands, forcing Mark and me to step back, and looks down at me with a grin that floods my panties.

He holds out his hand and maintains eye contact, eyes glinting with a challenge. I slip my hand in his, then smile up at him, then Mark, and then Matthew; all now standing as if it's already been decided.

With more bravado than I have ever felt I raise an eyebrow, issuing my own challenge, "Let's see what you've got Gospel Boys."

13

~

Annie

Stepping onto the dancefloor invigorates me. But walking behind three super hot, very tall guys, is intimidating as hell. It's not even their demeanor, it's the looks in their eyes and their apparent unwavering confidence.

As if sensing my thoughts, Mark takes my hand and turns me to face him once we reach a good spot with plenty of room. "It's just a dance, Pretty Girl. Even without the red bracelet, we would still have a conversation before anything crossed a major line." The sincerity in his eyes startles me and makes my heart beat faster; now for a completely different reason. I look towards the other two and give a shy smile, nodding my head to show I understand.

The opening lyrics to Earned It by The Weeknd travel through the room and I smirk at how utterly cliche it is. Mark steps up to me and takes one hand in his while tentatively moving his other hand to my waist. I can tell he's trying to not spook me so I grin and step into him, placing my other arm around his neck. Our bodies mold together and a fire ignites deep inside me. I should be freaked out but, in a place like this, on a night like tonight, I'm determined to let go.

Mark leans in, his stubble raking over my cheek, before whispering in my ear. "These guys are my best friends, partners in business, and my only family. We share *everything*." The emphasis glitches my brain while simultaneously flooding my panties.

Before I could ask him to clarify, he continues, "Can the others move in closer?"

I could see John in my periphery. He was standing back just enough that I didn't feel boxed in. Raising my head away from Mark's, I turn the other way to see Matthew, playing with that damn lip ring; grinning and hopeful.

"Yes. That's fine," I rasp. Mark puts his finger and thumb on my chin and squeezes gently, enough for me to return my eyes to him. "What's fine, Pretty Girl? We need your words."

I'm not sure why I'm getting all flustered. It's just a dance. But, *was* it? It's a dance with three insanely hot guys. Who cares if it's bullshit and they're just passing the time? I'll happily soak up the attention for one night.

"Please, dance with us." I lift my eyes to look at each man and tilt my lips in a grin that I hope conveys my sincerity.

The other two move in behind me. Each tilts to the side enough that half of their bodies press closer against my backside and the other half I can see in my periphery. We start moving to the music and I wrap my arm back around Mark.

I feel Matthew press in closer as he leans around me, causing me to look over at him. "Is this ok?" The rasp of his voice carries over the music and my nipples tighten without my permission. He looks like he's genuinely concerned about how I'm feeling. Before I can figure out what he's asking about, his right hand slowly, deliberately slides onto my hip, rubbing my side with his thumb through my shirt.

"Yeah," my voice takes on a breathy quality as I grin at him. I swivel my head in the other direction to look up at John, my smile still stretching across my face. I then return to look back at Matthew. Before second-guessing myself, I blurt "You can hold on to me. All of you. It's fine."

I watch as a wide smile takes over Matthew's face, his eyes glinting with amusement and something akin to a promise. I turn and press further into Mark, closing my eyes and embracing the warmth of their bodies pressing up against mine.

Our bodies move together, making our own rhythm. I can't even hear the music above the sound of my heart beating in my ears. John slides his hand on my left hip, just above Mark's, rubbing slow circles. Mark weaves his arm around my waist, below Matthew's hand, and pulls me in closer. My breasts press against his chest as John moves his hips against my side.

These men, these beautiful men, are surrounding me and filling me with much more than desire. Lust burns through my veins as John moves the hair off my shoulder. My head moves on its own accord, presenting my neck to him. My off-shoulder shirt already gives him more than enough access but I suppose my brain decided he deserves more. *Or I crave more.*

Mark smirks before glancing at his giant of a friend. He subtly squeezes the top of my ass just as John dips down and licks my collarbone straight up to the spot behind my ear before giving a gentle kiss. I shoot up to my toes, brushing my ass against Matthew and a gasp leaves my body. Matthew grinds himself into my backside, his height putting *it* just above my waistline. And oh gracious, it feels huge. And hard. And huge. *Oh God! I'm overstimulated. Something's not right. Why am I trembling and why is my pussy throbbing like th...*

My mind shuts off when he moves the hair off the other side of my neck and begins to leave slow, torturous, open-mouth kisses at the bottom of my neck. He then leads all the way up to my ear before nipping my lobe. A throaty moan escapes me and my entire body quakes.

I open my eyes and look up at Mark. He takes that moment to lean in and press a soft kiss to my lips, bringing his other hand to hold the side of my face, positioning my head where he wants. His tongue sweeps across my bottom lip, gently nipping at it. I open my mouth greedily and he pushes his tongue into my mouth; exploring the area until I lap at him with mine.

With a growl, he presses into me harder, his hard cock pressing against my belly and he brings his other hand from around my waist and places it on the other side of my face. The movement pushes me further into the other two men as we sway together; no longer keeping any kind of rhythm.

John takes my lobe in his mouth and nibbles on it before lightly biting down. With a yelp, my hand leaves Mark's neck and finds John's forearm. At some point, his hand had slid up to rest just below my breasts. *When the hell did that happen?*

I dig my nails into John's strong, wide forearms and give myself over to the sensations around me. I can feel my panties soaking even more as another moan is ripped out of me when Matthew and John press their tongues at the nape of my neck and slide them all the way up to my ears in perfect synchronization.

Mark and I tangle our tongues, fighting for dominance. Where my confidence is coming from is beyond me but, I'm here for it. As a new rush of pleasure jolts through me, I can't help but grind back into

Matthew before subtly shifting to catch John; the move earning me the most delicious surround sound experience as they groan out.

Someone's hands begin to fondle my breasts and I find myself leaning against the two men behind me. Matthew's hand travels from my hip, towards my stomach. I find myself jolt with anxiety. He must sense my discomfort as he moves his hand back to my hip and squeezes, just briefly, before latching onto my neck again.

Someone loudly clears their throat and breaks me out of my lust-filled haze. The guys all drop their hands, making me shiver from the drop in temperature, and turn to look at the security guard behind Mark. With an amused grin, the guard looks at the guys before saying, "You guys helped create the rules. You're not supposed to break them." With matching looks of confusion, they all take another step away from me.

His grin widens as if he's in on some kind of secret. The longer we stand in silence, the higher my anxiety climbs. My heart may actually explode out of my chest. My hands are sweating and I'm starting to feel dizzy with the impending attack.

Before I can lose myself completely to the 100 ways I could be in trouble, and possibly get Lana in trouble, the guard tips his head towards my wrist. The guys all look down at my red bracelet and a variety of groans and "fuck" rings out. Matthew steps back, tugging the ends of his hair, John's eyes flash with guilt and shame, and Mark looks like someone just kicked his dog.

"I'm confused. What did I do wrong? I'm, uh, I'm new but everything that happened was all on me. Please don't take it out on them." The guys' shoulders all relax and all four chuckle. *They're laughing at me, now? What the fuck? I'm such an idiot. I should have just stayed at the bar until Lana was ready to go. Of course, I was some kind of game to them. Something to mess with to pass the time.*

"Woah there, Siren. I can hear you overthinking from here." Matthew steps forward to put himself in front of me. He molds his hands to my face gently before lifting my head to meet his eyes. "You're not in any trouble. You just made us forget ourselves for a moment. Red bracelets are no play. Dancing is allowed, but we crossed the line when we put our mouths on you." His eyes seem to implore me to believe him. His thumbs rub the sides of my face gently as he maintains eye contact.

John clears his throat and his deep southern voice fills the space. "He's right. Sorry, Angel. We got carried away. We do know better but we just couldn't resist you." He runs a hand down the back of his head and...is that blush? He gives me a self-deprecating grin that immediately disarms me. I take a deep breath and step back again.

Seeming to take that as a sign that I'm ok, Mark faces the guard, apologizes, and thanks him for keeping such a close eye out. He then steps just past me, offers me his bent arm, and asks if I would like to join them for a drink. I'm not sure why, but I really want to. And, not just because they destroyed my panties without even trying. No, something about them makes me feel... safe...seen? I don't know. But, just for the night, I can enjoy the time I have left with them, and pretend to be desired by the most-devastating men I have ever encountered.

* * *

Mark slides into the rounded booth while Matthew slides in beside me. John takes the other side of Mark and glances up when another man approaches. *Wait a second. Is that?*

My eyes widen like saucers as I realize the man who has approached the table is the same one I had spoken to earlier. The one I accidentally laughed at when he gave his drink order.

Mr. ManBun stutters to a stop when he notices me sitting there. I bite my lip, something interesting in my lap having suddenly caught my eye as my cheeks blaze with heat.

"Well," he drags out the word slowly, teasingly. "If it isn't the kamikaze hater." I feel the other guys shift. I am sure they are now uncomfortable. *Shit. Maybe I could fake needing the bathroom and run out of here before this becomes a problem.*

The deep voice that responds tells me John has decided to answer. "Wait, you know each other?" I glance over at him through my lashes to see his face contorted with confusion. "Yup," Luke answers, popping the p cockily. "But unfortunately, I never got her name. She called me old and ran away."

Somehow that pulled a scoff for me as I looked up at him incredulously. "I didn't run away. I went back to my friends."

"Ah, so you do think I'm old."

"Wh-what?" I swear his grin grew to match the rising level of my anxiety. "I didn't. That's not what I meant. I didn't mean to offend you."

My hands are flailing all over the place, revealing my heightened emotional state. Matthew's hand slowly slides onto my thigh and gently squeezes, effectively stopping my rant.

"He's messing with you, Siren. He came back and told us all about the girl who blatantly rejected him. His poor pride is wounded." I look at Matthew, seeing the mischief and amusement in his eyes that match the smirk on his face.

Glancing back at Luke, I see him dramatically clutching his chest and pretending to wipe tears from his eyes. Realizing he's full of shit, I glare at him and roll my eyes, relaxing more in the booth. "I'm sure he'll be just fine. If he can't handle little ol' me, he has much bigger problems." My voice came out steadier than I thought and I'm quite pleased with the sass I was able to inject. *Where the hell did that come from? Go me, again!*

Their laughter covers me from all sides and I find myself soaking it up as Luke slides in beside Matthew. Luke reaches over the table to pass out the shots. Tequila gold judging by the scent.

"I don't know, Sweetness. That was a pretty hard blow to my ego.

But, I think you can take this drink with me to make it better." The challenge I see in those deep green eyes is obvious.

I notice he and the others are prepping their hands or wrists with the salt and make a show of pushing it away when it comes my way. Smirking at the surprise in his eyes, I raise my glass for a toast and the others follow. "To mending wounds and shattered egos, and making new friends." All four guys cheer as we clink our glasses together and down our shots.

The others grab their limes and squeeze the sour juice into their mouths. Piling the supplies back onto the tray, they all look at me expectantly. "What?" I said, my eyes darting around the table. Mark clears his throat and points at the time in front of me, "Aren't you going to take the lime?"

I find myself chuckling and shaking my head. "No. Real tequila drinkers relish the burn." They all freeze and share glances of disbelief before laughing, again. *Man, I could get used to that sound.*

We spend the next thirty minutes chatting about nothing overly important, or too personal. They talk about how they all met and share stories about each other as they throw out insults and jabs. I occasionally chime in but genuinely just loved to be in their presence. Reveling in the bond they have. It's clear they are very close, and not just for naughty purposes.

When I notice Lana walking up, I find myself feeling sad that I won't see them again. I quickly introduced them to "Elle" before scooting out of the booth to leave. When I stand, I look at each of them before thanking them for an amazing night.

Just as I turn to walk around, I hear Mark call out "We'll be seein' you, Pretty Girl."

Feeling light, and much braver than usual, I look over my shoulder and call out "Better start prayin' for it, Gospel Boys," before winking and following Lana out of the club.

14

⸎

Vince- 5 Days Later

I'm sitting at my desk getting fuck-all done. I still can't believe I spent the evening with Annie and she didn't have a clue! I wasn't in my uniform, and we had masks on, but once we got closer, I could see the tattoos on her arms and the same earrings adorning her ears. I wanted to tell her but it's supposed to be anonymous. And I know she's timid so I didn't want to make her run.

As soon as she departed, I broke the news to the guys. After my revelation, we all sat in stunned silence. How is it that the woman I have been tasked to help with a potential threat and the woman that pulled all of us into her web are the same?

We spent 20 minutes talking about our different experiences with her, including the hilarious realization that she was the one Nick had been watching when he creamed himself on the couch. It was evident to all of us that we were each drawn to her. Those curves, her eyes, the sass, and bravery she threw at us even though it was obvious she was nervous and fighting her initial responses.

The erotic images of her losing herself to the spark of pleasure on the dance floor play through my mind. Her lips parted, blush coating her cheeks and chest. I wanted to follow it down to see just how far it went.

I started thinking about how perfectly she fit in with our banter once we moved back to the booth. She followed the conversation intently, even throwing her own sassy remarks in there. It made me imagine what it would be like to wrap her hair around my fist and see what else she could do with that smart mouth.

Groaning, I adjust my pants as they have become unbearably tight. *Dammit.*

She may need some time to fully be comfortable with what we have to offer, but to see her blossom and take hold of the power she already has over us... Mmmm that would be worth every-fucking-thing.

Unfortunately, we were all too caught up in surprise and disappointment when her friend came to get her so they could leave. None of us had the wherewithal to get her number. We all just stared in awe as she tossed out her final remark of the night and sauntered out of our lives. *Idiots. We haven't all been drawn to a woman like this in a very long time and we blew it.*

Shaking my head clear, I sigh and rub a hand down my face. I have actual work to do and I will never be able to track the Black Thorns down if I keep my head in the damn clouds.

As I stand up to make myself another cup of coffee, my phone buzzes with an incoming message.

Nick- Hey Everest. Need a lunch break? The dipshit twins are thinking about hitting that Chinese place around the corner from the station in an hour.

I look up and see that it's already 11:00. Filling up my mug, I take it back to my desk before responding. I have been here since 3 this morning and have fuck-all to show for it.

Me- Sounds good to me. I just realized I think I have been living on caffeine for 2 days. Probably a good idea to step out for a bit.

Nick responds with a thumbs up and I set my phone aside. Opening up the file on my desk, I see that our forensics guy, Larry, finished up the analysis of the materials and liquid substances we recovered from the warehouse we recently raided.

At first, everything seems boring and normal. Nothing new. But then, I see a word that rattles in my mind. *Where have I seen that before?* Digging through the recesses of my mind, I come up empty. Jiggling my computer mouse, the screen wakes up and I type the word into the search bar. After staring at the screen and clicking through dozens of medical files, I pick up my desk phone and dial Larry.

"Mad scientist lab. What can I do you for?" He jokes. "Hey, Larry, it's Vince."

"Hey. I dropped the report of the substances found on your desk a few minutes ago."

"Yeah, I wanted to follow up on that. Speak stupid to me. Can some of the liquids we found be used to induce short-term paralysis?"

I hear the furious clicking on the other end before he sucks his teeth and responds, "They sure can. I mean, there were broken bottles everywhere but there are definitely substances that can block receptors. Tetracaine itself is frequently used in conjunction with other medication in spinal anesthesia for cesareans."

"Fuck." I grunt out. "Do you remember that case we had a couple of months ago? The body we found with missing organs. Can you compare their tox screens?"

"What? You think it's related? That was a body dump. The recent one was from the warehouse Black Thorns vacated. I thought they focused on stealing and moving drugs and guns?" I sigh and scrub a hand down my face. "I know. Let's just double-check. Just to make sure."

"You got it, Vinnie. I'll get that right up to ya."

"Thanks, man." I hang up and lean back in my chair, blowing out a ragged breath. If these two are related, that means there's a lot more cases to add to the Black Thorns' file. *Fuck me.* We have to track these bastards down. But, I have a sinking feeling that tells me we are far from close. And things are about to get a lot messier.

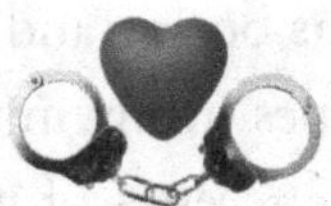

While walking up to the Golden Palace to meet the guys, my head is filled with uncertainty. I am beyond frustrated at the lack of progress we've made on this case. I feel like someone dumped a five thousand piece puzzle across a table and trashed the box before anyone got to see what the picture was. We are continually one step behind them and it's starting to piss me off.

Before leaving the office, I decided I would revisit the Black Thorns warehouse we found and the dump site of the body that was found a few months back. I took a quick shower and changed into street clothes so I was less likely to be noticed. If these two are connected, we don't want anyone to know we've made the connection. It may be the break we need.

Finding the guys is easy enough. Those jackasses stick out like flowers in a garden full of weeds. "Hey, Vince. How's it shakin'?" Jenson asks before biting into his crunchy egg roll.

"All good. Have some recon to do after but this place smells like heaven." I reach across the table and grab a dumpling, dipping it in some sauce and shoving the whole thing in my mouth. The groan I release is filthy enough to heat Nick's cheeks; and my own.

After a beat, we all start laughing. I reach under the table and squeeze Nick's thigh. We haven't been able to spend much time together recently. Life and work keep dragging us apart. But, I want him to know I am still here, for him, for us.

Sylvi pops over to the table and slaps me on the shoulder. "Where you been? You no come see me no more. Jackface." The guys all laugh at my pain and the fact this wisp of a woman pushes us around. I just flip them all off.

"I'm sorry Sylvi. We've been busy. How's Bo? Haven't been knockin' him around, too, have ya?" I smirk as she rolls her eyes.

"No. He a real man. He more a man than you big ox." The guys all lose it, again, and I can't help but laugh at this woman's fire.

I met her and Bo three years ago when some gang-banger wannabes forced their way in right after closing. They fired off shots around the little hole-in-the-wall Chinese restaurant, but it was more to scare than to hurt. When you're dispatched to an armed robbery in progress, we never know what we're really walking into. But I can absolutely say, *nothing* could have prepared us for what we walked into.

We came in guns armed and ready and completely froze. Sylvi, a little Chinese woman at least 70 years old, was yelling at them for being disrespectful little punks while slapping them repeatedly with a chef's towel. She already had the teen bangers sweeping up the mess they made.

Our response time was ridiculous that day. 3 minutes from dispatch to breaching the premise. And in those 3 minutes, she had those teens whipped into shape. She told us they didn't need charges, they needed discipline. Since they had no priors, were both in the foster system, and didn't point the weapons at anyone, the judge agreed. That little spit-fire had convinced the judge to saddle them with community service working in her restaurant, catering to her every need. By the time their 6-month probation ended, her entire restaurant was completely renovated and better than before. She paid for the materials, and they had to figure out how to do all of it.

Now, both of those boys have full scholarships at the university they attend *and* come back to work, for pay, at the restaurant every summer. Sylvi and Bo act like doting, albeit pushy, grandparents and those boys are definitely better for it.

Once she takes our order and hustles back to the kitchen, I feel my work cell ping with a message.

Larry- Looked into similar cases to the woman whose body we found. Had a buddy in the department in the next town over check their files too. Unofficially, we have 14 similar cases. It was just a quick search so digging deeper may find more or less. The earliest case in the whole group was 18 months ago.

18 months? Holy shit. This may be WAY bigger than we thought.

Me- Thanks man. I'll check it out. Send what's ours to my desk. I'll bring you your favorite kolaches in the morning. I owe you.

He responds with fireworks and I shake my head before putting my phone back in my pocket.

The guys and I spent the rest of lunch catching up on their business happenings and laughing about some inter-office drama I saw play out.

I know this case is about to take an ugly turn but here, at this moment, with my family, I'm at peace. And that's not something I've been able to say recently.

15

Annie

Once my kids get on the bus, I log in to my online platform. I have three English lessons this morning and nothing else until this evening. My to-do list for the day includes errands and grocery shopping. I may even get in a mini-nap before the kids get home.

My lessons pass quickly, the smile never leaving my face. Afterward, I move to the laundry room and begin pulling out a load of towels from the dryer before folding them and stacking them on the dryer. I switch over the washed clothes into the dryer and blush when I see the outfit I wore out on Friday.

Dancing with Lana was amazing but the time I had with those

sinfully delicious men had given me a confidence boost I didn't know I needed. I can still feel their kisses on my skin, see their eyes showing off their mischievous intentions, and... *Dammit, I'm wet again.*

After I put the towels up, I quickly change out my now dirty thong because I have way too much to do and don't want to walk around feeling *that*. It's not like I will ever see them again.

Lana just about combusted when I told her what had happened. For some reason, seeing her proud of me for talking to new people, that she didn't specifically know, made me feel good.

We shared stories, hers way more exciting than mine, while we finished off a pizza in her living room. The next morning, I took her to get her truck and we ate at a cute little restaurant that makes the best beignets. I then spent the rest of my free weekend cleaning and enjoying some time with my naughty book boyfriends.

When my mother dropped off the kids, I felt lighter, happier, than I had in a long time. So, on a whim, I decided to have them help me make muffins for the week. We ended the weekend giggling and curled up on the couch as we watched Disney.

I'm just re-filling the washing machine when my phone pings with a message. Adding detergent and softener, I close the lid and turn it on. I find my phone in the kitchen next to my laptop, the sun shining through the front window. But my good mood is instantly shattered when I see what was sent.

Unknown- Looks like someone had an eventful weekend. Did you find some drunken fool to fuck you right?

I jump when another message comes through.

Unknown- It's ok, kitten. I know no man can erase your desire for me. I'll be seeing you soon.

What. The. Fuck. No, no, no. This can't be. I close the messages and pull up the number for the Victim's Services Division and begin pacing. I give the operator my information and wait as she pulls up the information.

The news I get brings me to my knees. My vision tunnels, blackness swirling around. Two things are crystal clear. *He got out early. And he found me.*

An hour later, I whip into the parking lot of the gym. I usually go on Tuesdays but I desperately need an outlet for all of these emotions. I refuse to cry. The last time I let myself cry was 4 years ago. It was then that all the memories of my ex came rushing back and I remembered that crying was pointless. *At least I learned one thing from that prick. The prick that's back. Fuck.*

One of my favorite things about this gym is that it has a separate kickboxing studio. Equipped with bags of all shapes and sizes. When there isn't a class here, it's open to members. If no one else is around, you can even connect your music to the studio speaker. I'm not used to being here this early, or this day of the week, so I'm not sure if it will be occupied. I can usually squeeze in 30 minutes alone on Thursdays but I guess we will see what happens.

I greet Cathy when I come in and scan my member card before walking straight to the back where the studio is. I don't even bother with the locker room.

Once inside, I breathe a sigh of relief when I see that no one is here. The space is large enough to hold 30 people with plenty of room to kick, jab, and move. The wall across from the door is a full mirror, top to bottom. The far left wall has multiple punching bags including 6 hanging from chains, 4 free-standing ones on wheels that can be easily moved around, 4 Bobs, also on wheels, and 8 speed bags spaced out about 3 feet apart, mounted on the wall. The audio system that connects to the speakers in the studio sits in the storage closet on the right wall of the studio. I turn that way, and slip in, dropping my bag on the floor to fish out my phone.

After connecting to the Bluetooth, I shuffle through my playlists. I have a 'general workout one' and a 'fuck off' one. I close my eyes and breathe deeply, trying to identify what emotion I wanted to focus on.

Stupid fucking cunt.

Do you really think you should eat that, kitten?

God knew you would make me happy. And he knew only I would be able to handle you.

SMACK

Disgusting slob.

WHAP

If you didn't want it, you wouldn't have dressed like that.

RIP

Shut your mouth or I'll make you.

I've got a message for you.

Two voices, two men. One hell. My hell. I begin trembling with the memories. I've always been so weak. What if something happens now? I couldn't protect myself. How can I protect my kids?

That thought. That's the one I hang onto. Fuck them. How dare they think of me as useless trash. How dare they take things that I didn't freely give. I've worked hard to give my kids everything I can in life. And I'll be damned if someone thinks they can take that away.

Closing my eyes, I choose anger. I reach deep down and grab hold of it with both hands. Before I push it aside, I click on my 'fuck off' playlist and choose Middle Fingers by Aston to warm up to. I make my way across the studio, wrapping my hands on the way. A grin plays on my smile as confidence I usually do not have filters through each line of the song. *Pull up your big bitch panties and fake it 'til you make it.*

I begin stretching out my limbs and letting the lyrics wash over me. Once my hips start swaying to the music, I know it's time to start moving. I begin walking around the perimeter of the studio. After the first lap, I pick up the pace. By the time I finish the third lap, the song is coming to an end. My heart rate is perfect, not too demanding but I feel loose and ready to take some anger out.

The speakers play out the first few notes of one of my favorite songs and I grin. Not just because it references one of my favorite movies and books but because it's just so fun. Mad Hatter by Melanie Martinez lifts my mood just enough to focus instead of just jabbing the bag like a crazed person. I don't have great form since I haven't been formally trained but I definitely know how to prevent a sprained wrist.

I get in position and immediately lose myself in the familiar beat of the music, the weight of the bag resisting my force, the burn in my muscles and the clarity that comes with a good workout. No voices, no panic, no past or future. Just here and now. And damn it feels good.

Jenson

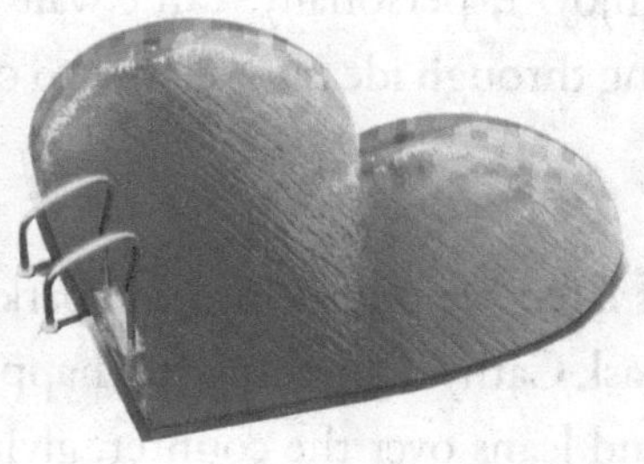

The guys and I walk out of the restaurant, still laughing at Sylvi calling Vince a big ox, slapping him on his back when he lifts her up for a hug goodbye. Vince even called out to her husband, Bo, to save him when she continued slapping him. The old man just waved him off, muttering something about crazy women.

Once we reach the cars, Vince waves goodbye and heads off to do something for work but says he will see us at home tonight. Nick, Cory, and I slide into our blacked-out SUV and take off for the gym.

Usually mid-day during the week is pretty slow but we had a meeting with a local youth organization. They recently had an investor interested in funding different kinds of martial arts and boxing classes for some of the kids and wanted to discuss pay scales and the options we may have.

We don't currently have much that caters specifically to youth but we all knew immediately that we wanted in. We told them to give us a month to talk to our staff, do some research, and figure out what we could provide and when. We left the meeting, hopeful and excited to be able to make a difference in our community.

Now that lunch is finished, we'll go back to work and split up the tasks to begin researching options best to offer for kids. We want to offer as much as we can since 1 or 2 options may not be enough to entice the kids. Even the four of us have different workouts we prefer and activities we enjoy. I, personally, can't wait to get started. I've already been running through ideas for classes to offer.

* * *

Fifteen minutes later, we pulled into the parking lot and walked inside, stopping to ask Cathy if anything fun happened while we were gone. She giggles and leans over the counter, giving us a view of her breasts, spilling out of her bright orange sports bra.

Nick grunts and pushes past us to head back to the offices. The man is still an enigma. Similar to high school, he keeps to himself in most situations. He can make eye contact like a big boy now but, socially, he still prefers to observe and loathes conflict.

However, when he loves, he loves big and loves hard. He'd take a bullet for any of us if needed. We're family and that's not something he takes lightly.

As for women, he basically doesn't bother trying. He either fears rejection or fears having to reject, possibly hurting them, and creating conflict. The latter happens the most as only 2 women have ever truly captured his attention. *Or, maybe it's 3 now.*

At home, or in the club, Nick is a totally different guy. He's still reserved and loving, but he's able to safely explore his need for control and pair it with his overwhelming need to cater to and protect those he loves.

Once I finish chatting with Cathy, making it a point to stare in her eyes as to not give her any hope, I head back to the offices with Jenson in tow.

The 'back offices' is really one giant office space that we partitioned into 4 separated spaces. Walking in, we have our main meeting area to the left behind a frosted glass window. It has a large enough table to fit 8 people. We were able to grab the gorgeous cherry red table and chair set at a local auction house for a fraction of what it's actually worth. A projector screen can be pulled down on the far left end with the projector we use attached to the ceiling. On the right, sits the laptop stand and all the outlets we may need.

The rest of the office space is 3 segmented areas. Each houses the same black desk, ergonomic office chair and dual monitors; with the exception of Nick's that has a huge multi-level, multi-monitor setup to keep our little tech geek happy. We each have our own files that pertain to the different areas of the franchise we oversee, and being the founders overseeing hundreds of locations, we have a lot of information we need secured.

"Uh, guys?" Nick calls out from his room. "Yeah, man? What's up?" Cory calls from his office.

"You have got to see this." We pause for a moment to see if he's going to explain but, knowing Nick, we should probably go in there.

Cory and I open Nick's office door and go to stand behind him. He has the feed from Studio 4 playing on the largest monitor. I squint my eyes, not believing what we're looking at. "Is that...?"

The question hangs in the air as we all stare; completely entranced by what we're seeing. We all stay frozen in disbelief as we watch the powerhouse of a woman wail on a hanging bag.

-*Nick*-

The camera in the studio is placed in the far right corner. We can see the entire room and have the perfect view of the front and storage doors. This helps monitor people who come in and out both doors in case of any issues that may arise.

When we first got back from lunch, I logged in to my computer system and began combing through emails. My focus was on the bottom right monitor as the security feeds looped through different views of the gym on the other 5.

It's typically pretty quiet this time of day. Most people are either here early in the morning or late in the afternoon. In my periphery, I see a few people utilizing the cardio area, a guy in the weights section, a couple of younger guys using the ninja course, and the aerial teacher practicing for her next class.

When I go to stretch, before looking into some classes to add for the youth group, I notice someone is in our kickboxing studio. Her hair is pulled up in a messy blonde bun. I know it's not the instructor; who's undoubtedly male with ripped muscles everywhere.

The feed loops to the next studio and I shake my head at the brief distraction, pulling up a search for physical activities that kids may be excited about. My goal is to utilize the instructors we have and find activities that don't need special licensing. The cheaper we can keep the programs, the more we can offer. However, we know that some of the programs we are already wanting include specific instructors; like Martial Arts.

I'm just about finished compiling my list of programs I want to dig into when the studio monitor flips back to the kickboxing feed.

I'm not sure why but it catches my eye and I can't seem to look away. I'm not even sure what I'm specifically drawn to but I just can't stop watching the woman on the screen. She's wearing a baggy shirt that is hanging off her shoulder, showing some kind of patterned sports bra strap. Simple black capris hug her legs and her white Asics are splattered with color.

Her form could use some work but the intensity pulsing from her body is mesmerizing. She keeps working combinations around the bag until her right side is facing the camera. Something on her arm catches my attention and before I can second-guess myself, I zoom in a little. *Why does that tattoo look so familiar?*

Although I can't zoom in much more, I can see her face, chest, and arms are all red with exertion. She looks frustrated, yelling out something between breaths. I go to click the audio on and immediately have to turn it down. Been to Hell by Hollywood Undead is blasting from the studio speakers. I watch as she sings, or screams, along to the song. It's like the song is speaking to her and the more it does, the more her rage spills over.

Just as that crosses my mind, she drops her stance and begins pacing with her fists on her hips. Her chin is tucked against her chest as she walks around. She gets about mid-way through the room and just as the song ends, she lifts her face towards the ceiling. "Fuck!" Rings out around the studio before the song switches. Popular Monster by Falling in Reverse begins streaming through the speakers. As Ronnie Radke raps out the first few sentences of the song, her face pinches in, pain, resolve...something. But when she shakes off that look, rolls her shoulders back, and breathes in, I realize who this woman is.

"Uh, guys?" I yell out. I heard the other 2 walk in a moment ago so I know they're here. A muffled response is returned, drowned out by the lyrics now vibrating through the speakers. "You have got to see this!"

I can't believe it. It's her! The woman from Friday. *How the hell is she here? And how did we not know that she's a member? Have we seen her before? Surely not or we would have all noticed.*

I can hear Jenson ask a question but he falls silent as Annie gets into the song. In perfect time with the beat drop, she begins attacking the bag. Jabs, uppercuts, hooks. She yells out some of the lyrics as she treats the bag like it personally wronged her.

One thing is glaringly obvious, she's starting to spin out. During the last song, she had some kind of form, some kind of control. But not anymore. "She's too worked up. She's going to hurt herself."

Jenson steps back and tugs at his hair but Cory and I don't move a muscle. Too focused on Annie wearing herself out.

During a few parts, she screams out the lyrics in agony; head tipped towards the ceiling. "Do we go in and stop it? What if she recognizes us? You remember how timid she is. She may freak out." Cory rants. He's not actually talking to us. His organized, planner mode doesn't like 'what if' scenarios. He chooses every action and word carefully after weighing every option. *Usually.*

The song fades to an end and she drops her stance, her shoulders, her everything. Hopefully, she just exorcized all of her demons and will start her cool down. Judging by the sweat dripping off of her, she's definitely been here a while and that song took the last of her reserves.

The collective sigh of relief we have is immediately interrupted by the next song in que. Apparently, she has a thing for Falling in Reverse because Voices in My Head begins to play.

She steps back from the bag and begins pacing the room, shaking out her arms and starting her cool down. Her sweet but pained voice carries just enough over the song since the instruments haven't fully joined in, yet. Her voice contorts with so much raw emotion that I have the overwhelming urge to go hold her. Even if it means watching her fall apart so we have to help pick up the pieces. *Why does someone I've barely spent time with make me feel like this already?*

Just when we begin to relax and step back to do, whatever it is we're supposed to be doing, the rhythm gets faster. Not only that; *she* gets louder. The pain, the fury, the hurt; it all plays out across her face and body. It's like the lyrics themselves are speaking to her; no, *for* her.

As the chorus begins, she runs back to the bag and unleashes. She's screaming, tears cascading down her face. She's no longer following the lyrics. I can barely catch some of the words over the music.

"Asshole."

"Worthless bitch."

"Hate you."

"Why?!"

She goes from hitting to flailing as sobs begin to wrack her body. And that's when I lose it. I'm out of my chair and running from the office before I can even register that I've moved. *Hold on Siren, I'm coming.*

17

~

Annie

All the fear, all the voices, all the pain. It bursts through and out of me like a dormant volcano suddenly blowing its top. I don't think I can pinpoint exactly what set me off but the more exhausted I became, the louder the voices got.

The voices of the past. They cycle through my mind like a broken record. My vision begins to tunnel, my chest constricts. I can't breathe. The harder I try to fight them, the louder they get. My surroundings begin to fade as I'm transported to my worst memories; reliving my greatest shames.

Useless whore.

Stupid cunt.

Slap

Swallow like your life depends on it, cuz it does.

Can't you do anything right?

Crash

Stay still dumb bitch.

Rip

Lukas has a message for you.

A sudden pressure wraps around my body. I can't hear, I can't see. I just feel. I feel too much. It's too much. A scream rips through my throat as agony overcomes me. I try to run but I can't. My muscles are weak. My body is so tired.

"Ssshhhh. It's ok. It's ok. I'm not going to hurt you."

"No, they found me!" I fight with all I have, but it's never enough.

My breathing increases. But through the fog there's a voice. "I think I can help but you gotta trust me. You're safe Siren. You're *safe*. But I *need* you to let me help."

I don't know who's talking. Those aren't the men. Those awful, terrible men. No, this one is sweet, sure, steady. I can't see but comfort and warmth begin to settle deep into my bones.

"Siren, breathe" The command shocks my system. It doesn't bring me fear, like it should, but I do have an overwhelming urge to obey. So I take a shuddering breath.

"Good girl," the man purrs. "Again". The authoritative tone should probably freak me out but it doesn't. It calms me. In some distant part of my brain, I know he's saying it with pure intentions. Meant to care for me, not control me.

I take a deeper breath and slowly come back to my body as the tremors begin to slow. "Good girl, Siren. Good girl." I feel myself preening from his praise as my heart rate decreases and the voices fade away.

I realize his arms are wrapped tight around me upper body. I'm leaning back against his chest, with his face tilted towards my neck. His body stays steady, sure, holding the pieces of my soul together while gluing them back with whispered praise.

It takes me a moment to realize a man is holding me. And I'm letting him. And it feels...good.

But, the good feeling shatters the moment reality catches up. *Holy shit. I just had a level 5 anxiety attack, in public, and a strange man is holding me.*

Oddly, I'm more embarrassed by showing so much emotional damage in public than having someone holding me.

Clearing my throat, I desperately try to swallow now that my throat is raw. "You can let go now. I'm sorry," I whisper to the kind stranger.

"You sure?" His voice comes out raspy and his breath tickles my cheek.

"Yeah. I'm good. Sorry to interrupt your workout." As he begins to loosen his hold, I take a deep breath.

"No problem at all. We all need to fall apart sometimes. Cleanses the soul." I huff out a laugh and shake my head. "Not me. And definitely not so publicly." *Dammit, I'm going to have to find another gym now. I'll never be able to come back here again.*

I lean up and out of his space to slowly stand. "Easy, the crash from an attack can be rough. Add that to wailing on that bag for who knows how long, and your body's likely to shut down for a while."

There's a pregnant pause before he clears his throat behind me, clearly having stood up. "So, um, do you need a ride home? Or I can call an uber or something? You really shouldn't drive. You'll need lots of water and then you'll probably sleep for a good long while."

"No, thank you. I'm good. I don't live far and can get in a nap before my kiddos get home. But, I..." I turn to look at the man who helped me, first noticing his black Metallica hoodie that is almost eye level with me. I trail my eyes up to meet his face and a gasp as I take in the electric blue hair, chocolate brown eyes, and, *fuck me*, a lip ring on the right side. *What the fresh hell am I in, now?*

-Nick-

Her cries rip my heart in two. It's been a long time since I've heard such a broken sound. And that was coming from me; a very long time ago.

She's so consumed that I know her demons have brought on a full blown anxiety attack. I could tell in the club that she had an aversion to touch but seeing her on the floor, trembling and crying out, I immediately knew she needed a firm, calming squeeze. Obviously, I didn't know her well enough to bind her so I chose the next best thing. I pressed her full back against my front then moved so I could lean against the wall. Once situated, I wrapped my arms around her chest. When she started fighting, I figured I'd add gentle commands as well, hoping to override whatever was in her head.

I won't lie, there was nothing sexual about the interaction but when she had obeyed my command to breathe, and shuddered under me when I called her a "good girl", my cock took attention. *Needy bastard.*

Calming her, having her respond to me, sent a strange flutter through my heart. I wouldn't have changed anything but, in this exact moment, I realized I may have reacted without fully thinking. Something that is not at all like me.

Her ocean-blue eyes are so much lighter under the harsh fluorescent lights of the studio. At the club, they were more the color of the deep ocean, now I'm reminded of the water you see in pictures of Bora Bora resorts. Bright, shimmering, and pure paradise. *Shit focus numbskull.*

She's looking at me like she's shocked to see me here. Which, I mean, same. I can feel the heat rising in my cheeks. "Uh, hey. Um...Small world, huh?" I let out a self-deprecating chuckle.

She gapes at me. Mouth opening and closing, head shaking in disbelief. "H-How did you find me? Did you follow me here?"

"No! No, no, no, no. I, uh, I work here. This is actually my gym. Our gym. We own it. Well the whole franchise really. And not just me, the guys too. They're somewhere." At this point I am full on rambling and my cheeks are heated. I can no longer look her in the eye. *Oh God. Now,* I'm *spiraling.*

I start to tug at my hair, feeling like the walls are closing in. But her words pull me from my own pending attack. "Oh, really? Um, that's really cool. Huh. Small World." She steps back and silence descends around us.

"Oh Nick-Nack! Where're you hiding?" Jense sing-songs out in the hall. I peek up through my lashes and chance a glance at Annie. The horror on her face is undeniable. She definitely recognizes his voice.

"Wait, Mark works here too?" She asks incredulously. I rub a hand through my blue locks and bite my lip ring. "Uh, yeah. And Luke. John's the only one who doesn't actively work here but he owns part of the company, too. And works out here, obviously."

Her cheeks and chest are still pink from the workout but I can see her pale slightly at my words. "Oh my God!" she gasps. "I'm so sorry. I gotta go. Thank you, again. I, I gotta go."

The loud scratch of the velcro as she unwraps her hands echoes around the room as she all but runs to the storage closet; her ass bouncing as she goes. But I am rooted to the spot. I'm sure I should calm her or something but conversations are hard for me. This whole situation is overwhelming me and I can't help but start pacing.

"Hey man, you ok?" Jense steps into the studio, eyeing me with concern. I notice his eyes flit around trying to spot my siren.

Before I can get a word out, she practically runs out of the closet and towards the door. She's stuffing things into her duffle and not paying attention. "Thanks again. I'm so sorry," she throws out towards me, right before smacking straight into Jenson. His arms come down on her shoulders, preventing her from toppling over, as she yelps in surprise.

"Fuck! Today is not my day." She mutters. Almost in the same breath, she begins apologizing again. She goes to sidestep him, her head down, and he chuckles while gently squeezing her shoulders.

"Sweetness, you never have to apologize for running into me. Even if it *is* a shock that you're here." She slowly peers up at him, searching his face like she expects him to be upset or something. His brow is lifted and the grin shows he's trying to loosen her up. He's using his low, calming voice and I see her finally inhale deeply.

He gently releases her shoulders before filling in the silence. "Today must be our lucky day! We had a fantastic meeting this morning, a damn good lunch, and now we get the pleasure of running into you far sooner than expected. Hey Nick," he shouts at me, pulling me out of my daze, "Maybe we should hit Vegas. Keep the good luck going and all that." He waggles his eyebrows dramatically and grins wider. He always knows how to get me out of my head when I begin to check out. Usually by saying something ridiculous.

"Ha" I huff out. "That's a hard no, man. We have actual responsibilities and big projects we need to get done. Besides, I don't think Vince will ever go to a casino with you after what happened the last time."

As we both start laughing, I see Annie's eyes flitting back and forth between us, eyebrows quirked up in interest. Her breathing has returned back to normal and she's just taking us in. What the hell she sees, I don't know, but she's not running so I'm counting that as a win.

"Who's Vince? And what happened at the last casino?" Her mouth is curled up, showing her genuine interest.

Jenson's mouth curls up like this was his exact plan. I shake my head and chuckle. Taking a few steps toward them, I keep my hands in my pocket and my pace casual. His voice has officially taken on his playful, flirty tone.

"Well sweetness, that is a long story. Guess you'll have to join us for dinner if you want it." Her face falls a little, "Oh um, I can't. I actually, um, have kids. In elementary. So, yeah. But, thank you."

Jenson doesn't let that stop him. "So, they'll be gone tomorrow during lunch, right? I think I can answer your question in that time. But, I have to warn you, the other three can gossip like teenage girls. Do *not* get them started on the couples in Married at First Sight".

She releases a laugh that is so pure I almost melt. She cuts herself off, furrows her brows, and looks between the two of us. "Wait, three others, as in..." She trails off and bites her lip.

"Yes, Sweetness. The other two shitheads you met on Friday would kill us if we took you to lunch alone."

She looks at the floor and clutches her hands. "Of course," I start, tilting my voice mischievously, while looking at Jense, "You and I *are* faster than the other two. I bet *we* can get her to lunch and back before the bozos even know we left." Her laughter bubbles out and she shakes her head at whatever visual is currently in her head.

Jense and I wait as she weighs her options. She tugs her lip into her mouth and I want to walk over there and untuck it for her. *Focus dickhead*.

We watch as she wars with herself for a moment before standing a little taller, rolling her shoulders back, and plastering on a smile. "Ok. We can all have lunch tomorrow. Besides, I'm pretty sure I owe

Matthew for pulling me from my private hell." She grins mischievously but I can't figure out why.

We make a plan to meet tomorrow at noon at a diner around the corner. I ask, again, if she's really ok with all four of us coming along before she quickly confirms and walks off out of the studio. Jense and I stand there, following the sway of her ass and grinning like the dumb assholes we apparently are.

"What the fuck just happened?" I breathe out, my voice definitely sounding huskier than it did a bit ago.

"No fucking clue man, but I'm here for it," Jense responds quietly.

We stand there, like idiots for another beat, before he slaps my shoulder and pulls me back towards the office. "Alright, let's go find Cory and get Vince on the line. Then we can get back to work. Maybe." He shakes his head and I follow behind him.

Maybe is definitely right.

18

Annie

I crashed hard when I got home but at least was smart enough to chug almost half a gallon of water before passing out. Thankfully I had the wherewithal to set my alarm for the bus drop off, just in case. The kids ate dinner while I finished some laundry and then we had our nightly reading time.

The moment I shut the final door and said my last "goodnight," I called Lana. To say she was ecstatic about today's events seems like an understatement. I swear her squeal rang through my ears long after we hung up. I skipped the part of the day that included my embarrassing meltdown and jumped straight into the fact that our collective anonymity was now blown. Well, sort of. I technically only heard Matthew's actual name; Nick. *Yeah, that matched him much better.*

She talked my ear off for fifteen minutes; gabbing about everything from their reactions, where we were going, what I should wear, and, of course, if I wanted them to take things further. I scoffed at the idea. It's been almost a decade since I willingly let a man touch my body. Less time for the other...way. *Bastard.* What no one knows is that sick fuck Lukas sent for me is actually my kids' father.

After leaving Lukas, I stayed with my mother for a while, knowing the police had arrested him. Almost a year later he was sentenced. With all the charges, he got 15 years. I changed my name for the first time and felt like I could finally move on.

Four months after, I got my first in-person visit with a message from Lukas. 8 months after that, my twins were born. Fear kept me from speaking out. I allowed my mom to believe it was some random hookup. And while she was disappointed in me, she still showered me with love.

When we came home from the hospital, there was a pink gift basket and a note attached. It was dropped-off from "Daddy Lukas". I still didn't bother telling my Mom. I mean, the timeline made it more than obvious he is fucking crazy as he was in jail at the time of conception. Regardless, it freaked us both out enough that we both changed our names this time, then moved to the next town over.

A year and a half later, the same man showed up with a similar message. Reminding me I will always belong to Lukas. 8 and a half months later, Josh arrived. And, just like before, Mom and I came home with a gift basket on the porch. This time in all blue. The onesie on top read "Daddy's little man".

For the next three months, Mom and I worked on changing our names, again, and stayed in one of her friend's empty rental houses to lose our paper trail while we came up with another plan. Eventually, we moved clear across the state. Closer to the gulf and further from danger.

When the girls turned 6, Mom met a fantastic man and I knew it was time to move on and let her live her life as she should. It had been about 4 years since our last 'visit' so I was comfortable moving out by myself with the kids.

The weekend we moved in, I was in the driveway watching my kids run around in bubbles, kicking a ball around. The ball rolled into the street and in front of Lana's truck. She stopped before I could even move to stand. She hopped out of the truck, told Josh to "go long" and punted the soccer ball across the lawn. My kids followed after the ball, giggling the whole way. She introduced herself and we immediately clicked. After thirty minutes of us chatting, she invited us over for a cookout with the neighbors near her and the rest is history. She's been one of my best friends since.

Today, though, she irritated me. I had to *beg* her to call me with an out while at lunch, just in case. This bitch made me swear on my life that I would FaceTime her so she could approve my "lunch date attire". When I finally agreed, reminding her that it's *not a date*, she agreed to call me twenty minutes after I get to the diner. We decided she would pretend to be calling from the school to make it plausible.

Now, I'm sitting in my bath, the scent of Epsom salt and eucalyptus, surrounding me. I'm not even sure why I decided to do this. Probably to keep my mind off of this lunch date... meeting...chat?

Either way, I have four outfits set out for Lana's approval. Not that there's much variation. I don't leave the house much, I always dress for comfort, and I honestly spend most of my money on kids clothes and sports. Their wardrobe definitely has more variety than mine. Even their shoes! But, that's just fine with me.

I take a big gulp of water, a deep breathe, and submerge myself under the water. I allow the echo of nothingness to surround me and submit to the feeling of safety and solitude, hoping it keeps my anxiety down long enough to get through this lunch.

Which reminds me, I still need to find a new gym.

I talked with Lana and the guys the whole ride to the deli on market street. When I called her to approve my outfit, she apparently dialed James, Connor, and Jose.

Once we decided on an outfit, *ok, they decided*, we bantered back and forth. Most of it was them giving me "the talk" and the rest was our usual sarcasm and jabs. I laughed at their ridiculousness but I knew what they were doing. They all know I don't date and the kids' dad isn't in our lives. Either way, "a decade is way too long for a sexy MILF to not be ravished." At least, that's what James said. Our back-and-forth had allowed me to finish getting ready and make it to the deli with a smile on my face and not an ounce of anxiety in sight.

I start saying my goodbyes and am hit with a chorus of "Yassss bitch," and "That's our girl." Lana reminds me she will call in about twenty minutes but supposedly has a feeling I won't need it. I suck in a deep breath, check my hair in the mirror, and step out.

The sun is in full-force today but there was just enough breeze to toss my hair. Texas summers can be brutal and I was already dreaming of fall. It's definitely my preferred time of year.

I walk into the deli and scan the inside. The space held 20 square tables and about 5 longer ones. The counter where you order was directly in front of me; their menu above on a huge virtual display. Little caddies line the short wall that separates the dining area from the front walk-in. Each caddie has a handful of laminated menus so guests can grab one and take it back to their table.

I peer out into the dining room and see a few couples eating, and a group of, what appears to be, business men, all dressed in fancy suits. In the far corner, next to giant open-windows, three men sit. I immediately draw to Nick and his vibrant blue hair. His shoulders are rigid and he keeps biting his lip ring. One I have the overwhelming need to pull out and suck on. *Now those are the types of intrusive thoughts that cannot win.*

It takes me a minute to realize that the guy on his left is "Mark". He has black rimmed glasses that frame his face in a sexy, book nerd type of way. I suppose he wore contacts Friday since he had to wear a mask. But, I'm glad he wore his glasses today. They completely elevate his whole aura and I immediately regret not bringing backup panties.

He starts laughing at something "Luke" is saying. "Luke" flips him off and throws something at "Mark", laughing in return. As if feeling my perusal of the group, they all pause and look at me.

Nick's eyes show interest, and worry. *Dammit don't go there.* Mark and Luke look equal parts relieved and surprised as they both take me in. I give them a shy smile and before I can chicken out, I walk over to their table. They all stand as I approach but then pause, unsure of what to do.

"Um, hey. Nice to see you again. Well, not *again* since part of your faces were covered. Well maybe not Matthew and you," I point to "Luke" as I continue my anxiety-induced word vomit. "I saw you yesterday but, you know what I mean." I spectacularly end with a strained chuckle then run my fingers through my hair. My face begins heating up before Luke graciously pulls me out of my head.

"It's good to see you, too, sweetness. Come, sit and figure out what you want. I'm starving!" He slides out the chair between him and Nick, and motions for me to sit. With a start, I join them, sliding into my seat.

Nick slides me a menu over to me and they all chatter about what their favorites are. If I didn't know any better, I would think they are trying to override my anxiety with light conversation that I don't necessarily have to respond to. It's definitely working.

After a moment, I settle for a club sandwich on a flaky croissant with guacamole added. Luke states they always order the chip and dip appetizer so I didn't need anything additional.

As soon as it's decided, Mark stands, takes my menu and goes to order at the counter. I tried handing him the cash I have but he said "pretty girls aren't allowed to pay" before dropping a panty-melting grin and sauntering off. *Fucker*.

I turn my attention to the other two before taking in another deep breath. "So, *Luke,* do you have another name or are we sticking with club names?" I ask with a teasing grin.

His eyes meet mine, the bright green sparkling even brighter with the sun shining through the windows. "I don't know, sweetness. Do you *want* our real names?"

My smile grows and I quirk my brow before answering. "Up to you. I have no problem with calling you the Gospel Boys" I chuckle. "But, *Nick* might be uncomfortable if the only person's name I know is his." As the words leave my mouth, Nick's eyes widen, and Luke's face contorts in confusion. I keep my mouth as straight as possible for as long as I can.

I only make it about twelve seconds before I start laughing. "Easy boys, I'm not a stalker. I overheard you call out for him at the gym yesterday." I explain with a giggle. Their shocked expressions morph into grins as they shake their head at me.

"Oh Sweetness," Luke says, "You are a sneaky one." I roll my eyes at his comment.

Luke glances at Nick and then back to me before sticking out his hand and saying, "My name is Jensen and the handsome bastard that's grabbing our lunch is Cory." I smile, returning his handshake, "Annie nice to meet you officially."

His large hand engulfs mine and he squeezes, just a little, before smirking back. I find myself unable to let go. For just a moment, I lose myself in the idea of what those large hands can do.

Pulling myself out of my head, I ask, "So where's the fourth Gospel Boy?" Nick leans in a little and clears his throat. He looks around, before meeting my eyes, again. "He, uh, he's on his way. He...he texted me a while ago telling me he left work."

"Okay. That's fine," I say in a low voice. Cory returns with our food and a sexy grin. There's enough food here to feed a small army but these guys are so huge, I guess it makes sense.

Jensen lets Cory know that anonymity has been shattered and reintroduces me as Annie. Cory's wide smile faces me and shakes my hand before placing a delicate kiss on my knuckles I can't help but blush. I tried to look anywhere but at him so he doesn't see just how much he affects me. Cory graciously ignores me and unloads the tray of food. He even sits down a basket of food for their missing friend.

"So you all and this other guy," I begin, taking a drink of my tea before continuing. "You've all been friends for a while?"

Cory responds since the other two have just taken huge bites and their mouths are very full. "Yeah, we've all known each other since high school. Became fast friends, brothers even, before deciding to open our own gym. The gym and all of its amenities became such a hit that we started getting calls about opening it as a franchise. Within the last couple of years, we've opened over 100 locations around the US.

"Wow! That's impressive." I say before taking a huge bite out of my sandwich. The croissant is absolutely perfect and the flavors of the sandwich explode on my tongue. I didn't realize that I had moaned out loud until I open my eyes and find three pairs of eyes boring into me. My face reddens but I try and giggle it off before continuing with my line of questions. "So all of you own the gym but only the three of you run it?"

"Yep," Jenson responds. "We are all equal investors. But only the three of us oversee day-to-day operations."

"That's awesome! So, what does the other guy do?" The moment the question leaves my lips the sun catches and draws my attention to the door opening across from us. Suddenly the room grows much smaller and I can't seem to get in a full breath. What are the odds that Officer Daniels is here at the same time I am?

I take him in and his fitted uniform and don't realize I'm staring until Jenson jumps up from his seat causing me to flinch. "Nice of you to take time out of your busy day, boss man." Jenson jokes. He pulls officer Daniels into a bro hug before leading him back to our table. *Okay…did I hit my head last night and am passed out somewhere? Is this a strange dream?*

As they approach, Cory clears his throat and begins to rub the back of his neck. "Annie, we forgot to tell you that John from the club is Vince. And apparently you two have met before."

With those words, the world around me begins to crumble. I can feel the panic rising inside me. *How can those two men be the same person? Did he know? Does it matter? Do I want it to matter? Is this some kind of setup?* He seemed nothing but professional every other time we have talked, but the events that took place in the club on Friday were not professional in the least.

Vince and Jenson approach the table. Vince looks like he's not quite sure of himself, which is a far cry from how he usually holds himself.

"Hello Annie, it's nice to see you again. I'm so sorry I couldn't tell you before. Club rules are pretty explicit but I assure you that our professional working relationship is still intact. Anything job related, other than me knowing you, hasn't been shared."

At first, I breathe a sigh of relief. That means the other guys don't know about the creepy messages. Then again, Officer Daniels, Vince, doesn't know about yesterday's either. Then the rest of what he said processes.

"Wait, you knew who I was on Friday?" He scrubs his head before rubbing his neck and glancing away almost bashfully. "At first, no," he admits. "But when we started dancing, I saw the tattoo on your arm and the rest of it clicked. But like I said, club rules are very explicit. I didn't know how to approach the topic outside without freaking you out or without getting in trouble with the club. I also never would have imagined seeing you this quickly. Not that I'm upset, of course. I've been thinking about you since Friday but... I just hope you don't think I deceived you purposely. I really did have a good time Friday and I enjoyed hanging out with you. I can also assure you that this will not affect anything with your case."

Looking into his golden brown eyes, I see sincerity with a side of guilt. I remember how he was when we first met, how helpful he has been since then, and how truly wonderful I felt being with all four of them on Friday.

I decide to push it back, smile my biggest smile, and wave my hand towards the chair so he can join us. "No big deal, I get it. The club paperwork was crazy so I understand how that must have been difficult and I appreciate your honesty." Vince sighs with relief and takes a seat at the chair.

Suddenly, Jenson is moaning loud and long, directing all of our attention to him. "Oh my God, you guys, you *have* to eat the spinach artichoke dip. It's like a party in my mouth."

We all stare at him, shocked into silence at how random he is. Then, as if we orchestrated it, we all busted out laughing. Based on the smirk he throws my way, I'm pretty sure that was his intention. I have to say, I'm very thankful as the tension bleeds out of my shoulders.

19

Vince

I can't believe she is still here. I can't believe she forgave me for leaving out that I know her. I watched as every emotion flashed across her face. From horror to embarrassment, confusion to irritation. Then, finally, settled on resignation, then acceptance.

I can't even explain how relieved I am. Something about this woman has interested me from the moment I knocked on her door.

But, seeing her on Friday at the club and watching her lower her walls little by little; absolutely intoxicating.

Once Jenson relieved the tension, being his usual, goofy self, we steered towards slightly safer topics. The guys talked about their new project, partnering with a local youth center, and Annie's eyes lit up with interest and, what I think may have been pride. The more the guys threw around ideas for programs, the more Annie relaxed. Soon, her excitement bubbled out of her and she was giving her own ideas and even talking about partnering with other organizations; like a local science lab for kids and the art place around the corner that lets you paint your own sculptures and canvases.

It became clear that she has a lot of experience working with kids, other than her own. "So," I began once there was a pause in conversation "You seem to know a lot about this kind of stuff. Have you worked with kids before?"

My question seems to catch her off-guard. I can see her walls slowly sneaking back up, as if talking about herself is not something she is comfortable with, or used to. She takes a deep breath before glancing at all of us, then returning her eyes to her plate.

"Um, yeah. I worked in a school a lot when I was younger. Was an aide in a special education class when I graduated high school, put myself through school, and began working as a teacher the moment I graduated. When I got pregnant with my twins, I was high-risk and had to go on bed rest. I found an awesome online school and taught 3rd, 4th, and 5th graders almost every subject over the next 4 years. I then switched to teaching middle school science for a year but it still took too much time away from my babies. The girls were in school and I wanted to do all the things; Parties, Field Day, spoiling the teachers with lunch or snacks. So, I switched to something more flexible. Now, I teach English to students on the other side of the world once the kids go to school, then make the rest of my money as a book editor and reviewer." She shrugs like it's not enough or doesn't matter.

Before I can comment, her phone rings out, making her jump. She recovers quickly and pulls it out. We all stay quiet but try to not listen-in too much. But, come on, we're all sitting at a small table together.

"Hello?" she responds. "Yes, this is her." She listens for a moment, slowly smiling at whatever is being said. Her cheeks pink, just a little. Then as if she realizes what she's thinking about, she suddenly shakes her head, drops her smile a little and says "Thank you for your call but I'm not interested. Have a great day."

She shakes her head, trying to hide her smile before putting her hand in her purse. "Was that Elle?" I asked. Her body jolts like I slapped her and she looks at me incredulously.

"Wh-what? Elle?" Her brows frown in confusion. "Elle, your friend from the club?" It takes another moment before she starts giggling. It's like the tinkling of bells wrapped in a warm-embrace and I can't wait to hear it again.

"You caught me, *Officer*," She states, giving me a sassy head tilt after emphasizing "officer". *God damn it.* If picturing her as a naughty school teacher hadn't already made my dick hard, her saying "Officer" like Nick says "Sir", sure the hell would have. Now my dick is punching uncomfortably against my zipper. If the fucker had hands, it would unzip my jeans for me.

Nick's chuckle has me snapping my eyes to his. I didn't even realize I had been staring right at Annie's mouth. The fucker smirks, eyes sparkling with mischief and clearly biting the inside of his cheek to prevent from laughing out right.

I finally get hold of myself and lean back in my chair, resting my right arm on the side while rubbing my lip with my thumb. I can see the moment he catches the moment, his eyes filling with heat instead of mischief. Just when I know I have him, I smirk and tap 2 fingers to my mouth, signaling he has now earned two punishments.

His eyes get darker and he subtly adjusts himself. Clearing his throat, he shoves his seat back and mumbles that he needs a refill. I chuckle under my breath as he walks away, trying his hardest to maneuver himself away from prying eyes. *Yeah, we're both looking forward to that punishment.*

-Nick-

Damn bastard.

I was already hard enough thinking of the moan Annie had made earlier, then seeing her so excited about helping out local youth. Now, that prick just made it worse. Promising me a double punishment. One we will both enjoy, no doubt.

Annie, though, she's something else. Her pretty, soft pink lips, the giggle I want to record and play whenever my past tries to pull me under, her obvious strength. She's clearly lived through hell yet she continues to find reasons to smile and laugh and make the world around her just a littler brighter.

I can admit that it's been a while since I was interested in a woman. Amber fucked us all pretty badly. Before her, no one really caught my eye. But Annie, she has caught much more than that. And judging by the others' expressions and how enrapt they are with her, I know I'm not the only one.

I was a little worried about today for that reason. We were already so taken by her at the club but I wondered if it would be the same once we were out in a normal setting. The lights are brighter, our minds are free of alcohol, and we definitely don't have the sensory overload that come with just walking into Sky's the Limit. Without all of that, there's bound to be differences in perception; reception too, I guess. But, judging by the way conversation is flowing and smiles are being shared, I think it's safe to say that no one's interest has changed.

I walk back to the table with my drink re-filled, a pep in my step, and my heart full of hope. As I step up, I hear Annie's muffled laughter. It appears she has a mouthful. Cory puts his hands up, pleading his case, "I swear! I didn't mean to do it. I think she took more than she was supposed to. Ol' witch pulled out this giant horse needle, stabbed me with it, then started moving it around like she was Harry fucking Potter waving a wand around."

Jenson and Vince are roaring with laughter. Annie finally swallows down her food and states, "Ok so how did *that* lead to you giving her a concussion?!" Oh, I love this story. It's one of my favorites.

Cory scrunches up his nose like he really doesn't want to relive the whole ordeal. He exhales dramatically. "After she was done, emptying my body of its power of life, I wanted out as quickly as possible. Apparently you're supposed to sit there for a while and eat a cookie or some shit but I wasn't waiting around. I remember standing up and the world spinning." He rolls his eyes to the ceiling like he's praying to get out of having to tell it. With a sigh, he lowers his voice just above a whisper. "Next thing I knew, I was waking up to the sounds of people asking what happened, running back and forth from the room. I realized I was lying on a hard-ass bed and saw that lady was sitting on the chair next to the bed, the back of her head getting stitched up and some other nurse or whatever shined a light in her eyes. I groaned, because my head hurt and reached up to feel four stitches at the top left side of my head."

Annie gasps, completely engrossed in his story. Leaning towards him, eyes wide, and chest raising with every breath she takes. *And, I'm hard again. Shit.*

Cory chuckles before wrapping up the story. "Apparently I passed out on her. Literally, *on* her. She was facing away from me but by the time she turned around and saw me standing, I was already toppling forward. This woman was barely 5 foot tall and older than my grandma. When I went down, she did, too. She smacked the back of her head on impact and I smacked the top of mine. Apparently it took 3 guys to get me off of her."

By this point, we have all fallen over in laughter. Annie's face is bright red with exertion. Her whole face transformed by pure happiness. She looks light, happy, unburdened. *Would it be weird if I took a picture? It would. It definitely would.*

Jenson rolls his eyes towards Annie, smirking and stuffing a chip in his mouth "And that's how he took out a poor, defenseless old lady. Every time he goes to give blood, we have to go with him. Just so he doesn't try to kill anyone else." He chuckles.

Annie gives Cory a look that promises something sexy and sarcastic is about to leave her mouth. "Hm, welp," she pops the *p*, and tilts her head, giving way to a naughty grin "You know what they say: the bigger they are, the harder they fall," she leans in, lowering her voice a little and quirks her brow, "on you."

Cory drops his mouth dramatically, gaping at her before smiling so wide, I'm afraid he might break his face. *Have I ever seen him smile that big before?*

"Oh you naughty girl. I'm going to remember that." He says with a lifted brow and she meets his stare with a grin of her own.

"Oh no! What ever shall I do?" She matches his dramatics, clutching her chest like she's clutching pearls. A ridiculous southern woman accent coming out to play. "The big sexy man is going to remember little ol' me laughing at his blunders." *Is that* brat *I'm detecting?*

I see the moment Vince and Jense have the same thought. They both subtly shift in their chairs, eyes swirling with desire.

Cory lets a beat pass before grinning. "Did you just say I was sexy?" Annie chokes on her drink, trying and failing to keep it in as she grabs at a napkin and begins cleaning her shirt up.

"I didn't say that. I said "scary"." She takes a moment, clearly going over her words. "I meant scary. Just a slip of the tongue." Her face is getting redder by the second, and she is blotting at her shirt like there's anything more she can do about the wet spot she now has.

"Slip of the tongues are my favorite." Jenson mumbles, causing Annie to snap her eyes towards him before laughing out loud. Thank God for Jense. Always knows when to bring his humor out to play.

Vince glances at his watch and curses. "I gotta get back. Cases won't solve themselves." He throws a wink at Annie and she quickly stands up, piling all of the trash to throw away. Before she can step away, I reach for the tray. "I got it, Siren." I throw out a wink before she drops her head and whispers a light "thank you."

We all pile out of the deli and walk her towards her car. Once she is next to the older model SUV, she turns, looking almost as unsure than she did when she first arrived. "So, um, thank you, again for lunch. I appreciate it."

Not a single one of us boneheads can even respond. She gives us each a small smile before fiddling with her keys. "Thanks, again."

Her turning and pressing the key fob, unlocking the doors, at least kicks Vince into motion. "Annie, thank you, for meeting us. Um, we'd like to do it again, soon, if you want." He rubs the back of his neck and actually looks nervous for once.

"Oh?" She turns around, clearly surprised. "You would?" She looks confused and twists her lips as she considers her next words. "Like, *all* of you want to hang out?"

Well I guess now's the time to rip off the band-aid before we get in too deep. I step forward, pulling her hand in mine. "No, Annie. Not to hang out." Her brow wrinkles in confusion. "We want to date you. Get to know you."

Her confusion grows deeper as we give her a moment before I start again. "So, we've been a unit, a team, a family, basically since high school. We live together, and we share, um, everything."

"Everything?" She questions, searching each of our eyes.

"Yes, pretty girl, everything. We've only had one real, long-term relationship with a woman but it's definitely something we all want. And, right now, we really want to get to know *you* more. If you want."

"If I want." She whispers more to herself than to us.

"I don't know guys. I don't really date. I don't have a lot of time for it and, I'm," she breathes and gulps, "I haven't actually dated anyone in the last decade. And my last relationship was like, bad-bad. And that was only *one* guy that I couldn't keep interested. I don't think I'd be enough for all of you. Besides, you guys are solid. You *deserve* someone solid and I can't be that right now; for you or anyone else."

I choose to let her little comment about keeping guys interested slide; for now. I can see the disappointment on everyone's face, including hers. They mirror my own. But, I know, deep in my bones, this is right.

"Ok then, Siren. No dating. How about we stay friends? We can all use more of those, right?" I ask, trying not to sound as desperate as I feel.

"Friends." She rolls the word around in her head, fighting whatever inner battle with herself before she glances at each of us, then smiles. "Ok. Friends is good. But just remember, single Mom with three kids. I don't get a lot of what's known as free time."

Vince responds by reassuring her, "S'all good Angel. We are *great* friends. We have lots of experience."

At that Annie laughs and turns back, opening her door wide. Before she can step in, Jenson stops her. "Wait. Can I have your phone, Sweetness?"

She looks back, confused by his question. Reading her face, he flashes her a charming smile. "I'm not trying to steal your secrets, love, but it's hard to prove how great we are at being friends if we can't contact each other." She immediately smiles, shaking her head and hands him her phone.

We wait in comfortable silence. A moment later, all of our phones ping before Jenson hands her phone back. I notice that he's holding it in a way that she has to brush her fingers over his to take it. We all take note of the way he tightens his hold, for just a moment, before slipping his hand off. I roll my eyes at his antics before she can catch it.

Then, we all watch in silence as she gets into her car. She says "Bye guys," before closing the door and driving off, with one final wave and a smile that could melt Frosty.

"We are so fucked aren't we?" I ask. And they all respond with a resounding, "Yup.

20

~

Annie

Turning out into the street, I decide to use this time to decompress. No thoughts of the creepy messages, no thoughts of the guys or how they make me feel... But, to do that, I need to jam out a little.

Flipping through my playlist, I decide that screaming at my past is the best way to handle this. The first words of Jax's Victoria Secret ring out. But, instead of the general feel good, own your body version, I choose the re-mixed version.

After her original dropped, she connected with a little girl who has aspirations of becoming a metal singer. The girl absolutely loved the message of Jax's song so, they created a metal version. It has the power to simultaneously boost my confidence and bring a smile to my face at Jax and Harper's story.

Women empowering women, older empowering younger; we need more of that. So much more.

I sing, scream, and move to every part of the song, letting myself relish in this moment of freedom; one where I can just be me. Not mom, daughter, teacher. Not ex, ruined, and broken. Just. Me.

I spent the rest of the day yesterday doing laundry and trying not to think about the amazing men I that have taken up residence in my head. Even in my dreams, apparently.

Waking up with a smile on my face was a nice break from the panic-inducing nightmares that usually plague me. I rolled out of the bed with an extra pep in my step, ready to take on the day. *What the hell is wrong with me? I barely know these men.*

Shaking my head to clear the thoughts of *them,* I begin outlining my day in my head. First, I need coffee. Then I'll wake the littles and get them ready for school before hopping on the computer for work.

It's a whirlwind of activity from the moment their little blue eyes pop open until they climb on the bus. Once the bus disappears from sight, I login to my English lessons for the day and lose myself in the familiar flow of work. Pride and unbridled satisfaction thrum through my body, as it usually does working with these kids.

After my lessons, I have plenty of feel-good reserves leftover so I decide to get some reading done so I can get ahead in my editorial notes. After about fifteen minutes, my phone pings with a message. I'm so wrapped up in the story I'm reading, I choose to ignore it. I figure it's my mom wanting to see the kids. *Heaven forbid she goes longer than 4 days without seeing them.*

I roll my eyes and chuckle to myself, secretly loving her love for it. We may have had a rough time growing up, but I couldn't even begin to ask for a better grandmother for my kids.

Before I can finish the next line, my phone pings again; then again; then again. *What the hell is going on? This is ridiculous.*

I grab my phone and immediately laugh out loud at what I see.

Gospel Boys is showing in the notification bar. I can feel my smile grow as I shake my head at the ridiculous group name Jenson must have created.

Ping
Ping
Ping

I swipe my phone to unlock and read the ridiculous banter that has now taken over my messages.

Jenson- Morning Sweetness. Cory said I have to wait 3 days to say hi but, we're just friends, so I don't have to abide by the rules, right?

Of course he would be the one to start up a conversation. He's so carefree and filled with light, always knowing when to be serious and when tension needs to be averted. He's going to be a handful but I can't help but crave his light. I also don't miss the flutter I feel in my stomach as he points out the "just friends" piece. Almost like he's pointing out it's more for me than them.

I'm not even sure how I feel about all that. They totally caught me off guard. I don't even want to go down that rabbit hole.

I'm pretty sure they just want to share me in a sexual way. There's no way they actually want a real relationship with me. After what happened last Friday, I get it. I have thought about it more times than I can count. But, sex isn't really something I do. Not anymore. And knowing that's all they are really after, it's best to just lock them firmly in the friend zone. No hurt, no heartbreak, no feelings. *Right, none at all.*

Cory- That's not what I said and you know it. Stop twisting my words around. Oh, and good morning, Annie. Hope the rest of your evening was as great as our afternoon together.

Well damn if that's not equal parts hilarious and sweet. These guys are way too much but I love it. I mean, I like it; a lot. *Down girl. You have kids and no room for drama. And there's four of them! Four beautiful, perfect, drool-worthy specimens. Shut it down, now.*

Nick- Annie, I'm sorry my brothers are apparently choosing to go with childish for the day. I suppose you and I are the only adults working today. <winking emoji>

I find myself laughing out loud. I'm not sure what their offices look like but I can picture them all sitting together, bantering with each other, texting me, while Nick is busy doing, whatever he does.

Vince- I'm working, Nick-Nack. And just because I'm not there doesn't mean you can stir shit up, Jense.

Another message pings as I finish reading Vince's comment.

Jenson- I'm doing no such thing! I am simply trying to make our new friend feel welcome.
Nick- Maybe stop while you're just now getting behind. Much more of this and she'll never talk to you again.

I can't help the laughter bubbling out. They are all so ridiculous. As I begin typing a message, another comes through.

Jenson- Nah, Annie adores me. I'm her favorite. If anything she will see how mean you all are and ONLY talk to me. <laughing emoji, smug emoji>

Me- You guys are far too much! I'm trying to work and I can't do that if I have to keep controlling my laughter.

Jenson- Exactly! Laughter makes the heart grow fonder.

Vince- That's not how that line goes at all. <Eye roll emoji>. Annie, Angel, please save me from these clowns.

Annie- No can do. I have my hands full with my own kids. I don't think I can handle grown ones.

Cory- Oh, I think you can handle us just fine pretty girl.

Panties, ruined, again.

Annie- <Eye roll emoji>. Whatever. Thank you for giving me a reprieve from work but I have to silence you all now. I have got to get these edits done.

Nick- Ok Siren. I'll steal Jense's phone if needed. Have a great day.

Me- You guys too. And try to behave.

Cory- Not likely with this crowd but we will do our best.

I silence my message notification, just in case, and get back on with my work for the day. By the time the kids are getting off the bus, I have managed to completely finish all of my editing tasks and even got my lesson plans ready for next week.

The kids are all telling me about the friends they are making, what their favorite subjects are, and everything in between.

As soon as we sit down for our nightly reading time, my phone rings out. It's then I remember I silenced the notifications hours ago. *Oops.*

Mom wanted to ask about taking the kids to some interactive exhibit this weekend to which I obviously agreed. Anything to get them away from the house is a plus; at least to me.

Once we hang up, I check my messages. I have a few from Lana and a couple of other friends I talk with. Mostly TikTok videos which I save to watch later when the kids are in bed.

But, at the end of the unread section I see it. I don't want to open it. I don't want to know what is being said, but I can't stop myself from clicking on the message.

Unknown- Heard my little kitten is dating. And four men? I knew you were a filthy whore. But, it's ok. I forgive you. I know it's been hard not having me around but there's nothing I won't do to get my family back. Tell the kids Daddy's coming home. See you soon, kitten.

Fuck. My. Life.

21

~

Annie

I pace, then turn, then I pace some more. I numbly put the kids in bed and weigh my options. I didn't tell Vince about the last messages because I went to the gym, and fell apart and the guys showed up. I don't know what is with them but when they are around, I suddenly feel like I can breathe, like I can be me, like I'm safe.

I scoff at the idea. I'm not safe. Apparently I never was. But what do I do now? Vince is, well, Vince. And even as friends, there's a connection there, a line. What if he finds out just how truly broken I am? How badly I'm damaged? What if he convinces the others I'm not worth having as a friend. Do I really think he would? I mean, it's Vince. Gentle giant with a smile that could convince a nun to sin. *Shit, shit, shit. What do I do?*

Fifteen minutes and a glass of wine later, I'm dialing Vince's police number; attempting to at least put that boundary in place. He picks up on the second tone, "Officer Daniels."

"Um, hi, it's Annie."

"Oh, you could have just called my personal cell, Angel." The now familiar nickname rolling off his tongue.

"Yeah, but, this is, uh, not a personal call." I can literally feel him shifting position, all playfulness in his tone gone.

"What happened? Are you ok? Where are you?" His rapid fire questions make me feel both protected and overwhelmed.

"No, I'm ok. I think. I mean I'm not but I don't necessarily need rescuing, physically, so to speak." Why can I not talk normal? I did so good at lunch the other day and now I'm a bumbling basket case.

I blow out an exhausted breath before continuing. "So, I didn't get a chance to tell you because of, some other stuff," hoping the guys hadn't told him about my epic meltdown, "And I have had a couple of more messages from the unknown number. The good news is, I know who it is. The bad news is, I don't know how to find him, and he is *really* bad." I pause but continue on before he can say anything else. "Look, I know that we accidentally crossed the whole professional line and now we're friends so I'm not sure if I'm even allowed to talk to you or if you will get in trouble but," my voice gets quieter as I swallow my pride and admit the one thing I didn't want to. "I'm scared."

After admitting my fear, Vince insisted on coming over. He needed to talk to his Chief first, to tell him about the change in our "relational status." He had also planned on grabbing ice cream on his way home and said he could pick some up for me.

I brushed him off, at first, but when he promised me a banana split made with Vanilla Bean, Mint Chocolate Chip, and Very Berry Strawberry ice cream, how could I refuse? I told him we could hang out in the driveway since the kids were asleep and he agreed with no hesitation.

Twenty minutes later, I have the garage open and the lawn chairs set up. I'm pacing the driveway as a Ram 2500 pulls up. It's already dark out but with the lights shining above the garage, I can see that it's a dark blue color.

After a couple of seconds, the truck turns off and the big man hops out of the cab, strutting over with a bag full of goodies. *Screw what's in the bag, I want the man. Holy shit how does he get sexier every time I see him?*

Vince greets me with a warm smile as he approaches. When he comes to a stop in front of me, he slowly leans down towards me. His sweet smile turns into a sexy smirk like he knows exactly where my mind went. His minty breath skates over my cheek as he asks, "May I please have a hug?"

The question is phrased so damn politely that a laugh bubbles out before I can contain it. "Yes, you may." I tried to keep my response firm but sweet. Instead, it came out husky and breathless.

He moves slowly, like he's testing my reaction. His arms wrap around my shoulders as my arms wrap around his mid-section. After a moment, he pulls me in closer and hugs me tighter. His huge frame engulfs me and his scent clouds my brain. Sandalwood and lavender. Odd combination but, very him. Strong and soft, bold yet understated.

We stay that way for God knows how long. I'm pressed against his huge chest and allow myself to drown in the beating of his heart. *This man is like a drug and I may be getting addicted.*

Eventually we pull apart and I offer him a seat. Thankfully I have what my Mom calls "bougie" lawn chairs. They are thickly woven, can hold up to 350 pounds and recline almost completely flat. As an added bonus, there's a little pillow you can move that rests at the top. Vince sits in the chair and hands me my banana split.

At first, we stick to safe topics. The guys, my job, even comparing our favorite workouts and food.

After our desserts have been discarded, he breathes in deeply before pushing it out. Then he turns his chair to face me head on. "I want you to know that I talked to the Captain and he says I can still work on your case but only if that makes *you* feel comfortable. If you want me to pass on your info, a couple of my buddies would absolutely treat this right." His eyes shine with equal parts sincerity and genuine concern.

I take a moment, looking down at my lap, to gather my thoughts. I really do feel safe with Vince. With all the guys for the matter. But he has been great since the first moment. Kind, respectful, attentive. And that's just Vince the police officer. Vince the man is all of those things and more.

I look him square in the eye, wanting him to see me and the truths I hold. "If *you're* ok with it, I'd like to keep working with you. This whole situation is bad. But, it *has* been worse. More so than anyone knows. I..." I trail off, coughing lightly to prepare myself for what I know I have to do.

Baring myself to him so soon after telling them I want friendship is terrifying. He needs to know just how bad my past is, how dark it is. And he needs to know how much they all mean to me already; how much I want to protect them from my past. No matter the costs.

I send up a silent prayer that once my story is done, the parts I can give him without destroying myself in the process, that he will still want to be around. Even if it's just as a police officer, helping a citizen.

I take a breath and let it loose before I have another second to reconsider. "I really like spending time with you. And the other guys, too. I feel, things. Things I can't explain but I am not one for casual hookups, I don't really date, and I don't have a lot of time to go out so my friendships are numbered. The handful I have are there for me in every way *I* have allowed. They truly understand I am by myself. It's me and my littles so I can't just drop everything and go to the beach for the weekend. Sometimes I have to cancel plans, even if I haven't seen them in weeks, because a kid gets sick. And they have never, not once, made me feel bad or guilty for that. They accept me wholly. It took a long time to really let them in but, they let me take that at my own pace, too.

"I guess, what I'm trying to say is, I don't want this case, this bull-shit, to ruin the new friendships we're all building. Friendships that I feel so strongly about already."

I pause my rant, trying to get a breath in. I can't bring myself to look him in the eye as I whisper, "I don't want to lose you all. And this stuff, this guy; he will try to destroy everything. My baggage, my burdens, my brokenness; it's a lot.

"I'm not asking you to take it on, but consider what staying on this case means for us. We are barely starting out. Are you ready to see my demons? Are the guys? Is my friendship worth it?" I breathe again before looking back at him, fighting back the tears.

"*You* let *me* know what you want to do. And I swear, I will respect whatever decision you make. I just... I just needed you to know how ugly it is, I am, before you make that decision."

I look back down in my lap, squeezing my fingers and eyes shut. *Breathe in for 4; hold for 4; breathe out for 4. Breathe in for 4; hold for 4; breathe out for 4.*

I open my eyes back up and lift them towards Vince. What I find almost knocks me back. His eyes are swirling with more emotions than I can name or identify. Anger, despair, pain, longing, and even determination are like fires lighting and swirling together in his chocolate eyes. The lights from above the garage hit him at just the right angle that the gold flecks in his eyes seem to dance.

Without a word, Vince slowly rises to his full height and looks down at me. He seems to be studying me so I brace myself for impact. *That was the shortest friendship ever.*

As I plaster on a fake smile and try to not reveal my disappointment, he kneels down in front of me. His chest rising and falling between my bent knees. He slowly brings his hands to either side of my face and locks eyes with me. We sit there, frozen as we search the other for God knows what before his shoulders drop just a smidge and he leans in. *Holy shit he's going to kiss me!*

I'm drawn in to him, matching his slow pace until we are centimeters apart. There, he holds my stare and waits for me to make a move. My brain shuts off completely and I finally let myself just go, just feel, just be in this moment with this mountain of a man. I close the distance so fast, it catches him off balance. He gasps in surprise before closing his eyes, and kissing me back. His lips on mine are soft and firm and utterly amazing.

I scoot forward in my seat, arms drawing up behind his neck and widening my seated stance to make room for his broad body. Just when I feel like I can't get close enough, his mouth opens just a little, and his tongue sweeps out across my lips, requesting entrance. I obey immediately and the groan that rumbles up his chest sends lightning to my core, instantly making my clit throb. Our tongues duel for dominance before I officially submit to his silent demands, allowing him to take control. He moves my head to the side, positioning me as he wants and I let him. I become both pliant yet strung so tight, I may combust without him even touching me.

He moves his hands from my face, down to my waist and before I can register what's happening, he's lifting me out of my chair and I let out a little yelp. He carries me like I weigh nothing while our lips finding each other once more.

The bite of cold metal has me gasping as he pushes me against his truck. The change makes me realize he's holding all of my weight and I suddenly feel guilty. I weigh a ton! I break the kiss long enough to plead with him, "Put me down. You're going to hurt yourself."

The next thing that comes out of his mouth takes me from needy to downright desperate. *This man is going to be the death of me; and all of my panties.*

-Vince-

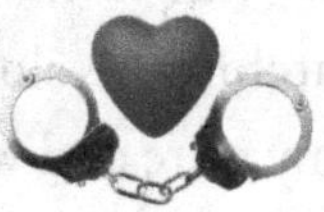

Dear Lord Almighty. This woman tastes of minty chocolate and sin. I can't get enough of her. Once she poured out her soul, I knew I needed more. More of her, more of this, just more.

My cock throbs hard as it presses against my jeans. It wants her as badly as I do. Hearing the sweet little sounds she makes, taking in her gasps, and knowing just how vulnerable she is trying to be with me is my absolute undoing.

But then, she makes that comment. One I couldn't let slide. For just a moment, I let my dominant side slip.

I rear back, locking my eyes with hers. Once I see that I have her undivided attention, I implored her to hear, feel, every word that I say. "Angel, don't you dare say anything negative about yourself like that again. I know what I can handle, and, right now, it's you. Now wrap your legs around my waist and know I want this, I want *you*." I emphasize the last word with a thrust of my hips.

Her mouth parts on a gasp as she searches my eyes, probably looking for a lie. But I know she won't find one. I see the moment she believes me, the moment she submits, as her arms tighten around my neck.

I grab both juicy ass cheeks and lift her up as she wraps her legs around me. Her breasts are pushed up against my chest, rising with every pant, and I can feel her wet heat scorching me through our pants.

At first, she's tense, even when I lean her back against the truck. But when I devour her mouth, again, I feel her slowly relax, allowing herself this moment with me. Her submission, seemingly so small, is every-fucking-thing. I know whatever she needs to tell me, is going to be hell for her. I also know that she is strong, fierce, and I will make it my life's mission to bring those sides out of her.

Our tongues tangle and she thrusts again, trying to gain friction where I know she is throbbing. For me. It's such a heady feeling and I thrust back against her letting her know I want it, too.

She gasps on a moan as I break the kiss, and thrust against her, trailing kisses down her jaw, and to her neck. I suckle on her throbbing pulse point and her moan lets me know I have hit my target. But, I'm not done.

I gently drag my teeth over her pulse point, making her groan at the sensation, bucking up into me. I bite down, just enough to spark pain but not so much to draw blood. Her small yelp morphs into a throaty moan as I lick the sting away.

"You are perfect, Angel," I murmur between kisses leading up to her ear.

Today she has a looped earring in her bottom lobe and a simple stud right above it. Her industrial bar is still the same from the other day. I take my tongue and flick her lobe, before gently tugging the loop. "Oh God. Vince," she responds in the sexiest tone I have ever heard. My name on her lips has me leaking precum, my cock pleading for attention.

I trail my tongue up her ear whispering, "I love the sound of my name coming from your mouth, Angel."

She's grinding into me shamelessly, chasing the feeling of euphoria I know she needs. Her breaths are harsh pants, synchronized in bliss and sexual need. "Vince," she gasps.

"Yes, Angel, tell me what you need." She grinds against me again, releasing a moan and tilting her head back. I capture her mouth in another kiss, reveling in the minty chocolate flavor as my tongue commands her attention.

"I need your words, angel. Use,"

thrust "Your"

thrust "Words."

I stop my body. It trembles with the effort it takes to keep myself contained. I want to give it all. I want to give her everything. But she needs to know she holds all the power of me, of what we do, and over the others should she ever decide that.

She groans in frustration, her body seeking friction. I grip her chin loosely so it doesn't hurt, but firm enough she feels the silent command. Her eyes open, pupils blown wide in heavy lust. Her cheeks are flamed red, even in the shadows of darkness I can still see it.

"Tell me what you need, Angel. I need your words." I emphasize the need so she fully understands the line of consent I am drawing for her.

Her panting breaths push her breasts against me and I can see the war raging in her mind. I hold her in silence, my hands gripping her waist, knuckles almost white. I implore her silently, trying to show every ounce of vulnerability and restraint as possible; trying to get her to truly understand that this show is hers, and I'm just along for the ride.

Her mouth opens and closes a few times, indecision warring all over her face. Then I watch as she pushes it all back. I can see it in her eyes. The moment she takes control of herself, of her body, of her desires. Determination sparkles in her dark blue eyes. Whether they are dark because it's night, or dark with lust, I'm not sure. But I can't wait to find out.

She clears her voice, talking just above a whisper, "Vince, I need y..." and then her phone pings with a message, effectively breaking the spell. She shakes her head like she's just remembering where we are and what we may or may not have been about to do.

She chuckles a little, gives me a smile that could melt glaciers, and taps my shoulder twice. I slowly slide her down to the ground, ensuring that my achingly hard cock stays pressed against her; flexing it a little when it rubs on her stomach. The grin on her face tells me she knows exactly what I'm doing.

Once she's on her feet, she looks up at me with those big blue eyes, blush tinting her cheeks. "I, uh, I guess I should check that."

I chuckle in response, grinning like a fool before stepping back and letting her walk back to her chair.

I watch as she bends down to pick her phone up off the ground; her big peachy ass in the air. I have to bite my knuckles to hold in the groan that wants to rip from my throat. *Fuck.*

She turns my way and unlocks her phone. The driveway lights

shine bright behind her and casts an ethereal glow around her. My angel.

My heart already feels like it's going to explode right out of my chest. But then, her sharp inhale pulls me from my thoughts. Her face has completely transformed. No longer needy, no longer determined. No, she is terrified. Her eyes wide, mouth dropped open as if in disbelief, and I can see her hands begin to shake.

"Annie, what happened? Everything ok?" I rush toward her, stopping just in front of her and waiting with baited breath.

"He texted me again." Is all she whispers before collapsing into the chair. She stares out into the darkness with a look of hopelessness that completely wrecks me.

Instead of asking her to repeat the message, I hold out my hand. "May I?"

She snaps her head back to me, glances at my hand, then looks back into my eyes. "Are you *really* sure Vince? Once you know, you'll be in danger, too." She all but whispers.

"Annie. I'm *here* and I'm not going anywhere. Whatever is happening, we can get through it, together." She scans my face for any hint of deception or maybe fear before sliding her phone into my hand.

"You can read the others too, since I didn't get a chance to catch you up." She says with a tight smile before her cheeks pink back up. Good, I'd rather her think about what just happened than this jackass.

I look at her phone and read the latest message.

Unknown- Oh, kitten. Look at you whoring yourself out while my kids are left all alone. Guess we have more lessons to learn. Don't worry, I'll be seeing you soon and I will fix you.

The fuck?

I read through the messages he has sent since they started. Exhaling deeply, I put the phone down by my side before extending my hand. She notices the movement and looks back up at me with fear, trepidation, and so much damn worry. I flip my fingers upwards a little, in a silent command. She takes a breath before sliding her hand in mine. I pull her up to standing before wrapping her up in a hug that I pray expresses all of my thoughts. *You are safe. I am here. I won't let anything happen to you. You are not alone.*

She relaxes into my embrace and we just stand there, holding onto each other. One needing strength, the other willing to give it all. I know I need to get started on this and get more information from her but, for now, she needs this. So, I will stand here and offer my physical strength until she is ready.

Then, I'm going to burn the world down just to end this fucker.

22

Nick- 3 Weeks Later

The last three weeks have been a blur of activity. We've taken Annie to hang out 11 times. Most were lunches but we did fit in a few breakfasts. Vince told me what happened when he brought her dessert. Well, the part that had him blushing like a kid with his first crush. He told me he was working a case for her so he couldn't say more. I completely respect that. Not just professionally, but personally.

I keep waiting for the moment she opens up to us about whatever is going on. Hoping she will trust us to be there for her. The good news is we have spent three weeks texting, talking, and hanging out. Her walls have definitely come down. Seeing her blossom from being shy and timid, to sassy and full of life has been everything. We're finally getting the Annie her friends have. The Annie we are all slowly falling for.

But, Annie isn't the one on my mind at the moment. She's not the one that has me pacing around the house. It's Vince. Vince hasn't been home in 2 days. Not completely out of the ordinary with his job but he usually checks in, or at least responds to messages. But it's been radio silence for two whole days. My anxiety is getting the best of me, always thinking the worst. *What if something happened? What if he died? Can I live without him? The one person I have ever truly loved?*

I'm now pacing the kitchen, completely forgoing any pretense that I'm going to get any work done today. My hair is a complete mess, having run my hands through it repeatedly over the last day. I'm not even sure when the last time I ate was. *I can't sit here and do nothing anymore. I have to do something, but what?*

I know Cory and Jenson are just as worried but they still went to the gym, knowing there was nothing we could do at the time.

Suddenly, I get an idea. I run over to the kitchen island and pull out my laptop. I begin searching for numbers of every hospital and emergency room in a 20 mile radius. Just as I lift my phone to my ear, I hear the front door open, then click shut.

I immediately shoot up to my feet, running out of the far opening of the kitchen, closest to the foyer. The tile floors make way for wooden floors as I step into the foyer. Dark cherry and perfectly polished to Cory's standards. The sound immediately echoes in the foyer, alerting anyone there to my presence.

I round the corner but already see Vince's retreating back. I exhale roughly, finally able to release some of the tension stored in my shoulders. But, something still isn't right.

Vince begins heading up the stairs, thumping loudly with each step. His body is so tense I can literally feel the irritation rolling off of him in waves. "Vince." I call out, my voice betraying my worry. The only sign he heard it was a slight flinch of his body and brief pause. He shakes his head and continues up the stairs.

"Vince, stop!" I yell out as I begin walking towards the stairs. He doesn't respond, not a single part of his body.

"Vince!" I call out again, dashing up the stairs behind him. He reaches the stairs at the top of the landing and continues walking down the hallway. "Vince, wait! Please. Stop." I can hear the tremble in my own voice as the panic rises inside me.

He ignores me completely and just keeps making his way down the hall; I assume to go to his room. My steps quicken as I jog towards him. As soon as he's in reach, I reach my hand out and squeeze his shoulder. "Vince, stop!"

Vince abruptly whirls around, his hand wrapping around my throat, and backs me up against the nearest wall. The slam on impact forces me to grunt but I don't care in the slightest. What I do care about is the man in front of me. The man whose heart is larger than his shoulders. The man who has seen every broken, jagged piece of me and used his goodness and extraordinary patience to make me feel loved, cherished, special.

I stare, unblinking, into his big brown eyes; whiskey and sunshine mixing together. But the anger, the pain, the helplessness swirling in them, almost brings me to my knees. He leans in and grits through his teeth, "Leave it alone Nick. Back. Off."

I can feel his entire body trembling as he moves to release me. "No!" I snap. "I'm not leaving it alone. Talk to me Vince. What happened? Where have you been?" I practically beg. My eyes search his, back and forth, as if the answer will suddenly be written on his skin.

"I'm going to shower," is all he grunts before releasing me and turning away.

"No. You talk to me. We talk to each other. Don't you dare turn your back on me. I haven't heard a word from you in 2 fucking days! Give me something." My words slowly rose louder until they echoed around us.

Vince whirls around with a roar, backing me against the wall again, this time keeping his hands to himself. "I said drop it!"

"No. I won't let it drop Vince. You don't get an out. I'm your person and you're mine." My eyes plead with him, fire coursing through my veins.

"I c-can't." His voice breaks, chest rising rapidly. His eyes close and he leans his forehead against mine, breathing rapidly.

"You can, Vince, you can. I'm right here. Always have been. I can take it." I reach my hands out, cupping his cheeks and pouring all of my love into it.

"N-no. I literally can't tell you and it's killing me. I don't know what to do. I don't know how to help her. Why do I feel so much for her already? How can I protect her?" His voice breaking on a sob.

"Is this about Annie?" His head nods, keeping in contact with my forehead. His eyes are still closed but I keep mine open, needing to be able to read anything beyond his words.

"Ok, so did something happen between you two? I mean, we've all been talking and you know I love you. We agreed bringing in someone wouldn't mess with us. I'm not mad. A little jelly I couldn't watch, but not mad."

He huffs out a laugh but it's far from humorous. Shaking his head he says, "No nothing like that. Nothing more than the kiss I told you about."

I filter through his words, trying to piece together what he's not saying. "Is this about her case? About the reason you two met."

He sighs heavily before nodding and I continue. "So, you literally can't tell me because it would invade her privacy, and you can't talk about an active case, right?"

Again he nods. His shoulders begin to relax but his eyes are screwed tight.

"Ok. Is it bad?" Another nod. "Worse than you originally thought?" Another nod.

He takes a shuddering breath, before speaking in a low grumble. "Yeah. She only skimmed the surface. She knows who is bothering her and we finally got a hit on his activities. It's bad, Nick. So bad." His entire body trembles along with his lips as he speaks his next words. "Nick. How do I tell her? What this guy is wrapped up in..." He shakes his head and pulls on his hair.

I can see him starting to unravel as he steps away from me, pacing from wall to wall like a caged lion. The fear, the anguish, the turmoil. It's all overloading his body.

He can't do this anymore. He's going to give himself a heart attack.

Just as I have that thought, my mind supplies me with the answer. Without giving it a second thought, I step in front of him, and use all the strength I have to shove him up against the wall.

"Enough!" I bark. He flinches at my tone and his eyes widen. I'm not usually loud or outspoken. I tend to be reserved with my words and almost never raise my voice. And I definitely have never raised my voice at him.

I drop my tone a little, now that I've caught his attention, "Enough, Vince. You can't help her being this worked up. I don't know what's going on and I hope she will trust me with it one day. But, the good news is, she *does* have you. You are the best man I know, the best officer I know, the best friend I know. But you can't be any of those things when you're not thinking straight. You can't be there for her if you can't care for yourself." I can see each word hit its mark as his body slowly relaxes, understanding slowly seeping in.

I take my hands from his face, slowly bringing them down to take his in my hands. I squeeze them once, seeing the pain and helplessness in his eyes.

Slowly, oh so slowly, I sink down to my knees, keeping eye contact the whole way. I move my hands to his jeans, rubbing briefly over his half-hard cock, before squeezing once. The grunt he releases has me exhaling the breath I didn't know I was holding.

I unbutton his jeans, and roll his zipper down, shifting his jeans just enough to expose his black briefs. His length hardens and I can see it pulsing through the fabric. Looking back into his eyes, I see his pupils expanding, lust slowly pushing aside fear. I grin at him before freeing his cock.

I'm greeted with a hiss of pleasure as I pump his velvety smooth link; once, twice. Then I rub my thumb around the reddened head, smearing his pre-cum. His cock jumps in my hand as I fist the base and lick the tip, sliding my tongue through the slit. His musky, sandalwood smell is all him, and is utterly intoxicating.

I hear him growl before he grabs the back of my head, his hand engulfing it. "You gunna suck me better, Pretty Boy? Make all the bad feelings go away with the warmth of your mouth?"

His voice has taken on the husky quality that I beg for every day. The one that rattles through my body, deep in my bones, and causes my cock to stand at attention.

I hum around his cock as I take him deep into my mouth. I suck the entire length on my way back up while keeping my fist wrapped around the base.

His breathing has picked up and I feel his body shudder, relaxing the rest of the way. I take that as my cue to up my tempo. I begin slurping his cock, twisting and tugging from the base in a brutally rapid pace. Spit is sliding down my chin but I don't care.

Another grunt and I push him all the way to the back of my throat, relaxing as much as I can and breathing through my nose. I hold it as long as I can before retreating to gather a breath and repeat.

Vince groans loud and deep, sending electricity straight through my cock. I moan around his length and I feel my eyes roll to the back of my head, relishing in making this man feel good.

Suddenly, he pulls back, panting out his breath. I look into the eyes of my Vince, my man, my God. He may wreck me, but I wreck him, too.

His voice turns from anguished to dominant. "Open your mouth, Pretty Boy. You want me to give you my all? You want all of me?"

A groan in lust-filled agony. "Yes, Sir."

His responding groan is absolutely sinful as he tilts my chin until my head is back, almost completely resting on my neck. "Stick that tongue out for me so I can fuck your mouth." I immediately obey and he taps his cock on my tongue a few times, pulling on it with a rough grip as he does.

"That's what you want, right?" I nod as best as I can with his cock sliding over the tip of my tongue, smearing his pre-cum. "You want me to fuck your mouth so good until all you can feel is me?"

He finally stops teasing and thrusts his mouth down my throat. I can feel his cock bulging and pulsing. "You want me to pump your mouth full of my cum and make you swallow every drop?"

He brutally thrusts into me, making me cough and sputter. A mix of cum and spit leaking out of my mouth but I don't care one fucking bit. I'm so hard that my dick feels like it's going to explode. But, I know better that to reach for it. I know I can't touch myself until he gives me permission. So I kneel there, tears streaming down my face, eyes wide and blown with lust and I watch this beautiful man come apart for me.

Just when I become overwhelmed by the sensations, Vince pulls back and I gulp for air. "Good boy." He says as he wipes my chin. "Is your dick hard for me? Is it throbbing in time with me fucking your mouth?" I groan so loud I'm sure the neighbors hear it.

Vince loves orgasm denial. I love and hate it. Especially since I'm the only one that gets denied or edged repeatedly. Sexy *bastard*.

His next command has me submitting so fast I get a little dizzy. "Get your dick out pretty boy. I want to watch you come for me as I fuck your throat so raw, you won't be able to talk for the rest of the day." I barely let him finish his sentence and I've already got my sweatpants tugged down and fist around my cock. I begin pumping my thrust roughly as Vince slides back into my throat.

He grunts loud as I moan around his length. The harder he thrusts, the more I suck. The louder he pants, the harder I tug on my cock. It's absolutely intoxicating.

Before I know it, my balls draw up, my vision blacks out, and stars explode across my vision. I feel my release shoot out and I cum and I cum and I cum. I can't be sure but I think I'm screaming, the sound muffled by his cock.

That sets him off. He releases his warm, sticky seed into my throat. I swallow jet after jet until there is nothing left, licking my lips when I finish.

He leans against the wall, catching his breath. Before I can put my dick away, he pulls me up by my arms and crashes his mouth on mine. Tongues battling, the taste of coffee from his mouth mixing with the taste of his cum is perfection. Our kiss slows to languid and loving.

He pecks my lips once before leaning his forehead against mine and whispering, "Thank you, Nick. Thank you for loving me. Thank you for pulling me out of the hole. Just, thank you."

He pecks my lips one more time before I respond. "Any time, any place. It's you and me. Always has been."

I step away from him, casually perusing his body and taking it all in. He still has some tension but he looks a lot more relaxed than earlier. I hold out my hand for him to take and drag him to the en suite in his room. I turn on the shower, and set it to skin-melting, like he likes it, before slowly undressing him. He leans down to kiss me with a chuckle. "I thought I was in charge of after-care?"

I look into his eyes and smile softly at the man I love more than life itself. "Usually, yes, but today is for you. Let me care for you. Then we can nap and talk later. Please?"

I look at him, unsure if he would object to the latter. He thumbs my cheek, grins slowly and kisses me again before closing his eyes and whispering, "Okay."

I lead him into the shower and begin our aftercare ritual like he does for me. He's always taking care of the rest of us and the community. He gives and gives and so rarely receives. Sometimes though, you need to let someone else take care of you. Even if only for a moment.

23

~

Annie

It's been three weeks since Vince came over. After we were interrupted by my shitty ex, I finally broke down and gave him the basic outline of who Lukas was, and apparently is. I also let him know I changed my last name three times already. I didn't go into detail about everything I went through, and definitely didn't bring up the kids. Thankfully, he didn't push for more, but I'm sure he'll read about most of it once he starts digging.

He promised to let me tell the guys in my own time. Based on their continuing banter on the phone, and when we go out, I can only assume he has kept his promise.

But, I also haven't heard from Vince since our last lunch outing. Not a peep. I have texted a few times. I could tell something was up while we were eating. He spent the entire lunch barely touching his enchiladas. I mean, it's not like we're dating or anything but it doesn't stop the sting I feel in my heart when I think about him retreating from me all of a sudden.

I shake my head to clear out the thoughts of all the crap happening around me and force myself to focus on my lesson plans for next week. I may or may not have also been looking up ideas to help the guys with youth center programs. I haven't told them yet but when something pops in my head, I dive right down the rabbit hole and bring up statistics, finances, and anything they may need to make a decision. *It's for the kids. I'm doing it for the kids.*

Yeah, the argument sounds weak even in my own head. But, I can't help it. Watching them all get so excited about providing the kids with opportunities they may not otherwise get, it hit me hard, right in the feelers. It's clear this isn't a simple "make more money" or "look good for the press" kind of thing. They are all genuinely excited about it. More than once I heard Nick and Vince say they wished they had a youth center for them when they were younger and it made me want to dig deeper. To know them more, and uncover all the things that helped mold these incredible men.

My phone rings, dragging me from my daydreaming. I see it's Cory and I can't help the smile, and blush, that graces my face. "Hello Cory." I try to keep my voice steady so why did it sound like a girl getting picked up on her first date?

"Well hello to you, too, Pretty Girl. What's got you so happy today?" I hesitate to answer but decide to throw it out there. I mean, if Vince is running, I may as well stop over-thinking every word that comes out and let them see me.

"Well, you, of course. I was just wrapping up some work for the day and was pleasantly surprised to see you calling."

I swear I can hear him smile through the phone as he chuckles. "Oh Pretty Girl, I'd call you all day if it made you sound like that."

I start blushing and right before I can over-analyze how I sound, he cuts in. "I was actually calling to see if you wanted to get together for lunch, again? I know you're probably tired of your phone vibrating all day. Or maybe you're not." His voice tilts playfully. "Maybe you don't mind it *vibrating* all day." The emphasis he put on the word paired with his voice dropping has the stupid blush spreading through my body like a wildfire.

I gather myself as quickly as I can and try not to sound affected, but the breathiness in my voice kind of gives it away. "I don't mind it at all. I mean, I like hearing from you guys. You're all really good at making me laugh and y'alls ridiculous conversations help brighten my day."

He laughs out loud and collects himself before continuing. "I'm glad we do that for you, Pretty Girl. So, lunch? Jense is driving me nuts about some stupid smashing room idea and I have to get out of here before I smash him with something."

He lets out an oomph before laughing. Then I can hear Jenson's playful tone in the background yell, "That's what you get. It's a good idea. Annie would agree with me right, Sweetness."

I hear some shuffling and start laughing at their antics. I have no idea what is happening on the other line but eventually Cory gets back on the phone, panting, "See what I mean. He's driving me nuts! Please take pity on me and meet us for lunch. My treat."

I bite my lip as I think it over. The kids won't be home for 4 more hours and I really am ahead on all of my work for the week. "Ok, when and where."

"Whoop! I'm so excited. I've missed you." He clears his throat before starting again, "I mean, I'm happy we're hanging out again. Right, ok, how about Burger Heaven? Just a block over from Main. Near the popcorn place."

"Oh I love that place! But I'm definitely hitting the popcorn place on the way out. They have a zebra fudge that is better than sex. They also have a popcorn where they make the fudge but right before it hardens, they drizzle over the popcorn." I groan, rather indecently, "best thing ever!"

"Well if I get to hear you make more sounds like that, pretty girl, I'll buy you the fudge popcorn every week." I giggle, like an idiot, before saying goodbye. Then I rush to take a quick shower, throw on a pair of ripped black skinny jeans, my black Chucks, and a Beautiful Badass t-shirt that hugs my boobs just right. *Really, Annie? What happened to just friends?*

I'm learning that my inner voice can be a bitch and can kill my mood faster than thinking about my ex. A startled laugh erupts out of my mouth as I realize just how screwed I am with these guys.

I grab my purse, keys, and water for the way and prance out to the car. Feeling happy, giddy and hopeful, I decide I need a song to match. After scrolling for far too long, I finally find what I need.

The first chords ring out and I turn it up, knowing I don't want to just listen; I want to feel. I want it to thrum through my veins until I'm floating. Beautiful People from the Burlesque soundtrack filters through my car. It's still super hot out but I need to feel the wind. I need to let my body move as much as it can; while still staying safe of course.

The song proves to be exactly what I need. The rhythm flows through me, the smile never leaving my face, as I release everything. This song has a way of making me feel fun, free, and confident. I let the boost it gives me wrap through my body before locking it in place.

About ten minutes later, I pull into the burger place and park next to a big blacked out Suburban. All black wheels, lifted, and definitely new. At least the last 2 years. The tint is the darkest it can legally be on all sides but the outside is CLEAN. Like, too clean for this area. But, I shrug it off and walk into the restaurant.

I am barely lifting my glasses off my face before a body comes barreling into me. The person wraps their arms around me and spins me around. At this moment, I am thankful that my body's defense in flight or fight mode is to freeze. My brain catches a free laugh, equal parts mischievous and playful. *Jenson.*

"Put me down you goof," I chuckle out and pat his shoulder for good measure. And, he does.

His laughing subsides, but the mischievous smirk doesn't leave his stupidly handsome face. He slowly, oh so damn slowly, slides me back down to the ground. Every part of my front is touching something against his body the entire ride down. By the time my feet are on solid ground, I'm dizzy and, *dammit*, blushing.

His smirk kicks up a little more, probably knowing exactly the effect he just had on me, and I glare at him. "What?" He tries, and fails, to not laugh. "I missed you. And Cory's been mean to me all day so I needed a hug."

He puffs out his lower lip in the most ridiculous pout I have ever seen. I can't help but smile at him and shake my head. I step back to him and reach around his waist for a hug; for real this time.

His scent is intoxicating. I breathe it in, citrus swirling with leather, and it does naughty things to my lady bits. A throat clears behind us and I jump, remembering that I barely made it a foot past the door.

Reluctantly, I let go of Jenson, looking at him with a huge smile, before turning around. Cory is standing there, brow raised and a grin on his lips. "What? You just said you wanted to see me. Not that you wanted a hug," I sass with a pop of my hip and a grin.

His mouth drops open, I guess in surprise, but he recovers quickly. "Well, if I knew I'd just have to ask, I would have asked every day since we met." I roll my eyes. These guys are great for my ego, I swear.

He opens his arms and I smile so wide it hurts. Stepping into Cory feels different than with Jenson. Not bad. Just different. His scent is more eucalyptus wafting through a library. His arms are a little bulkier than Jenson's. They're both tall with lean muscles. Muscles that I feel ripple as I settle into the hug. *What would it be like to lick him; to outline the ridges with my tongue? Woah! Easy killer. No more Burlesque music for you.*

I clear my throat before my brain thinks any more ridiculous thoughts, and step out of his hold. He smiles down at me, dimples popping through his five o'clock shadow, and hazel eyes looking like they want all the answers to all the questions.

Jenson steps up behind me, momentarily making me flinch, before whispering "Sorry, Sweetness," into my ear and rubbing his hands down my shoulder.

"Alright kids, are we ready to find a table?" We all nod and head off to the back of the restaurant. We decide to grab the huge corner booth. I slide in and end up sandwiched between them.

We start looking through the menus and then give the waitress our drink orders. Jenson orders drinks for Vince and Nick, too. "So they're coming, too?"

I try not to sound too hopeful about seeing them all again. I didn't want Cory and Jenson to think I was bummed to just be with them but Cory hadn't mentioned the other two earlier.

Cory grins at me and says, "Yeah, they should be here soon. Vince went MIA for a couple of days and it freaked us all out. Nick more than us. I guess he showed back up at the house this morning in a bad way so Nick took the day off to take care of him."

I gasp at the revelation. "In a bad way? What do you mean? Was he hurt? Was he shot? They don't have to come here, we can bring them food." I'm rambling. My need to care for, to protect, to comfort, overriding anything else.

Jenson lays his hand on my thigh and softly squeezes. I didn't even have time to realize he touched me and I didn't flinch. My brain just latched on to Vince. "He's physically ok. Vince gets like this some-times. Especially if he has a particularly difficult case. He forgets to take care of himself, let alone check-in. He's good now. Just needed to relax and get some food."

I nod at him, finding some comfort in his words. The waitress comes back with our drinks and I take time squeezing my lemon slice in it before stirring it and taking a drink. Then, the rest of his words process. "Wait, did you say he was MIA for 2 days?"

Jenson nods as he takes a drink. "Yeah. We would have just driven by his work tonight and dragged him home if he wasn't back by then but he showed up, so, all good."

I get lost in my head. Thinking about all the things that could have happened to Vince. I mean, it makes sense. He hasn't responded to my messages but he knows he can talk to me, right? I mean I thought we were doing fine. I really thought we were all doing good. Just a group of *friends* hanging out all the time. Sharing laughter and ideas. They've become comfortable, familiar, safe to be with. I feel like I don't have to play chameleon. I can just be me. And they like that. Or, some of them do. *Maybe it's Lukas. Maybe he threatened Vince; or the guys. Maybe he's realizing I'm not worth this.*

Cory must sense something is off as he gently cups my cheek and turns my face toward him. "Where'd you go just now?" His eyes are searching mine, thumb rubbing my cheek. I lean into his warmth and decide I might as well lay it all out there. If Vince is running, they will too. They're a team. They do everything together. Might as well get it over with.

Just as I take a deep breath, I look between him and Jenson. Jenson still has his hand on my thigh, gently rubbing circles on it. It's calming; grounding. Cory takes my hand in his, threads our fingers together and kisses my knuckles. I open my mouth to reveal what's happening when two shadows cross the table.

"Well, doesn't this look cozy. Mind if we join?"

24

~

Jenson

I'm not sure what Annie was about to tell us but I have a feeling it wasn't good. Her entire body went rigid. Her resigned sigh told me she was about to tell us something we not only wouldn't like, but she fears we will judge her for; or maybe even leave her.

What she doesn't understand is we would never leave; could never leave. She has had us wrapped around her finger since that night at the club. The more we talk with her, message her, and hang out with her, the deeper we get.

Vince and Nick approaching the table clearly caught her off guard, even though we told her they were coming. Her eyes are wide in shock and wonder; searching Vince like she's waiting for him to do something. *What am I missing? Why is she looking at him like she's ready for him to destroy her?*

Annie struggles for a response to Vince's cocky little question. She doesn't make a move as his face morphs from a playful smirk to confusion. "What's wrong? Is everything ok?"

He rushes his words like he needs to know what's going on, like, yesterday. Her shock mixes with confusion before she responds. "Um, yeah, well no, but, are *you* ok?" *Oh, she was worried about his MIA stunt. Interesting.*

My thumb continues rubbing idle circles on her thigh. I'm not sure she caught it, but this time when I touched her, she didn't flinch. And nothing prepared me for how amazing it would feel for her to slowly relax under my touch.

Vince steps closer to the table, the confusion now setting deep in his brow line. He slides in next to Cory, leaving Nick to sit next to Vince. Nick's jaw tightens and his eyes focus on Annie like he's trying to figure out what's going on before she even says it.

"Why wouldn't I be?" Vince asks. I notice Annie's cheeks begin to pink, her eyes looking down at the table. "They said you went MIA for the last two days. And I, well, I..."

Vince gives her a moment before pressing her, "You, what, Angel?"

The nickname has her popping her eyes back to meet his and he sighs, lifting his mouth into a soft smile. "You thought it was because of your case?" He says it softly, but the words slap us all anyways; well us guys.

Nick pipes up first, "Did something happen? Are you ok?" Always the worrier in our group. He loves with the same intensity as his electric blue hair.

Vince turns to him. I can see him move his hand under the table before he smiles at us all... *Wait, that's not a smile, that's his smug look. Shit head.*

"No. *I'm* good. But I love that Annie was worried about me." He shrugs like he's the cat that got the cream.

Nick visibly relaxes, a smile matches Vince's. "Well that's good. Glad you're both ok. And Annie, please know, if you want to talk about whatever is going on with that," he swipes his hand between her and Vince before continuing. "We're here. No pressure but whatever's going on, you're not in this alone."

Annie looks over at Vince like he has the answer to whatever question is now in her head. Vince gives her a small smile and a shrug of indifference. Like whatever she is wanting to spill, is up to her. Her small smile tells me she not only wants us to know, but she's happy he kept her secret.

I'm just about to burst at the seams. I don't want to push but what the hell are they keeping from us? Just as I begin to shift and try to come up with something playful, she blurts out, "Vince and I kissed. The night he brought me ice cream."

Her muscles tighten, her back snaps straight, and she is looking everywhere but us. Her two sides are warring with each other. She wants to be bold, but she's also worried about our reaction.

Cory blows out a breath and smiles at Annie, which noticeably relaxes her. "Well that's a damn good ice cream party, Pretty Girl. Guess I need to find a way to top it." He gives her a playful smirk and kisses her knuckles which must shock her out of her mind because she started to giggle. Fucking giggles.

I'm about to melt into a puddle of goo. She's adorable and I need that giggle, every day, forever.

As her body relaxes again, she looks back at Vince in question. He's smiling so big that I'm surprised his face hasn't cracked. Nick looks like he just won the lottery but notices how Vince's face slowly morphs from pride to...support? He's looking back between them, trying to learn the code before anyone else but Annie clears her throat and we return our attention to her.

"That's not all. Vince told me that you know he's working on a case with me but you don't know why." She looks at each of us for confirmation.

She nods in satisfaction and continues. "Someone has been sending me messages. Creepy ones, letting me know he's watching. The day I, um, saw you at the gym, he revealed who he was." She takes a deep breath, her lips slowly trembling. I can see her hold on Cory's hand tighten, so I squeeze her thigh gently, hoping it gives her strength.

"My ex was, is, a bad man. He went to jail ten years ago and wasn't supposed to be out for another five but he was released for good behavior." She spits the words in disgust and outrage.

"He's back and he's angrier than ever. A part of me was worried that once you all found out, you wouldn't want to see me anymore." Her voice is barely a whisper by the end of her sentence, but it might as well have been a punch to my gut. *We can't have that.*

I bring up my other hand and gently cup her cheek, turning her towards me. Her eyes are glimmering with unshed tears. She looks so damn vulnerable and it makes me want to stab every mother fucker who has ever hurt her.

A tear escapes her eye. I wipe it away with the pad of my thumb before resting my forehead on hers. I need her to not only hear me, but feel the truth behind my words. "Annie, nothing and no one can take us from you, do you hear me? We haven't known each other for long but I feel it. I feel the magnetism that pulls us together, and I know you do, too. And I can speak emphatically about the others, they all feel the same. No asswad ex is going to prevent us from wanting to see you; your smile, your heart, everything you're willing to share. Your battles are now our battles. Even if you don't want us to physically fight or help, we will still be here, lending you strength, courage, and whatever else you may need until you can see the badass boss babe we know you are."

Her tears are steadily streaming down her face and the way she huffs out a laugh at the last part lets me know she at least heard it. Her eyes flutter open and she stares straight into my Goddamn soul with those big, deep ocean blue eyes.

The hand that was holding Cory's slips on top of mine on her cheek. She leans into it with a slight smile. "Thank you." She whispers. I grin and nod before placing a kiss on her forehead and moving back to my spot. She's looking at the others and they are all wearing matching grins of approval, nodding their agreement.

Her smile becomes shy for a moment before she wipes her eyes dry, takes a drink of water, and sits just a little taller, a little bolder, a little stronger. "So, can we eat? I know I didn't give you a lot of info but I will, soon. I just don't want to do it here. I want to enjoy my lunch break and we can talk later." We all nod our agreements and look back over the menus.

I'm about halfway through lunch section before she suddenly claps her hands, bouncing up excitedly. We all turn towards her and see this huge smile stretch across her face. *Damn she's beautiful.*

She reaches into her purse, pulls out her phone and starts clicking on the screen. We sit, suspended in time as we wait for her to, hopefully, share what has her so excited.

She stops clicking on the screen, and tugs her bottom lip into her mouth. She looks between all of us, a mixture of worry and excitement warring in her eyes.

"What's got you all excited, Sweetness? Please don't leave us in suspense." I give her my most charming smile and nod my chin towards her phone.

Her smile transforms into one that reminds me of when kids do something possibly wrong and their hoping their parents won't be *too* mad. "So, I did something. And, I don't want you to be mad. I just got so excited hearing you talk about working with the youth center and I looked around at some things that you all may want to look into. I have it all in a spreadsheet, contacted a few people and wrote as much information as I could find including price. There's about eleven ideas on there that could work but the top 2 seem to be the ones with the most favorable outcomes." She takes a steadying breath before looking at each of us, gauging our reactions.

Cory speaks up first, his brows furrowing in question. "You mean to tell me, you spent time, your time, researching ideas for us? To help the youth center?" He tilts his head as he assesses her.

She stays silent as she looks over at him. I can't see her face but the rigidity in her muscles tells me she has a lot of negative self-talk that we need to wade through.

"I, um, I'm sor..." Before she can even complete her thought, Cory's face splits into the biggest smile ever. It looks like he's going to cry. His hands come up to her cheeks and he closes his eyes as he leans his forehead against hers.

"Oh you dear, sweet, amazing woman. You realize we're never letting you go, right?" He drops his hands from her face and wraps her in a hug.

I barely hear her question, muffled against his chest. "So, you're not mad?"

Cor laughs, shaking his head as he leans back. "Why would we be mad? You wanted to help us; help those kids. That's amazing!"

"I just didn't want *you* to think that *I* didn't think you could handle it. It was just something I was thinking about and I looked up one thing and then, sort of, fell down a very long, winding rabbit hole." She chuckles before taking in a breath.

She looks at each of us, to make sure we all feel the same as Cory. When she's sure we do, she nods before looking back at her phone. "Okay, good. I'm glad. I get over-excited some times and rabbit-hole pretty regularly." She shrugs her shoulder before smiling.

We spend most of lunch talking about what she found. I soak up the light that shines from her as she talks about how each program could help kids in different age groups. Afterwards, we give her our emails so she can send the copy to us.

The rest of lunch is spent chatting about anything and nothing at all. The conversation remaining light and playful.

Oh yeah, this woman is perfect for us and we are perfect for her. This is right. I can feel it. Now, how do we get her to trust us fully so we can give her everything she deserves? And how big of a problem is this ex?

25

Vince

Lunch sits heavy in my stomach as I make my way through the station and knock on Captain's door. I've never felt so hopeless and torn, but I also haven't had such a personal connection to a case either. Sure I put my heart and soul into getting justice and taking down bad people but this, this is entirely different.

I hear Captain's grunt to enter and walk into his office, closing the door behind me. The man is old enough to be my dad, thick gray hair fills in his beard and his head is shaved smooth. The light from the outside window reflects off of it. He's gained a little weight in the last couple of years but he's still one of the toughest bastards I know. He truly cares about this city and the people who live in it.

I take a seat in the black leather chair across from his desk. Numerous folders are strewn about and it looks like he's filling out another completion form from a recent raid. Once he finishes and signs, he tucks it away before giving me his full attention. His light brown eyes begin assessing me, like I'm his new case. "Vince, what can I do for you?"

I prop my right foot over my left knee and sigh before leaning my head back and looking at the ceiling. After a beat, I bring my head back down and look directly at him, letting him see everything swirling in my mind.

"I need help, Cap. I don't know what to do, how to do it, who to talk to about which pieces..." I trail off knowing I'm making myself look like an idiot.

Captain leans back in his chair and folds his arms across his chest. "Ok, start from the top." It takes me a moment to figure out where the top is but I eventually find it.

For the next thirty minutes I talk about the Black Thorns and huff at how accurate a description it is. They are major thorns in my side. I begin to add in Annie's story and the information I found over the last three weeks about Lukas O'Brian. His rap sheet started way before he and Annie got together.

My reasoning for going MIA was the phone call I made almost two days ago. The one that filled me with so much dread I couldn't eat. I've basically been living on coffee since, going over every detail again, and again, and again until I knew, with absolute certainty, the connection I found was the real deal.

Almost 48 hours ago, I was following leads on a few guys we

believe are higher ups in the Black Thorns. I confirmed 2 of them, adding them to my ever growing pile of paperwork but the last one I struggled with. We really only had 'Joseph O' to go on. What pissed me off was it seemed like he bounced around a lot before eventually bringing his piece of shit ass here. It felt like I had spent forever trying to catch an address, a family member, anything. And then, I finally got a hit.

While it wasn't an address, it was a P.O. Box in West Texas, which aligns with everything else I have so far. It was difficult to find because he rarely had mail going there. And, it was registered to a woman; Jennifer Donahue. After the name popped up, I just stared at it. *Where had I seen that name before?*

Not wanting to waste any more time, I called up their local Chief of Police. It took him all of three minutes to pull up the information I needed. I took notes as fast as my hand could write.

Before I could ask anything else, he dropped the first of many bombs. His country accent was thicker than mine as he said, "Not sure why you need her info. She died a long time ago. Be 10 years in a couple of months. I worked that case, too. It was gruesome. We didn't have the evidence but we all knew her shitty son got one of his thug friends to do it. He was in jail, here, for being abusive to his girl. His mama told him she wanted nothing to do with him; never even came to the trial. The day his lawyer asked her to be a character witness, she told him to go to hell. She was found brutally murdered that same weekend."

"Holy shit," I mutter. "That had to be hard for her to go against her own son but, good for her. Anyways, it wasn't necessarily her I'm looking into. She shared a P.O. Box with a guy named Joseph O. We have reason to believe he's an enforcer or something for a local gang causing a lot of issues over here."

"Lil' Joey? Man, I haven't seen that kid in years. But, he was always glued to his cousin. Joey was a big boy but dumber than a bag o' rocks. Last name was O'Brian. Dad bailed on him when he was little. He was brothers with Jennifer's ex-husband. She took him in but they lived off the beaten path. No mailbox; hence the P.O. Box."

My brain glitched. *Did he say? No! There's no way.* "I'm sorry, Chief, but did you say O'Brian? What was the cousin's name? Do you remember?"

He didn't even have to think. He spit his name out like it was acid on his tongue. "Lukas O'Brian. Trashy prick. He'd been slingin' drugs all around. Had four girlfriends claim domestic abuse. Two mysteriously disappeared and the other didn't want us to press charges. She sounded so damn scared but we couldn't force anything, not when they hadn't shown us proof to take to the DA."

He exhaled heavily, giving away just how much this had affected him. "His last one, he was with the longest. Sweetest damn girl you ever did meet. Naive as she was beautiful. Definitely lacking in the self-esteem area. Anyways, she's the one who finally pushed charges. Got him for abusing her and both of their dogs. She even gave us access to hospital records. I'll never forget seeing the look in her eye when she realized just how fooled he had her. Poor girl honestly believed it was her fault, and some instances were just accidents." He sighs and pauses for a beat before adding, "I'm guessing if Joseph is there, Lukas is, too. He got out on some good behavior bullshit but he belongs in prison. *Or under it.*" He mumbles the last part under his breath and I can't say I disagree.

I realize I haven't even written half of this down. Seeing the path lineup so uncomfortably perfect had me sittin' stock still. Before I could process any more, he adds, "Joseph can break bones but Lukas controls him. He's bound to be high up on your totem. I'll give you anything you need. Just promise to take that bastard down."

I don't hesitate, I don't think, I just blurt out the only reasonable answer. "I need everything."

We swap information and he says he will get started pulling all the records they have on both guys.

Now sitting in Captain's office, I have all of that information and more in a giant folder. I hand it over documenting every detail I have found so far. It's clear to me, Lukas isn't just some dickhead who enjoyed beating, raping, and mentally scarring his girlfriends; yes, as in more than one. No, it appears that Lukas is the actual *leader* of the Black Thorns.

The timelines from past cases and trails all line up. His description, and mugshot images line up with what a few informants have given us, but he never uses his name. Shit, even the time when informants said the orders or information came from a second or third in command lines up with his jail time.

It's glaringly obvious that he's not just a bad man coming to mess with our Annie. He's an evil man and I firmly believe he has the ability to make good on his promises.

When Cap finally finishes looking through what I have and letting me talk through my thoughts out loud, he leans forward, rests his arms on the desk, and clasps his hands together. "Well son," his voice deep and rattled due to being a 2 pack a day smoker for the last 40 years. "It appears your little Annie is in some deep shit." He tilts his head as he considers his next words. "You need to tell her, warn her about what, and who, he is. Obviously, you can't give her all the information about the Black Thorns but you can give an overview. Just nothing that can slip out and screw up the case."

His words hang in the air as I swallow the lump on my throat. This is not the type of conversation I was hoping to ever have with her. "What about a safe house or something?"

Cap nods his head like he's already thought about it but his grim expression tells me there's red tape involved. "Only problem is we don't have evidence it's actually him. Other than a pet name for her, there's no evidence Lukas is messaging her. *We* know it's him, *she* knows, but the higher ups would need proof. Until then, we can have a few people add her street to their patrol routes but, past that, my hands are tied."

I exhale a heavy breath, knowing he's right, but still hating it. "Thanks Cap, I appreciate it." I stand, and shake his hand before heading back to the door.

The moment my hand reaches for the knob, he calls out, "I can see how important she is to you, son, I get it. I will do whatever I can to help. But, she need to know who he is. Right now, we have him tied-in as the possible leader of a dangerous gang that not only smuggles guns and drugs but, thanks to the information you and The Mad Scientist connected, humans, as well."

I sigh knowing he's right. I have to tell her all of it. This is going to crush her. But, if she will let us, I know the guys would join with me to make sure she knows she is cared for and protected. My heart pangs as I rub my chest. *Fuck, why does the thought of something bad happening to her feel so painful, already? And if I'm in with her this deep, how deep are my brothers?*

I head back to my desk and get back to work, knowing this is not a conversation to be had over the phone. I make a plan to call her later tonight in hopes of setting up a time to meet up and hang out. Then, I will have to reveal the monster that lurks in the shadows.

26

Annie

I'm more than ready for bed by the time evening rolls around. Lunch with the guys was fantastic. Jenson is such a goober. As much as Cory pretends to be irritated by him, I know he loves it. He's usually the one instigating.

Their friendship is so strong, familiar, and it feels amazing to be included in that. None of them ever make me feel like an outsider. But, that's part of my problem. The whole "just friends" line is dissolving before my eyes and I'm not sure I can hold out much longer. *Do I want to? What would it be like to give in?*

"Mommy, why are you smiling like that?" I swear I jump ten feet in the air. I clasp my hand on my chest, hoping to slow the now erratic beating of my heart.

I turn around to see Cheyenne standing behind me, hand on her hip and eyebrow arched like she's seen one too many Dwayne Johnson movies. I giggle at the sass radiating from her. *No idea where she gets that from.* I roll my eyes at myself, knowing damn well where she gets it from.

I go to rinse off the cup in my hand and notice the hot water has gone cold. Apparently I've been distracted for a while and only finished half the sink of dishes that were dirty. *Damn.*

I sigh, turn the water off, and rub my hands on a towel while smiling at my little clone. "I'm just feeling happy, Bug. I had a good day."

She appraises me, acting far too old for her own good, before releasing her stance and launching into a very dramatic series of events that took place at school today. I lean back against the counter and give her all the attention she needs. She explains how Brady threw a chair at Ms. Stone and called her bad names. We talked about the consequences of his actions, what he could have done differently including using the 'calm down corner' *way* before he got that angry.

But, let's face it, sometimes anger just ignites and kids, just like many adults, aren't self-aware enough to use restraint. Unfortunately, I can almost guarantee that kid will be right back in class tomorrow. It's actually one of the reasons I stopped working in a brick and mortar.

Fifteen minutes later she's working on a sympathy card for her teacher. I am so damn proud of her. Her heart is so huge and, mostly, untouched by the evil in this world. I just hope nothing dims her compassion and her empathy for others.

Just as that thought crosses my mind, my phone rings. I cross the kitchen and grab it off the table. My smile is just plain silly at this point when I see Vince is calling.

"Hey. Didn't you get enough of me at lunch?" I'm so proud of how I'm learning to be more comfortable with them; more myself.

His deep, rich chuckle comes through the phone and envelopes me. "Oh, Sweetheart," his voice low and almost predatory. A shiver runs down my spine. "I could never get enough of you." *Dammit. There goes another pair of panties. Asshole.*

I laugh off my own reaction but try to play it off like I'm laughing at his words. "So, did you need something? What's up?" I mentally high-five myself again for sounding so casual and not at all affected by him.

He clears his throat, and coughs a little. Like, what he was calling about isn't flirty or fun like I hoped. His voice steadies and takes on a hint of his professional tone. "I have some information, about your case. About Lukas." He growls, actually growls out his name. *Damn, why is that so hot?*

But then my mind catches up on processing what he says. "Oh, um, ok. Everything ok?" I've lost the ability to speak confidently. I heard the tremor in my voice and I know he did, too.

"No but," he lets out a deep sigh before continuing. "I talked to the Captain since, you know, we're hanging out more and he's given me the go ahead to give you some details. Actually, he insisted. However, I don't want this conversation to happen on the phone. I'd like to meet you sometime this weekend. The sooner the better."

The urgency in his voice has my panic rising and I can feel the trembles working their way through my body. "Um, ok, yes please. When are you available?" I start to pace but catch myself once I spot Cheyenne at the table still. I don't need her to worry.

"I have time tonight, after the kids are in bed. Or any time tomorrow. Like I said, the sooner the better."

I gnaw on my lip, wearing it between my teeth before agreeing to meet tonight. We make quick work of goodbyes and I start our evening routine.

* * *

As each of my littles climbs into their beds, I spend an extra minute just hugging them and sending up silent prayers. If I have to move them again, they will be wrecked. But I refuse to let Lukas come anywhere near them.

My resolve solidifies and I start the coffee pot for Vince's arrival. He knocks on the door shortly after and I can tell by the look on his face, this is going to be a rough talk. He wraps me in a hug so fierce, so safe that it takes my breath away. His hugs are so damn addicting. And by extension, so is he.

Not ready to have that talk with myself, yet, I quickly make our coffees and guide him to sit at the table. We each take a steady sip before he slides two folders across the table. I go to move my hand over them before he lays his on top of mine. "Annie, what I'm about to tell you, is probably more than you ever thought. But I want you to remember, you are not alone, I'm not going anywhere. And neither are my brothers. If you want, we can tell them. It honestly might be helpful for you, but you have plenty of time to think about that decision. For now, it's me and you. I've got you, okay? Can you trust me?"

Four words. How can four words be so simple yet so terrifying? Trust. That word itself can lead to life and death. Happiness and sorrow. Freedom and confinement.

But with him, with them, there's just something. I can't explain it but my gut says, yes. Yes, I can trust him, and them, with this. If my personality hasn't had them screaming for the hills, maybe this won't either. And if they do run off, at least they do it before more of my heart gets more involved. *Or my kids.*

Shaking my head at thoughts I do not need to entertain right now, I inhale a deep breath and blow it all out. Lifting my chin and squaring my shoulders, I give him my answer, my truth. "I trust you."

With that, he smiles, squeezes my hand once, and flips the folder open.

27

∾

Nick

It's Saturday night and I'm just getting home from closing up the gym. Cory and Jense are walking down the stairs talking about the programs we have lined up for the youth center.

I walk into the living room and plop down on our oversized black leather sectional. We've all slept on this thing more than once. It's like a fluffy cloud that always stays cool.

Jense takes the far left side of the couch and stretches his feet out while Cory stalks off to the kitchen. He comes back, hands us a beer, and takes the opposite end of the couch with his legs open wide and his feet planted on the floor.

I'm already cruising the channels but nothing sounds good. Not really in the mood to fight about it, I click on Dexter and we all settle in. It's one of the few shows we don't mind watching on repeat.

Cory breaks our silence first, "So, Vince is coming home tonight, right?" I grunt in affirmation and shift in the seat, trying to get more comfortable.

Apparently, he really needs to talk tonight because he then asks, "Has anyone talked to Annie today? I wanted to call or message her but I'm not sure what to say that won't mess things up. I mean, do I approach the asshole ex or leave it until she's ready?"

No one responds, all of us lost in our own thoughts of Annie. So, he continues, "I'm worried about her. And it seems like she's not used to people worrying, or caring for that matter. I mean we know she has Elle and a few other friends but she's always so busy. Then, she helps us pull more information about programs for the kids. For *our* company. Who does that for no other reason than just to help? And how can anyone be a dick to someone so pure and selflessly amazing?"

Jenson takes a pull from his beer before responding, "Yeah, I get it man. Annie is, well, she's something else. I don't want to be cliche and say 'different' but, yeah, she is. I mean, I never thought we'd want someone again after Amber but, fuck. I don't just want Annie. I want her to drop all the walls, for good. I want to see her with her kids, I want to come home to her. I want everything."

He rubs at his chest for a moment before downing half his beer. His next words are barely audible but the impact is like a nuke exploding; the waves fanning out across the house. "I think I'm falling in love with her. And what really scares me is she has us firmly in the friend zone."

His heartache is palpable. Of course, I'm feeling the same way. And, judging by Cory's face, he's right there with us.

The memories of our time with her filter through my mind. From the time at the club to our messages, our non-date dates and even the things we learned yesterday. Then, it's like a light bulb clicks on. "Or does she?"

I feel the other two staring at me but I'm too lost connecting the pieces, letting the codes run until they are just right. "Think about it. We were friend zoned pretty hard yet we definitely spend more time with her than she does her other friends. She even told us last week that Elle, Lana, whatever, was whining about not seeing her since the day after the club."

Now, I'm up and pacing in front of the couch, my mind working in overdrive. "Guys, I don't think we *are* in the friend zone. I think she feels the same way we do, but she doesn't understand that it, this, can really work. And she *definitely* won't make the first move now that her feelings have changed.

"She had a hot and heavy make-out session with Vince a couple of weeks ago but *just* announced it. *That's* why she was so nervous to tell us she kissed Vince. She thought the rest of us would be hurt and she didn't want that. She's expecting to be hurt and for us to run. She doesn't think we really mean that *all of us* are in, so *we* need to be the ones that make a move."

"Okay," Cory says slowly, "So how do we show her? How do we convince her to give this a chance, give *us* a chance, without scaring her off?"

"Well, Vince went for it. Maybe we need to follow suit. If the opportunity to move presents itself, we do it. We step up and stop letting her control it. She wants to relinquish control. We've all seen it. I mean, four weeks ago, she was so jumpy and skittish we could barely brush her arm unless she saw it coming a mile away. Now, she's let us hold her hands, cheeks, thighs, even hug her without moving at a snail's pace. She's ready. We just have to show her we are, too."

They look at each other and grin, nodding their heads in agreement. Before they can respond, we all get a message on our phones. "Well, that's convenient," I say as I read the message.

Vince- Annie has a kid-free night. I wanted to invite her over for dinner and drinks.

We all look at each other, then nod at Jense. He takes our agreement then types out a response.

Jense- Sounds good. We're all home already. Need us to get anything? What time are you thinking?

Vince- On the phone with her now. I'll be home in 30 minutes so maybe an hour? She says she's more comfortable driving herself here in case the kids get sick and she needs to leave.

Cory- Sounds good to us. We have plenty of wine, beer, and water. Does she want anything particular?

Vince- Chinese takeout? She said wine and water are good. I want you to know I talked to her yesterday about updates on her case. I couldn't give her a whole lot of info but, just know, it really rattled her. I'm afraid she's considering changing her name and moving again.

A chorus of "fuck" rings out around the room. Anger, desperation, and determination fills the room.

Nick- Thanks for the heads up Vince. We got this.

We get to work making sure the bathrooms and bedrooms look

presentable. We are usually pretty neat but the last few weeks have been crazy busy.

Once we're satisfied with presenting our home to Annie, we all end up back in the kitchen, deciding on dinner. Of course, we have so many favorites, and aren't sure what she likes, so we go way overboard. At least we'll have leftovers for tomorrow.

Just as we make our way back to the living room, Vince enters. He quickly shouts out that he's headed for the shower and shoots up the stairs. But before he did, I could tell that he's feeling what we are; excited, scared, on edge, but determined to keep her. Any way we can.

28

Cory

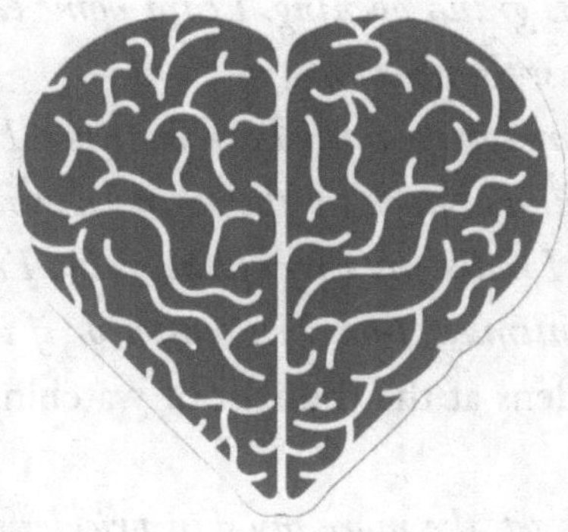

I can't get comfortable. My heart is beating out of my chest. I'm so excited to see Annie but the short notice has my anxiety sky-rocketing. I would have spent the day scrubbing had I known she would be coming. But, any time with her is better than nothing at all.

I also can't get Vince's comment about her leaving town out of my head. I can't take it. And I know the other guys feel the same.

Shit, did I even care about Amber like this? I mean to the point where I'm going insane thinking about her leaving?

We loved Amber, all of us. And we thought she loved us. Her betrayal hurt. Like heart shattered, thrown in the flames, and tossed into the trash kind of hurt. Finding out she was looking for a payday damn near killed each of us. But what she did to Nick and I, that was a whole other level of fucked. *Literally.*

Amber spent 2 years with us. Trying her damnedest to be our perfect submissive. She wanted to be the perfect wife. She implied it more times than I can count. But, we just weren't ready for that. We loved her, sure, but something kept stopping us from taking that step. Then, the night it all came out, she played out the ultimate betrayal and stomped all over us in her stiletto shoes.

Vince is still at work and Jense is out of town meeting at one of our new gyms for its grand opening. I cam home early, hoping to take Amber to dinner; just the two of us.

When I walk through the door, I can hear her. Her voice is muffled, traveling from behind a door up the stairs. Assuming Nick's having some fun with her, I make my way up the stairs. I'm just going to peek in to see if it's an intimate 1-on-1 encounter or if they mind an audience. My cock hardens at the thought of watching her in the throes of passion.

But, the closer I get, the more my skin prickles with unease. Something isn't right. *The sounds aren't right. I walk faster knowing deep in my gut something is absolutely wrong.*

By the time I reach Nick's door, my heart is racing. I can hear her muttering curses but not enough to make sense of it. I ease the door open and my body forgets how to move.

The scene playing out before me isn't adding up in my head. Nick's on his bed, head lolled to the side. He's handcuffed to the headboard his eyes are rolled back.

Amber's bouncing on his dick, almost angrily. "Come on asshole, cum already." She says it like she's irritated or disgusted with him.

I glance back down at Nick and realize he isn't grunting, submitting, dirty talking, anything. His wrists are just dangling in the cuffs. What the fucking hell?!

I move up beside her before speaking, "What the hell are you doing, Amber?"

She jumps and screams, toppling sideways onto her back. For a second, I can tell she's trying to come up with something to say. But the longer she flounders, the more I realize it's because what she was doing is sick, and so, very wrong.

I glance back over at Nick and he still hadn't moved. She's drugged him with something. Fuck. She knows what his childhood was like. Why the fuck would she drug a willing man?

Rage, disgust, hurt, betrayal, and confusion are at war in my mind as I meet her eyes. I watch as her whole demeanor changes. Like her whole persona had been smoke in mirrors.

She climbs off the bed and stares me down while popping her hip out. "I'm doing what I need to do to take care of myself," She sneers.

In that moment I see just how awful she is. Every moment, every single time we were together in a group, or just us two, she has worn a mask. A mask of perfection, of innocence. A mask of adoration and love. And she always wanted more. More, more, more. She was always asking for something. Always talking us into spending money, buying expensive gifts, traveling to events; anything she wanted. And we did it, willingly. We loved her. But it obviously wasn't the same for her.

My brain finally slows down long enough to speak. "What are you talking about? We give you everything your heart desires. We take care of you, Princess. We love you. What the hell happened? Why, Amber, why?" My voice started out sad and broken, and turned into angry and pleading. How did we miss the signs?

She scoffs at me, like I'm being a petulant child. "Oh please, you think any woman would want your faggot little nerdy friend or even you and your over-planning, analytical ass? Jesus. Two years, Cory! Two fucking years I've waited to become Mrs. Top Growing Business in the

U.S! Ugh! I couldn't take waiting anymore. So, I took matters into my own hands."

Her grin is downright evil as she glances over at Nick. "What. The. Fuck. Did. You. Do?" I roar, stepping towards her.

We're face-to-face, noses barely an inch apart. I can see exactly who she is now that her mask is now gone. The mirth, the evil, the fucking wolf in sheep's clothing.

She lowers her voice to a whisper, leaning right up to my ear and says, "I remember Nicky Boy whining about his Mommy shooting him up with drugs. And there was a special combination she favored. One that would make him compliant yet still get him hard for the customers. Well, since you all only fuck me with condoms, I knew this was the only way to get any of you to fuck me raw."

"But why? Not using a condom wouldn't get us to marry you." My anger is growing because I truly don't understand. I can't see the bigger picture.

She chuckles but it's void of any humor. "Oh, little Cory. Marriage isn't the only way to get access to those bank accounts."

Just as it clicks in my head, a sharp pain steals my breath away. I can't register what it is. Like, cold and hot at the same time. It stems from one point and expands throughout my body.

I look up at her, my breaths growing heavier, and peer into the eyes I once loved; cherished. Now, all I feel is my heart throbbing in pain as I slowly become more detached from her, from everything. All the questions, all the confusion just swirl around in my head. I just don't understand how she could do this.

I feel dazed, floaty, and find myself looking down at the place in my body that's radiating pain. As I look down at it, a gasp leaves my mouth. My mind slowly realizes there's a knife sticking out of me, or is it in me? I watch with floaty fascination as the blade is suddenly yanked out of my stomach before it plunges back in again.

Now, I'm just cold, shaky, confused. I'm no longer floating, just falling, as darkness surrounded me.

The sound of the doorbell ringing brings me out of the worst nightmare I have ever lived. My heart is pounding against my ribs and I'm definitely sweating from the shitty trip down memory lane.

I glance over to find Jenson strolling towards the door before searching the living room for Nick. He's sitting on the couch, staring at the door like he may be able to see through it.

Once he sees it's just the food, Nick sighs and takes another swig of his beer. When his eyes reach mine, he must not like what he sees. "You ok man? You look like you're gunna be sick."

I shake my head to rid it of the last pieces of the memory and stand abruptly. "Yeah, I think I'm going to take a shower." I walk away before he even has a chance to respond.

* * *

As I step out of my bedroom, feeling the lingering effects of the memory fade, I hear the sweetest laugh ringing out from the kitchen. I follow the sounds and aromas to the kitchen. As I enter, I'm hit with such a strong sense of family that I almost fall over.

The crazy amount of food we ordered is spread out across the huge island. Vince and Nick are on the opposite side, leaning against the counter by the stove. Jenson and Annie are sitting in the stools, cracking up over something. The air in here is light and happy and I just want to soak in it.

Vince must sense my presence, as he glances my way and nods at me in question. All I can do is smile and nod my head, letting him know that I'm good.

Annie must catch Vince's look because she whips around to see me standing in the corner of the kitchen near the foyer. "Cory! You're here!" She jumps up and rushes me for a hug. And I fucking melt.

That's it. I can die a happy man. She has never initiated contact and I'm so happy she did with me.

"Hey, Pretty Girl. Of course I'm here; it's where you are." I give her my best cheesy grin as she pulls back to look at me. But, I have always sucked at keeping my facial gestures blank. She sees right through me as she searches my eyes for what could be wrong. I don't want her to worry so I lean down and keep my voice just so she can hear, "It's ok. Just a rough day. I'm so excited you're here." I give her an extra squeeze before she hesitantly steps back, happy to let it go for now.

She holds my hand in hers and pulls me over to the stool on the other side of her, then hands me a plate. All of the guys can sense something's up but they at least have the decency to keep it quiet. The neanderthals are shoveling food in their faces like they've been starved for weeks. I actively have to fight off a grin.

Annie's happily chattering away, seeming to be completely comfortable in our space. I pick up the tail end of whatever story she's sharing, "And then Samantha turns to Josh, wipes away his tears, and says "Don't worry bubba. I'll kick his ass tomorrow." I was so dumbfounded I couldn't even react to her cursing or threatening to get revenge." Annie's face is lit up with so much emotion and unfiltered joy that I can't help but mirror her smile.

Vince chuckles around his mouth filled with food. Once he manages to swallow, he says, "That doesn't surprise me. Any kids of yours are bound to be filled with fire. I bet you were secretly proud." His brow quirks in challenge, daring her to say otherwise.

She stares him down, grinning so playfully that my heart swells. "Hell yeah I'm proud. I just hope she never loses that sense of justice and standing up for herself and others." She shrugs and takes a bite of her Orange Chicken.

Nick and I start talking about the meeting we have with the Youth Center Director and liaisons this week. Annie seems genuinely shocked that we incorporated some of her ideas in the plan. "Why are you so shocked, Angel? They were great ideas. Some of the outside businesses, like that science lab, were all too happy to jump in and work with us. What we can offer those kids is just so much more than we had hoped. And we definitely have you to thank for a lot of it." She blushes at Vince's compliment then shrugs it off. *Damn she's adorable.*

Everyone is chatting about the programs and my stomach growls loudly, earning me a glare from Annie. "Eat, Cor. You guys got enough to feed a third world country."

She taps a box of noodles closer to me and grins. Her need to make sure everyone is taken care of shining through. *I bet she really is an awesome Mom.*

Just as I'm piling my plate full of Lo Mein, dumplings, and General Tso's Chicken, a ping from a phone rings out. All conversation stops as Annie jumps. "Sorry guys, might be the kids." She tilts her mouth up in a gentle smile before digging her phone out of her pocket.

I take a bite of my chicken, relishing the heat that explodes in my mouth. But then, I feel Annie tense at my side. I turn my head to look at her. Her body is rigid, her hands are trembling, and if I lean over, and down, just a little, I can see tears forming in her eyes.

Not knowing if it's something she wants everyone to know, I slide my hand gently on her thigh and rub circles with my thumb. She slowly turns her head towards me and looks up at me. Tears are clinging to her lashes and her face is pale. Subtlety is out the window as I bring my hands to her face and force her to keep eye contact. "Pretty Girl, what's going on? What happened?"

By now, the others have clued in that something's up. The kitchen is completely silent as she stares at me. But, she's not seeing me, not really. She looks so far away. I rub my thumbs over her cheeks and lean in closer, "Annie, baby, talk to me. What is it?"

That seems to snap her out of it and she shudders an inhale before turning. I let my hands drop as she takes in the others, finally landing on Vince.

They stare at each other for a moment, a silent conversation passing through them. Eventually, he nods, sets his plate down, and says "I'll grab the drinks."

Jenson, Nick and I stay frozen for a minute, staring at Annie for a sign of what's happening.

Vince snaps us out of our staring and directs us to the living room. "Alright guys, grab your plates. Let's have this conversation in the living room."

Annie moves, almost on auto-pilot, and takes Nick's outreached hand. I grab my plate and hers and follow as he leads her into the living room. He asks if she wants the couch, the maroon La-Z-Boy recliner, or the gray, round, oversized chair. She lights up, just a little, at the oversized chair and plops down. She is so fucking cute as she wiggles around and finds the perfect spot to get comfortable.

I hand over her plate of food and Vince hands her a glass of wine. She thanks both of us with a whisper and a shy smile.

She sets her food down on the chair and takes a healthy sip of her wine. She then looks up and watches as the rest of us find our spots around the room. Each of us trying to mentally prepare for whatever awful conversation is about to take place.

Vince

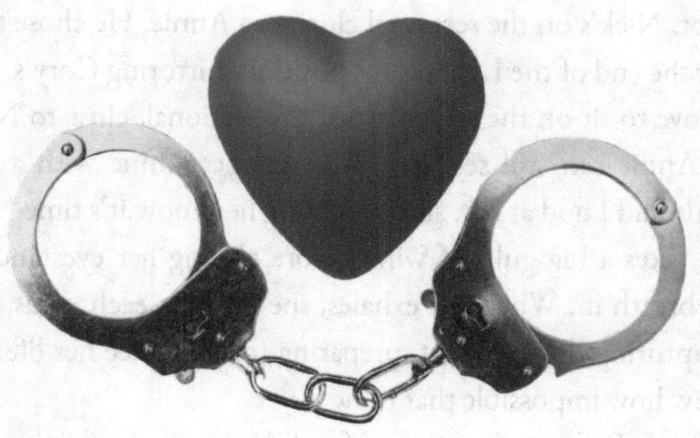

After passing out the drinks, I head back to my room to get the file I have. The much smaller one with the information I *can* share, if Annie so wishes. I'm not sure what just happened, but it seems she's ready to give the guys her truth. At least some of it.

I'm nervous, anxiety riddling my body. I want to keep her close, I want to protect her, and I know the guys will, too. I just hope she lets us and doesn't try to run. We are stronger together and I am determined to show her that. Somehow.

When I come back to the living room, Annie is curled up in the round chair, looking like a snug little bug with her knees tucked under her. She looks terrified. But I can't tell if it's from this whole fucked up situation or from her concerns over their reactions.

She was so sure I would just drop her and leave once I found out what was going on and who was harassing her. But, I'm pretty sure I've succeeded in showing her that I'm not going anywhere and I know the guys will, too.

Jenson is across the room leaning back in the recliner, trying to look like he's not freaking out. Cory is on the far side of the sectional facing Annie. His arms sitting on top of his bent knees, as he stares at the floor. Nick's on the sectional closest to Annie. He chose the spot right at the end of the L shape, his position mirroring Cory's.

I move to sit on the wide part of the sectional, close to Nick but where Annie can still see me. Her eyes meet mine with a look of gratitude and I nod at her, silently letting her know it's time.

She takes a big gulp of wine before closing her eyes and taking a deep breath in. When she exhales, she looks at each of us. It's like she's capturing this moment, preparing for us to flee her life. If only she knew how impossible that is, now.

"Okay," she starts. Every one of us is looking at her, giving her our full attention. "Vince is aware, obviously, but before I open up about this, I need you to know that no one but me really knows the full story. I don't share easily and, now that I know just how bad my ex is, I'm afraid he will start threatening you all."

Jenson scoffs, Cory's eyes shine with adoration, and Nick shakes his head like he's about to disagree. Before any of them says a thing, she moves on. "Look, I know we're friends, and I love hanging out with you but, um..." she trails off, not meeting any of us in the eyes.

Taking another gulp of wine, she shakes her head then continues her thought. "I really like you. All of you. I want you in my life but I don't want you in danger. Especially since we really just became friends and we hardly..."

"That's bullshit and you know it." Jenson didn't yell but his voice commands attention. Her eyes snap to his, brows raised to her hairline.

He leans forward in the recliner and looks her dead in the eye. "Annie, we've hung out a lot. Since the first time we met you, we saw you and wanted more. And that feeling has only grown. We want you to be *ours*. Today, tomorrow, and every day after. We're not going anywhere and I think, if you're honest with yourself, you know it's true. You feel it, too."

His head tilts to the side as if assessing her thoughts before adding, "We're in this with you, all the way. But only if that's what you want. We did the friends thing, and we'll continue with that, if it's truly what you want. But, Annie, Sweetness, you know damn well not a single one of us wants to be in that bubble. If you'll let us in, I promise that we'll support you, protect you, and care for you more than anyone on this planet. So, please, don't worry about us running or judging you by your past or the way it haunts you in the present. *We* are your future. We've just been waiting for you to accept it."

The room is filled with a tense silence. Annie's eyes flit to each of ours, trying to find any hint of disagreement or reason to bail. But I already know, she won't find any.

Her eyes begin to shimmer with unshed tears as she smiles and says the four words we've been waiting a month to hear. "I'm all in, too." Her smile brightens up her face; hell it brightens up the whole damn room.

Jenson doesn't wait another second. He's out of the recliner and across the room before she can barely blink. He reaches down to lift her up, palms the back of her neck and says, "Finally" just as he crashes his lips to hers. It's hard and desperate. Demanding to show every ounce of truth behind the statement he just made.

She hesitates at first, like she wasn't really expecting it but then gives in. Her body relaxes into him and she fists his shirt in her hands. He breaks the kiss and chuckles when she whimpers. His voice is now husky and low when he tells her "I can't hog you all to myself, Sweetness. But, don't worry. I'll be back for more." He kisses her nose before winking at her and stepping aside.

Cory appears just as soon as Jenson retreats and Nick and I stand together. Cory reaches his hands up slowly, cupping her cheeks and grins at her. They hold eye contact for what feels like forever. Like their souls are speaking. Then, he slowly presses his lips to hers, and I see her smile into it. Their kiss is the opposite of Jenson's. Cory's is sweet, awe-filled, but still pours every feeling into it.

Just as they break apart, Nick stands up and walks to her. I can barely hear him whisper, "My sweet Siren." He hesitantly wraps his arms around her waist and pulls her in for a hug. She wraps her arms around his neck, leaning her head on his shoulder and accepts his embrace. I see tears sliding down her cheeks but the smile of pure contentment and happiness proves they are good tears.

After a moment, he leans back with a smile and goes to release her but she stops him. She unwinds her arms from his neck and looks at him like he's her sun. She gently cups one of his cheeks with her hand, rubbing the stubble there with her thumb. She slowly lifts on her toes and places a soft kiss on his lips. I can see his hands flex on her waist but he doesn't move anything else. It's like she *knows* he struggles with touch. She knows he needs more time. She sees the demons in his soul and knows they are similar to hers. *How does she do that?*

The kiss is short but no less meaningful. She retreats from him and gives him the most gorgeous smile. Nick's face is bright pink and I'm pretty sure he just fell completely head over ass in love with her.

He moves back and I step beside him, grabbing his hand and

squeezing gently. His smile for me makes me want to slay every demon either of them ever encountered. But it also fills me with so much love that I feel I may burst.

When I look back at Annie, I see her studying the expressions on our faces, subtly glancing down at our hands, as she pieces together our relationship. I had already made up my mind that I wanted her to know before we had the relationship talk but, it's happening a little sooner than I thought it would. Which is awesome but I just hope it doesn't push her away. My brothers are all so happy. I pray she can accept this part of us, too.

She smiles up at me with a grin, like we are adorable little puppies and I chuckle. "So, in full disclosure, Nick and I are, also, together. So, taking that step with all of us, also means accepting this."

I don't know why I'm nervous, I can tell she has zero problem with it. I want this so bad I can taste it. Nick squeezes my hand a little tighter, his anxiety probably growing, too.

Then, Annie shocks the crap out of us, again. She lifts her brow while her smile widens and says, "I love that for you both. Happiness and love are just that. If you find it with me and with each other, all the more to celebrate. There's too much bitterness and hatred to put limits on love. And, I won't lie, it's really fuckin' hot."

She fans herself as her cheeks turn pink before continuing, "You know, I wondered. You all seem so damn close but you two… it's just something else. Something more. Like your bond went further into your souls."

She smiles at me again and I lose it. I drop down and smash my lips with her. Pouring every ounce of want, need, gratitude, and determination into it. She wraps her arms around my neck and I can't help but press my body into hers. My cock hardens in my pants. *Oh shit. Not right now. We need to have the other talk first.*

I reluctantly release her, both of us panting with need. I step back, and subtly adjust my pants. When I look back at her, the sly smirk she gives me shows just how subtle I wasn't. *Brat.*

I look at her one more time, reminding her of what we started. Her face changes from sheer happiness to determination. No fear in sight. *Damn I'm so proud of her.*

* * *

New beers are passed out and I fill Annie's glass up before we all settle in. Annie takes a drink before closing her eyes and inhaling deeply. When she exhales, she opens her eyes and a mask of determination and indifference settles over her face.

When she begins talking, it's like she's detaching herself from it. Like she's telling a story about someone else. "My ex and I got together about 12 years ago. Long story short, I became a woman I didn't want to be. I withdrew from family, friends, even myself." She huffs out a humorless laugh.

"Over the two years we spent together, his temper and my need to be good, to be loved, became worse. Throwing dishes, slamming me against walls, and just being a dick if I did the smallest thing wrong."

She pauses, swallows down a healthy gulp of wine, before lowering her voice and casting her eyes down to the pillow in her lap; Her fingers fiddling with the edges. "I have Clitoral Atrophy and Female Anorgasmia. Having one is pretty difficult but having both means that, on top of it being basically impossible to orgasm, I also need the help of lube to get wet. Lukas, he, uh, well he hated that. Would always yell at me for being too dry and, after a while, he just stopped trying to lube altogether. Especially when I had made him mad or he was drunk and wanted to act out some porn scene he had watched."

Her cheeks and ears are bright pink, and not because she's aroused. She's embarrassed.

This dickhead took a medical condition and used it against her. *I swear to God, when I find him, I'm going to...* my thoughts are cut off when Nick grabs my thigh, effectively grounding me. I guess he could feel my reaction.

She clears her throat and bats a tear at her face angrily. "Anyways, I had multiple doctor and hospital visits during that time. And, during every one of them, I defended him. You know, 'it was an accident', 'he didn't mean to', typical stupid girl bullshit." I scoff and Jenson huffs, shaking his head. Her head snaps towards us.

I can see her negative self-talk like it's a physical being on her shoulder. I can't have that so I cut off her line of thinking before it gets too far. "No, that's not stupid girl bullshit. This isn't on you. It's on him. Period. So get that through your beautiful head right now before you continue." She flinches like I smacked her, shocked by my absolute and unwavering belief in what I just said.

She then looks to the others, one at a time, and must see they're all thinking the same thing. I see the refusal on her tongue but she looks down, nods her head, and puts on her armor again. *Jesus. This prick did a real number on her. If I have my way, we will spend every moment for the rest of our lives showing her what a precious soul she is. No one will make her feel bad about herself again.*

"Thank you. I'm trying. It's just hard. But, I hear you, and I appreciate you all for being here, still." She takes a deep breath and blows through the rest of her shortened story like she just wants to get it over with.

"Anyways, one night we were all out and I saw him cheating on me. He flipped it around and had the audacity to tell me he thought she was me." She scoffs and rolls her eyes. "I mean, she was half my size and black. I may not always make the smartest decisions but no one could possibly buy that. So, one thing led to another and he convinced me to drive him home. My dog was there and my stuff so I figured it would be easier to just wrap it all up then. But, when we got back to his place, it's like he snapped, changed. Like he wasn't him anymore but someone, something else entirely. He'd accidentally hit me and hurt my dog before but he had never choked me. He had never threatened to kill me; never held his gun to my head."

She whispers the last part and then takes in a shuddering breath as she wipes away more tears. They're flowing down her face now and it's taking every ounce of control I have not to walk over and scoop her up. But, she doesn't need that now; not yet.

I glance between the others and see they are all fighting their bodies, too. Each of us is rigid, leaning towards her. Not a single one of us looks relaxed in any way.

I move my eyes back over Annie's body and take her in. She's snuggled up on the round chair. She went from sitting with her knees under her and off to the side, to having them pressed against her chest. Almost like she can make herself small enough to disappear. But, we'd still see her. Her light would still shine and we'd still help her fight her way back.

She sniffs as she finishes. "After what seemed like a lifetime of fighting and screaming and terror, I managed to free Mable and we ran. He shot at us but we got away. I drove to my best friend's house. I had barely seen her during that time because Lukas didn't feel comfortable with her." She rolls her eyes and shakes her head. "What a joke. Anyway, he went to jail. The lawyers dug through every picture I had, every medical document, even the recording I made of him beating his dog in front of me. He ended up getting 15 years in prison. I changed my name, going from Annalise Jones to Anastasia Fitzgerald and never looked back."

She pauses, letting us a brief moment to process. "But, I recently learned that he's no longer in prison and he's found me. He's been sending me messages from an unknown number over the last few weeks. Nothing too outwardly dangerous but enough that it has freaked me out. The only reason I really know it's him is because he called me "kitten". It was a nickname I hated, and I'm pretty sure that's why he stuck with it." She blows out another breath before wrapping it up, "Lukas is back, and he's pissed."

She downs the last of her wine and looks over at me. Instead of the look she had given before, asking for support, she's looking at me with shame and guilt, maybe? *Oh fuck. What else? I can't handle much more. But, I have to. If she's sharing more, worse, I have to handle it. For her.*

I give her my best reassuring smile and take a deep breath. I then nod, letting her know she can continue. That whatever it is, we've got her; granting her permission to lay her monsters at our feet.

30

~

Annie

The guys have taken my burdens and handled them pretty well so far. I can feel the anger and outrage pouring off of them. But, none of it's pointed towards me. No, it's *for* me.

I know I need to tell them this last part. Especially since we're trying to start a new relationship together. Taking that step with them is undeniably what I want but, I can't start this without them knowing everything. If they were to find out from someone else down the line, I know it would tear us apart. So, the only way to show them I'm all in, is to show them my whole truth. Even if it rips me apart in the process.

But, it seems like Nick already caught on to one piece. One piece of the fucked up puzzle that is my life. He looks over at me in confusion before asking, "Wait, you said you changed your name to Anastasia Fitzgerald when you left. Why did you change it again?" He tilts his head like he's trying to pluck the answer straight from my brain.

"Holy shit, I didn't even catch that. I'm not pulling off the whole police officer thing right now, I am?" Vince releases a self-deprecating chuckle and rubs the back of his neck.

His eyes land on mine and he grins like he's apologizing but I just smile and shake it off. Before I have a chance to answer, Vince nods his head to my glass. "Need a refill?"

I look down at my empty glass before deciding that I do, in fact, need more. He smiles as he takes the glass from my hand and stalks back to the kitchen.

While the living room is silent, my thoughts are loud. Lukas is back but he isn't my biggest secret. No, there's one thing I've never shared with a single soul; and it's time to let it go.

Hopefully the guys can handle it but, if not, it's fine. I've been on my own long enough, I can do it again. But it doesn't stop my heart from squeezing and tears forming in my eyes. *Shit. Why does the thought of losing them hurt so bad already?*

Vince appears with my glass and passes the guys their beer before they all turn to me, ready to watch me carve my heart out for them.

I take a sip of my wine, letting the light fruity flavor run off my tongue before jumping in. *Might as well get this over with.*

"After Lukas was sentenced, I moved in with my mother. Then, one night about 9 years ago, my mom was out of town with my aunt. I came home from work and all the lights were off. I knew the bills were paid and all the lights were on in the neighborhood so I went to flip the breaker. But, when I got there, I wasn't alone. A guy, I didn't see his face, but he sounded mean, awful; he was waiting for me when I opened the garage door. He, um, he threw me against the wall, held me there by my hair, and told me Lukas had a message for me. He smelled like cigarettes and Goldschlager." I release a gag as I swear I can still smell it.

The flashbacks that take over my mind assault me and I fight to catch my breath. The tears are crashing down but I am determined to get through this.

I don't know what the guys are thinking or feeling. I can't look at them; can't take on their feelings, yet. So I don't try. I just keep talking. "By the time he was done, he cut the zip ties and just walked away. I went to the hospital and other than some superficial cuts on my wrists, and some, um tearing, down there, he didn't do too much damage. He wasn't in the system, whoever he was, but," I choke on a sob, "But 8 months later I gave birth to my twins."

I do everything I can to gather myself to at least get through this. I'm almost there.

I swallow the giant lump in my throat and press on. "I never told mom about the attack and just said the girls were from a random fling. She was disappointed but supported us anyway." I shrug, and re-position myself on the chair.

"When we brought them home from the hospital, there was a pink gift basket from 'Daddy Lukas'." I spit his name in disgust and begin shivering.

"We decided right then and there that he was truly psychotic so, I became Anastasia and Mom became Andrea. We moved out of that town and into a larger one nearby. But, a year and a half later, Mr. Goldschlager came back with another message. This time, he left a few more bruises."

I've noticed that my words are getting quieter and it's becoming much more difficult to talk. I take a deep breath, picking at the pillow as the familiar feeling of numbness starts to blanket me. At this moment, I'm thankful for it. I'm almost there. But I don't want to feel this. Not anymore.

I swallow the last of my wine, and pull my legs back up under my chest. Staring at the floor, I complete my story. "My son was born 8 and a half months later. And another creepy package appeared. Mom and I changed our names, again, now becoming Annie and Melissa. We moved across the state, rented a house from some of my moms friends, leaving no paper trail, and we've been here ever since."

The silence in the room is oppressive, heavy, and highly uncomfortable. I can't look at them, the walls are closing in, and I can feel myself slipping into disassociation.

I can't be here. Not now. I gotta go.

31

~

Nick

I'm sitting here, frozen. Frozen in fear. Frozen in anger. Frozen in awe.

This woman has been through so damn much and yet, here she sits, allowing herself to be vulnerable. To us. But, how? Why? Who the hell are we that she would, could, drop her walls down?

If I wasn't sure she was strong before, I would know it now. *Strong. What a lame word. It doesn't even come close.*

I hear someone shuffle and I'm dragged out of my own damn head. I release the grip I have on Vince's thigh and my fingers ache from my hold.

I look over at Annie, and it's like I'm watching TV. Like, she's there, I can see her, feel her pain, but there's a barrier. I'm trying desperately to process everything she has told us. The weight of the world on her shoulders.

And her kids! Her damn kids that she does everything for; that make her whole face light up when she talks about them. *How the hell did she do it?* Three kids from a disgusting, evil monster. One I want to rip to shreds for having dared to scare her; touch her. But she loves them with her whole fucking heart. Like the memory of who their father isn't doesn't destroy her.

Suddenly, she's up and heading to the kitchen. I can see I'm not the only one who's tracked the movement, but we all seem to be frozen in shock.

A sob wails through the space and that's what does it for me. I'm up and running into the kitchen.

When I round the corner, I see that she's frantically searching around. She has her bag and curses while sobs wrack her body. "Annie." I say her name but it sounds small, hoarse, pained. "Annie, what are you looking for?"

She starts shaking her head frantically and I take a step closer. "Annie, please let me help." Another step and I'm right next to her but it's like she doesn't see me.

I'm close enough that I can see her shirt is soaked in tears and she's shaking so hard that she can hardly control her movements. She's thrashing her hand around the bottom of her bag while mumbling nonsense.

She's officially in mid-spiral. I have to stop this. I have to- "Annie, stop!" The command whips through the air. It wasn't a full yell but I definitely had to raise it so she could hear me over her sobbing.

"I can't!" She screams at me and it's so broken, so full of pain that I don't think, I react.

I step up behind her, wrap my arms around her, and press my front against her back.

"You can, and you will." I whisper the words into her ear, seeing some of her hair fan out from my words. Unlike at the gym, she doesn't fight me. She reaches her hands up, grabs hold of my arms and squeezes. Then, she shatters.

Knowing she needs more pressure, I turn us until my back is against the island and slide us to the floor. Once there, I go to move my arms but she grips them harder and yelps, letting me know some part of her understands that the pressure helps. "It's ok, Siren, pull your knees up for me. Then I can wrap around those too. It will help. Trust me."

Other than trembling and crying, she doesn't move for a few moments. Then, ever so slowly, she unclenches her fists from my arms and slides her knees up to her chest. I lean forward a little and wrap my arms around her legs, just below her knees, and grab back on to my own elbows, ensuring a tight fit. Her hands move up on the outside of my arms and squeeze mine. She bends her head forward and her sobs slowly start to decrease.

I'm not sure how much time passes but, with her in my arms, and my head leaning against her shoulder, I don't even care. Nor do I care that I'm pretty sure my whole ass is asleep. It doesn't matter.

Her sobs gave way to gentle crying and, eventually, the cutest damn hiccups I've ever heard. But, she's silent now. Not moving, other than the gentle lift that comes with each inhale. I'm just sitting here listening to the sounds of her beating heart and steady breaths.

I decide we need to get up and get some water in her. I roll my head so it's facing her ear and inhale deeply, letting her know something is happening. The last thing I want to do is scare her. "Ok, Siren, we have to get some water in you. Are you ready to start stretching out?"

The only thing that tells me she heard me is a slight squeeze of her hands. I slowly start unwrapping my arms from around her, careful to keep some pressure so it doesn't deplete her system too fast.

Once I'm untangled, I gently squeeze her arms and shoulders a few times. After another minute, she slowly releases the bend in her knees and slides them out in front of her. She rolls her head around, working out the kinks, before dropping it towards her left shoulder.

"Good girl." I praise quietly, snuggling into the left side of her neck. I see goosebumps flutter over her skin and grin before placing a light kiss to her cheek.

She giggles and turns her head towards me. Her eyes are swollen and her face is pink and wet but I don't think I've ever seen someone so beautiful. "Thank you," she whispers to me and I grin then kiss her nose. "Always, little Siren. Always."

We make our way into a standing position, shaking out our limbs. Once I'm up, I head straight for the refrigerator, trying not to make it obvious that a thousand tiny needles are running through my hips, down to my toes.

Grabbing a bottle of water, I turn and see that she has made her way closer to me. I reach out the bottle to her and she takes it with shaky hands. She eagerly gulps it down before setting it on the island.

I notice that she's biting the inside of her lip like the kitchen is the most interesting thing in the world. I mean, it is really nice. Deep blue cabinets, gray and white marble countertops and black stainless steel appliances fill the space.

When we first looked at this house, we didn't like that the kitchen has two openings with a wall between, blocking the view of the living room. But, the space itself is more than amazing. Heck, the whole house is. So, we bought it anyway.

One entry point, on the left side, is closest to the entryway. It has a section of 3 cabinets above and below the counter. Cory's fancy ass espresso machine, complete with grinder and frother, *insert eye roll here*, sits smack in the middle of the counter. The refrigerator is also right next to it so it's easy enough to grab out the beans or creamers and shit.

The walk-in pantry was one of our favorite things about the house. It sits in the corner of the kitchen past the refrigerator. Two people can literally walk in together, take a few steps and walk back. I mean, as long as one of them isn't Vince and his lumbersnack build.

On the long wall, across from the entry wall, is a line of 3 upper and lower cabinets, the stove/oven, and another set of 3 upper and lower cabinets. The stove/oven is a huge restaurant style with 2 separate oven areas and an 8 burner stove; 2 of which are covered with a griddle pan.

The area after the next section of cabinets opens up to a huge dining room area. A dark cherry wood table with a black epoxy river running through the middle of it sits in the center. It's large enough to sit ten comfortably and still leaves plenty of room to move around it. Cory commissioned some guy he met at the gym to make it. Apparently his family was going through a hard time and his wife had cancer. The table is literally a work of art. After buying it, we started leaving his business cards at the front desk and even made a little ad on our website.

Just past the dining room table is a door that leads to the backyard. It sits on the wall that opens into the living room. The stupid wall in the middle is just that, a stupid wall. Granted, the kitchen is huge but the wall serves no purpose. For now, it helps hold up the bar cart.

In the middle of the kitchen is a giant island. The oversized sink sits in the middle of the counter. To the left is a trash compactor, to the right is a wine/beer cooler. The counter behind the sink lifts about 5 inches and then continues out another foot. On the other side, we have 4 bar stools. The space is enough that we usually eat breakfast here, and the occasional dinner if we are in a hurry or there's just a couple of us.

I catch Annie lifting her gaze to the ceiling. Ah, yes, my favorite detail. The kitchen has recessed lighting that I hooked up to an app on our phones. We can turn the lights on, off, dim them, and even change the colors. Above the table also has a long truncated pyramid made with glass and steel. Five Edison bulbs hang through the middle of it, giving just the right amount of lighting.

Above the island is another industrial style fixture. This time, it has 3 separate units hanging down, equally spaced apart. Each unit has its own Edison bulb encased in a glass cylinder with black steel plates lining the tops and bottoms.

"I really love this kitchen," she whispers. "I didn't really take it in earlier because the food just hit me, and, I mean, who looks at cabinets when you have man candy?" A little grin tilts her lips and I am blown away, once again, by her ability to smile, even when she's hurting.

"I get it, it's the same way we all feel when you enter the room." I grin back. She chuckles before sliding her hand in mine. "Thank you, Nick. I'm so sorry. It was just so much and it was the first time I, you know, actually told someone all of that. Mom knows some but not the stuff about the kids. I just, I didn't want her feeling different about them, I guess. I don't know. They're mine and I love them. Even when I imagine killing the man responsible for so much pain, I just," she takes a quick breath in and out. "I just never want anyone to see them other than the crazy, silly, smart, compassionate little farts they are."

We both ended up laughing at that. *Do I just cut my heart out now and hand it over? I mean, it's already done. She owns me.*

I lean in, bringing my hand to cup her cheek before whispering, "You are truly miraculous. Even if you don't see it, don't know it, it doesn't matter. You are and we're the luckiest men alive that you decided to open yourself to us."

Before she can refute or anything, I lean in and steal a kiss. I can tell it catches her off guard but when I swipe my tongue across her bottom lip, requesting entrance, she opens for me. I slide my tongue over hers and the sweet tanginess of the wine mixed with something that is just, her, is better than any dessert I've ever had. I immediately want more. My hands slide down her waist and behind her back.

"Ahem, sorry to intrude but we didn't know the party moved in here." We reluctantly separate, panting for breath. Our eyes stay glued to each other and the smile that stretches across her face is every-fucking-thing.

And now I'm grinning like a dopey bastard.

32

~

Annie

Now that my panic attack has subsided, I'm feeling shaky and exhausted. But, my mind is clear enough to know that I can't run away from them. I need to pull up my big bitch panties and deal with whatever fallout that may be waiting. However, judging by Nick's kiss, and how he looks at me like I'm something precious, I don't think it will be all bad.

Tingles of excitement and hope ripple through my body as I consider the very real possibility that telling them was right; that my gut instinct to trust these men, was accurate. I'm already feeling lighter than I have in years. But, I know better than anyone how quickly that can change.

I finally step back from Nick and face Jenson. I'm not sure what I thought I would find but that shit-eatin' grin on his face, arms folded across his chest as he leans against the far counter, was not it.

I finally process the words he said before, about moving the party in here and I laugh, shaking my head at him. I shrug my shoulder and throw a smirk his way. "Well, it got kind of stuffy in there so we decided to migrate where the booze was kept." His booming laugh echoes around the kitchen.

He steps further into the kitchen, walking on the other side of the island before opening up a cabinet or something underneath. "Well Sweetness, if booze is what you want, booze is what you'll get. What would you like?"

I walk over to the other side of the island, confused as to why he's looking down there and not in the refrigerator. The cabinet in the island on the left side of the sink is a mini-fridge but with bottle holders instead of shelves. "Oh my God, that's so awesome! I need one of these. Or, maybe not, tiny humans and all."

Jenson chuckles and brings out a bottle of merlot before tipping it my way in question. I nod my head eagerly with a smile and watch as he grabs a clean wine glass and fills it up.

He looks at Nick in question but he shakes his head and says "No more for me. I'm good."

Jenson hands me the glass, his fingers lingering for just a moment on the stem as I go to take it. Sparks fly through my fingers and I let out a small gasp. His grin tells me he felt it, too. His bright emerald eyes bore into me. Searching, hopeful, like he's willing me to see everything he can't say.

I smile softly, before leaning up on my toes and pressing a gentle kiss to his lips. "Thank you, Jenson" is all I whisper before settling my feet back down and taking a sip of my wine.

I clear my throat and prepare for the second part of this conversation. "Ok. I'm sorry I freaked out. But, if you still want to know the rest, still be in this with me, then let's go back to the others."

Jenson's smile falters and his eyes grow wide. It takes me a second before I realize he may think there's more bad things about my story. There is but, I mean, the big things were covered. *Much to my relief and embarrassment.*

I reach my hand and tug the bottom of his shirt a little. He shakes his head and refocuses his eyes on me. "Hey, not any more of *that*. The reason Vince went MIA, was because he found some things. Things he didn't want to tell me, but that he needed to. He already told me most of it and it's my choice to share that with you." I look over at Nick across the island before adding, "All of you."

Nick gives me a reassuring smile and nods before heading for the living room. Jenson grabs my hand, kisses my knuckles, then says "We're still her, Annie. And we will be as long as you let us."

I'm pretty sure that's all I've ever needed to hear. I smile so wide that my cheeks hurt and simply respond, "Okay."

He keeps his hand in mine and intertwines our fingers as we walk towards the living room. When we enter, Jenson releases my hand and sits in the big round chair. I gasp in mock disbelief and stomp my foot as I whine, "Hey, that's my chair. It's my favorite." I even add a little pout for dramatic effect. *Yup, just like the girls.*

All of the guys start laughing before Jenson rudely points out it's my first time there and the only other seat I have been in is a stool. I stick out my tongue and before I can back away, he pulls me by my waist, turns me around like I'm a rag doll, and positions me with my ass directly against his right side, my back on the side of the chair facing the wall, and my legs draped over his lap. I sit in shock for at least ten seconds. *He just totally man-handled me. And, it was hot.*

"Whatcha' thinkin' about, Sweetness."

I squeak out, "Nothing," and take a big healthy drink of my wine.

He grins, winks, and turns back to the guys who are all apparently having some silent conversation.

With a nod, Vince clears his throat and leans forward, resting his arms on his knees. "You want me to pick up where you left off, Angel?" His tone holds no judgment, no pity, just compassion and an overwhelming feeling of protectiveness.

I realize just how much that really means to me. He has never once made me feel small, less than, weak, or stupid. Personally, professionally; it doesn't matter. He looks at me the same, treats me the same, and I realize that I'm *really* here, telling *my* story, braving *their* judgment, because of how this man has treated me, how he continues to treat me and make me feel. *I'm going to have to thank him somehow.* Until then, I smile and nod my agreement for him to fill them in with what he's found out about Lukas.

* * *

Ten minutes later, Vince finishes telling the guys about Lukas and his probable involvement with the Black Thorns. For the longest time, we just sit in the living room in silence. Contemplating, processing, planning out revenge. *Ok, I was probably the only one thinking of that.*

Cory stands up, catches my stare, and softly walks across the floor until he's standing right in front of me. His hazel eyes glimmer with unshed tears. Not pity, like I expected, but pain *for* me. He reaches his hand out to me and Jenson takes my wine glass, giving me a small smile before nodding back to Cory. I place my hand in Cory's and let him pull me up. His hands grip my face as he leans his forehead against mine.

Bringing my hands to his waist, I lock my thumbs in his belt loops and just let myself feel his connection. When he closes his eyes, I do the same. We stand there for who knows how long just sharing oxygen. Our hearts beating out the same tune.

It's not until I feel water on my face that I even realize I'm crying.

No, wait, he's crying. My tears are all dried out from earlier. My eyes flutter open, removing my hands from his waist, and placing them on his cheeks, rubbing away the tears streaming down. "Cor," I whisper, licking my lips before trying again. "Cor, are you ok? What's wrong?"

He starts laughing. Laughing!

I rear my head back, afraid he's lost his damn mind. His laughter goes from low and deep to loud and stomach-clenching.

My eyes dart around to the others, who are now standing and making their way over to me. Seeing them nervous about Cory makes me nervous. "Cory, you're scaring me."

That does it. He jumps like I hit him, widens his eyes, drops his hands from my face and backs up until he's across the room, his hands raised. "Oh, damn, no. No, no, no, no. Annie, I'm sorry. You just caught me off guard.

"You literally went through all 9 circles of hell and you're asking me if *I'm* ok? I mean, *you*, Annie, you are *everything*. You are brave, and smart, and strong, and funny, and sweet, and love kids. You're an amazing Mom, just by hearing you talk about them, and you're a pretty damn great *friend*." He lets out a little chuckle after his emphasis, shaking his head with a small grin. Tears are pouring down my face at his revelation.

His smile widens and the look he gives me takes my breath away. "We literally just started something more than that but, dammit, Annie. I know you're going to be pretty damn wonderful being ours, too." My eyes are so wide that my brows touch my hairline. *Ours.*

He's panting so hard and it makes my heart beat faster. Never in my life has anyone said half of those things about me. Sure, my closest friends like me, and my mother has always been great but, not like this. Not so much, so intense that it feels like he not only believes those things, but is begging me to believe them, too.

My face begins relaxing as I feel the words, and the emotions behind them. They are seeping into my bones and spreading through my veins.

With tears still leaking from my eyes, I make a decision. I don't second guess it, I just act, as I run across the room toward him. When my body crashes into his I fling my arms around his neck, stand on my toes, and crush my mouth to his. I pour every ounce of gratitude, peace, and appreciation into it. We hold the bruising kiss until we both need oxygen. I step back, our breaths mingling barely twice before he pulls me back in into another bruising kiss.

We finally break apart, and I soak up the colors in his eyes. Shining brighter than before. The perfect combination of brown and green swirl together in his hazel eyes, offering me a glimpse of eternity. I thank him, before pressing another small kiss to his lips. Then I step back into the middle of the living room.

I meet everyone's eyes, all filled with varying emotions, before offering a smirk and pop my hip out. "So, you know all my dirty little secrets. Sure you wanna stick around for the after-party?" My therapist always said sarcasm and dark humor were my defense mechanisms. *Hm, I guess she may have been right about that.*

They all roll their eyes before chuckling and shaking their heads. They take a moment, trading looks and silent conversations, before all looking back at me.

Vince stands first, making his way to me. He leans down, molds his hands to my cheeks, then meets his lips with mine for the briefest moment before retreating.

Nick steps up the moment Vince retreats, also leaning down and briefly kissing my lips once, twice, three times. He then retreats with a knowing smile.

Jenson steps up, wraps his arms around my waist before lifting me to his mouth, and gives me the gentlest kiss. Then, he kisses my nose before sliding me back to the floor.

Finally, Cory steps up, smiling so big, his dimples pop out and his glasses raise on his face a little. He leans down, puts his hands on my waist before leaning in to whisper, "In case you're wondering, we're in. We're *all* in." He bends down and captures my mouth with his. So brief, I whimper when he retreats.

There I am, heart filled to the brim, standing in a room with a bunch of guys; as in more than one. More than one guy I trust and care for. More than one guy I let myself be vulnerable with. And damn do I feel better than I ever have before.

I leave the guys' house a little over two hours later. We decided to pile on the couch and watch Dexter. Since we had all seen it before, we were critiquing his technique as well as every little detail about the other characters we could judge. It was silly nonsense but it felt so good.

I feel lighter, freer, happier than I have felt in a long damn time. I am so glad Mom wanted the kids tonight. It was good to just get all the shit out in the open. Now, I don't have to worry that they will leave before it gets started. They know my worst memories turned nightmares, the darkest parts of my soul, and yet, they still want this; want *me*.

I feel like I can breathe. Almost as if I'm finally letting go of Lukas and all his bullshit. Letting myself start truly healing from the pain. Even allowing myself to finally start a relationship with someone, *or multiple someones*, after a decade. They just lift this heavy weight off my chest and shoulders.

Naturally, a good song is in order. Starting Joke's On You by

Charlotte Lawrence, I smile my biggest smile, turn up the radio, and roll the windows down. Belting out every word, giving it my all, I sing out to Lukas. I let it all go right out the damn window and release my own version of goodbye.

He'll leave me alone eventually. He's wrapped up in gang shit now so he'll get bored and fuck off somewhere else. In the meantime, I'm going to enjoy every second I have with my kids, and *my* guys. That thought makes me giggle like a damn school girl.

Ten minutes later, I'm turning into my neighborhood when my phone rings. Lana's name flashes on the screen and I answer the call, rolling up the windows as I do.

"Hello lovely, what's up?" She says she's just checking on me since she hasn't heard from me much this week. So, I cave. I mean, it's not like she begged but I was bursting at the seams to share my news.

"Girl, I'm amazingly fantastic! I'm almost home after having dinner at the guys house and..." *dramatic pause for effect*, "We made our relationship official tonight!"

Her squeal of excitement echoes around my Suburban and I flinch as it bounces between my ears. She starts rattling off a million questions at once. Everything ranging from whether I had dusted the cobwebs out, who kisses best, and who made the first move.

I laugh at her enthusiasm for my love life as I pull up in the driveway. Before answering her questions, I ask her to hold on. My phone can be tricky when connecting and disconnecting from the car and I'd rather the whole neighborhood *not* know about my business.

Turning off the car, and sliding out, I look down at my phone to make sure the icon is showing the speaker on and Bluetooth off. I reach through the car and pluck my purse out of the passenger seat before leaning back out of the car. I back up so I can shut the door but instead of having nothing behind me, I hit something solid.

I scream out and try to turn towards them. Before I can twist my head around, one hand is around my waist, pulling me back, and the other is clamping around my mouth and nose. My hands immediately come up, trying to break the attackers hold. I stomp my foot, try to elbow his/her side, kick back, but nothing lands. Not hard anyway.

Just when I take a much needed breath, a sharp pain radiates from my neck. "Ow, what the fuck!"

The attacker's hands suddenly release me and I feel the warmth of their body leave. But that's not all I feel. *Or is it?*

My eyes grow heavy and I try to blink them, but opening again gets harder. When I finally do, it's slow and almost painful. Like I'm fighting it. *Oh, right, fighting. Wasn't I...*

Then it all goes dark.

Acknowledgements

First and foremost, thank you so much for giving this newbie author a chance. I have dreamed about this for years and I am so thankful I was finally pushed into releasing it. If you loved this book, please help spread the word by leaving a quick review and don't forget to follow me for updates on new releases.

A huge forking thank you to my BFF, partner in crime, and bestest Ohana Bitch, Kayla. I would have never gone down this rabbit hole without your enthusiasm. Thank you for jumping in with edits and suggestions, forcing me to hold on to hope that this could happen. Everyone needs a good hype woman in their life and I'm so glad you're mine!

Finally, thank you Elle Thorpe, Bex Dawn, Ames Mills, Heather Long and A.K. Rose. You don't know me but your books, your words, your stories made the best movies in my mind. They opened me up to a new way to deal with my own trauma, live out new fantasies, and rekindled my love for reading. Without your audacity, I never would have imagined writing my own book and allowing the catharsis that comes with it to heal me. Thanks to your bravery and abilities, I not only hit my goal of 100 books read this year, but I wrote and published my own. For that, I will forever be grateful to each of you.